A CREEK CALLED
WOUNDED KNEE

Also by Douglas C. Jones
in Large Print:

Hickory Cured
Roman
Rubicon One
Russian Spring
The Search for Temperance Moon
Shadow of the Moon
This Savage Race

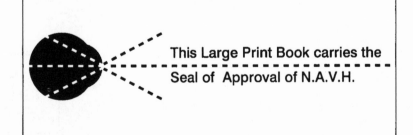

A CREEK CALLED WOUNDED KNEE

Douglas C. Jones

G.K. Hall & Co.
Thorndike, Maine

Published in 1997 by arrangement with Wieser & Wieser, Inc.

G.K. Hall Large Print Western Collection.

The text of this Large Print edition is unabridged.
Other aspects of the book may vary from the original edition.

Set in 16 pt. Plantin by Rick Gundberg.

Printed in the United States on permanent paper.

Library of Congress Cataloging in Publication Data

Jones, Douglas C. (Douglas Clyde), 1924–
    A creek called Wounded Knee / Douglas C. Jones.
     p. cm.
    ISBN 0-7838-8231-9 (lg. print : hc : alk. paper)
    1. Wounded Knee Massacre, S.D., 1890 — Fiction. 2. Dakota
Indians — Wars, 1890–1891 — Fiction. 3. Large type books.
I. Title.
[PS3560.O478C74   1997]
813'.54—dc21
                                            97-14523

This is a novel with some fictional characters, but all the words quoted from newspapers were actually written and actually read, I suspect, by some of the real people described here. All of it, fancied and historical, is dedicated to KEMM. And they know who they are.

Although the Indian's ancient way of life had never been as rich as they remembered it, that life had been one they understood. But now, it was gone. . . . And for them, the age of hope was ended.

Rex Alan Smith
Moon of Popping Trees

PART ONE
THE GATHERING

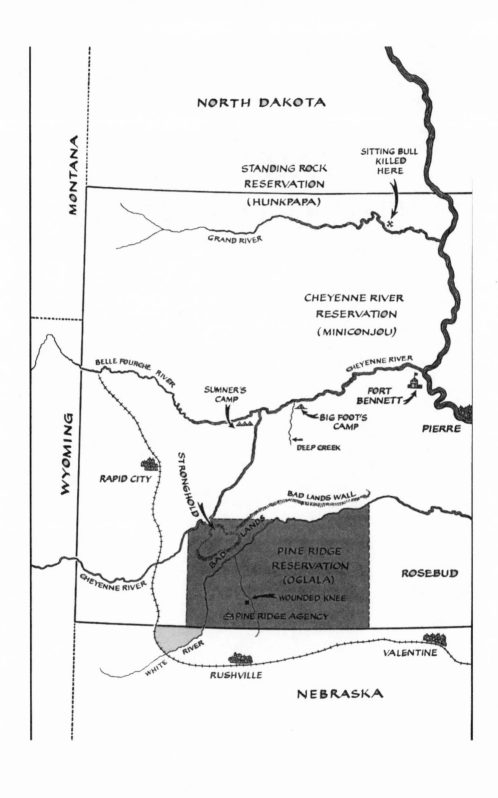

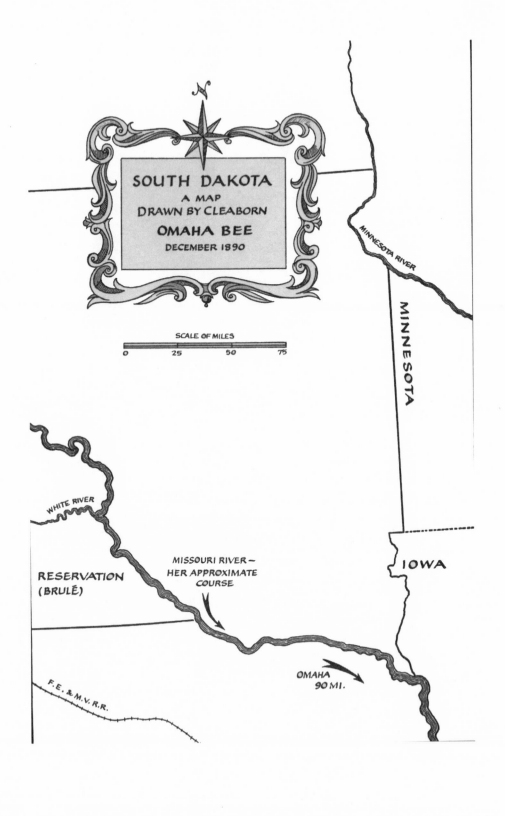

SOUTH DAKOTA
A MAP
DRAWN BY CLEABORN

OMAHA BEE
DECEMBER 1890

SCALE OF MILES

0   25   50   75

MINNESOTA RIVER

MINNESOTA

IOWA

WHITE RIVER

MISSOURI RIVER—
HER APPROXIMATE
COURSE

RESERVATION
(BRULÉ)

OMAHA
90 MI.

F.E. & M.V. R.R.

1

ST. LOUIS GLOBE-DEMOCRAT — There is no disguising the fact that hostilities with the Sioux and a general outbreak are imminent. . . . The greatest excitement prevails and it is feared that a massacre will ensue.

At first there had been the breath of hot new life across the land, blowing like a summer wind from the Black Hills to the Missouri, making the People alive again, even when their bellies were only half-filled with corn and flour gravy. Even when there was no meat at all. The promise of new beginnings made their passions rise and their eyes weep tears of gladness. Their spirits soared. They sang the songs the Teacher from the West had told them to sing. They danced the dance the Teacher from the West had told them to dance. And there were shining faces.

A bright day was near. In the season of *wétu,* the time of snows melting, it would begin, when the old ones would come back. The ones long dead, the ancestors whose bones had been scattered across the prairie from woodland to great rock mountains. All of them would come back to be alive again, to sing and dance with the

11

People. Near the villages would be the great herds, covering the land as they once had, bellowing and saying to the People, "Come. I am *wóyute ma hayápi*, I am your food and clothing."

The villages would be vast, stretching up and down the rivers for as far as a man could ride in a lifetime on a good pony. The tipis would be of buffalo hide, not canvas. The drying racks would stand in the sun bent with meat. The fires would be hot with fat buffalo chips, and there would be the smell of roasting ribs. Even the children would have plenty of *tapí*, the good raw liver, and camp dogs would be fat like Cheyenne puppies ready for the cooking pot. It would be a time for courage again, a time for lance and bow against old and honored enemies. The young braves would return from war parties against the Arikara, leading stolen ponies, and the young women would run out to them with cries of warmth and passion. The young men would return from hunting parties with elk and antelope, and the children would run out to them with cries of gladness and hunger. The land would be green, the water sweet. The hawk would hunt above, dropping his feathers for the People to wear in their hair. The wild plums would grow in great thickets and would be fat and juicy.

All of this would happen when the Messiah came. And the Teachings said He would come in the season of *wétu*, the time of snows melting.

Then some of the wise ones began to ask questions. Many of the Teachings were hard to understand. And so the questions were asked about the part hardest of all to understand — that the white man would become harmless, his weapons impotent, and he would finally disappear beneath the earth. The wise ones asked, "How will this happen?"

They searched the Teachings, but they could find no answer. Some of the men, and especially the ones with hot blood, said that no matter how it was to happen, they would help it. Some of them took out rifles that had not been used against men for more than ten seasons, and some of the rifles had never been used against men at all. And some bought ammunition. Many of the ministers of the Teachings gave the People shirts that would turn aside the bullets of their enemies. And these were called Ghost Shirts.

The white man watched the singing and dancing, and some were afraid. Stories were told in the white man's talking papers, and the stories said the People were dancing to make the white man disappear. So the white man asked the question, too. "How will this happen?"

Sometimes the white man answered his own question and said the People would fulfill the prophecy themselves. The People would come off the reservations with weapons in their hands to be sure the white man disappeared beneath the earth.

Some of the People said, "No! It cannot happen this way. Such a thing is not in the Teachings!"

13

But some of the People were stubborn and said nothing, except to each other. And then they said, "Let the dog face with hair around his mouth think what he wants to think." Because of this stubbornness, the white man was sure the Lakota, the westernmost tribes of the great Sioux nation, would use their weapons. But most of all, the white man was afraid about those Ghost Shirts that would turn aside bullets. "Who wants a bulletproof shirt," they said, "unless he intends to get into mischief?"

So Lakota men who were not young and hot-blooded brought out their rifles, too. Not because they wanted to act courageous before the People, but because they knew when the white man became afraid, it was a time for fear among the People as well. For they knew that two things caused white man's war: anger and fear. And most of all, fear.

The wise men said, "We will keep our weapons close in case somebody does something foolish. We will make no threat." But when the white man saw the weapons and thought about those Ghost Shirts, it was threat enough for him. He went to his government and said, "Send the Blue Coats to stop this singing and dancing because it is dangerous."

Many white man's talking papers told of the danger and asked for soldiers, too. Soon the white man's government told the Lakota to stop dancing and singing, and they sent the Blue Coats to be sure it was done. The People knew

14

that many other tribes were singing and dancing, and the white man said nothing. But with the Lakota it was different. Because of the rifles in a small way. Because of the Ghost Shirts in a large way. For the other tribes did not show off such things that made the white man nervous.

And so the warm breath of new life began to cool among the Lakota — among the Oglala, the Miniconjou, the Hunkpapa, and all the others who were Lakota. Many of the wise ones said that although the singing and dancing were good, frightening the white man was bad. And dangerous. But even as some of the wise ones said these things, others continued to dance because they were Lakota, and once they set their minds to a thing would not be put off from it. They would dance until the Messiah came and brought the new day, and they said, "Whoever tries to stop us will have terrible trouble!"

The Lakota had always been a fiery people. They had always enjoyed a good argument. When the Messiah thing grew dangerous, the arguments became serious. Because of the uncertainty, threats were made against brothers. Blows were struck between friends. And there was a struggle for power among the People, a struggle for the right to tell everyone what to do.

Some said, "We are Christians, and it doesn't concern us." Some said, "Tell the Hair Mouths we will fight to save our singing and dancing." And some said, "Nothing is worth having the white man set his Blue Coats on us like angry dogs, for then our religion will be destroyed and the People with it."

Now they are divided, the Lakota. There are the hotbloods who dance on a high mesa called the Stronghold in the Badlands, defiance replacing the love that made gladness two moons ago. There are the ones at the agencies in canvas tents, docile as cows who stand for milking. They think the white man is stronger than the new religion. And finally, there are those out on the reservations still, in their cabins and camps, most confused of all. They are afraid to dance, afraid of the white man, afraid of the Blue Coats, afraid of each other. In those bands, the young men hold their rifles and think of the old days when everything was simple and a man always knew who the enemy was and glory could be won by showing courage. The old men hold their rifles, too, but they think of Blue Coats marching through the snow relentlessly. And the women and children watch and wonder what has happened to the shining faces that were everywhere in the season of *ptanyétu,* the time of leaves falling.

2

RUSHVILLE [NEBRASKA] REPUBLI-CAN — To the satisfaction and relief of local citizens, it is not 1876 but 1890 and the Army can move its troops quickly by the railroads when an Indian outbreak threatens. Latest to arrive at the scene of disturbance is the ill-fated Custer regiment, the 7th United States Cavalry, coming all the way from Fort Riley, in Kansas.

Where the Republican and Smoky Hill join to form the Kansas River, the wild plum and hornbeam and black willow trace patterns of brown, blue, and black against the light sandy soil of the high banks where they grow. It is a quiet place, here at the edge of the high plains, where even sounds do not diminish the silence but seem only to emphasize it. And the wind is so constant that after a while it has no voice at all but is simply a part of the land.

The water is low, but it runs clear and cold. With the spring, moisture held as ice and snow in the high country to the west will be released, and the rains will come, too. Then the crest will rise dramatically, and the streambed will over-

17

flow. The water will be filled with silt, as it has been for centuries, after running off the sandy flats. But in the late fall the silt is settled, and the water has cut its way through the sandbars to make channels that are deep and regular. Now the river flows for miles without increasing in size, because as much water seeps back into the loose soil along the way as runs into the stream from the land.

In east central Kansas the land was once an ocean floor, and the sediments were laid down over the centuries, forming strata of rock in reds, ochers, and siennas lying one on the other like layers in an ancient cake. Then the whole thing was thrust upward to form a huge plateau, and the sea ran off and disappeared. When rains began to form rivers, the water searched for the low ground, running generally to the east, cutting down past the strata of rock and sand, exposing each successive level that had at one time been the sea floor until it, too, had been covered by those above. The water cut broad valleys and sharp canyons, their shape and size dependent on the resistance of the rock. Before they were called Republican or Smoky Hill or Kansas or before they were called anything or had been seen by man, the rivers trenched the plains and at their juncture left a broad valley surrounded by sharp hills topped by striped bluffs. The rimrock. In the center of this broad valley, on the north bank of the Kansas River and east of the confluence of the other two, is Fort Riley.

The buildings are long and low, the parade grounds extensive to accommodate the convolutions of mounted cavalry drill. The stables are sandstone, each end marked by a large, arched doorway like the entrance to a railroad tunnel. They stand empty now, except for a lame or sick horse unfit for campaign, and the stalls are cleaned and scrubbed. The tack rooms are empty, extra bridles, bits, cinches, and saddle blankets gone. Across the wide parade fields only the wind raises dust. A few children play along the sidewalks in front of Officers' Row, and women go back and forth to visit. At the post headquarters is a corporal's guard and the bugler who still sounds all the calls for the day from "Reveille" to "Taps." But the fort is empty. The Seventh Cavalry Regiment has gone out on Indian campaign once more, to do the job it was originally formed to do in 1865.

Now the crows sit in brazen lines along the gables of the barracks buildings and hurl harsh, insulting calls at the large claybank gelding that grazes in one of the choice pastures. This is a very old horse named Comanche, the only Seventh Cavalry survivor from Custer Hill at the Little Bighorn. Found on that battlefield, he was set out to pasture with honor, and now is almost dead of old age. He ignores the crows, for he has seen many things more dangerous than birds, and, besides, he is stone deaf.

But on the day the regiment marched out, the place was sound and movement and expectation.

19

It was gleeful anticipation that was somehow fearful, too.

Alongside the stables that morning, teams had been hitched and waiting. These were the regimental trains, and the men assigned to their operation moved among the vehicles and animals, testing trace chains, pins, and canvas. Across the parade grounds, troopers were moving horses into line, stationing themselves before the proper guidon, first sergeants shouting their instructions.

The regiment would entrain in two places. Most of them would load east of the main post at sidings built specifically for the military along the Kansas Pacific Railroad — the old Union Pacific Eastern Division line. These units had moved early, leaving only two troops and the band and trains to march the two miles west directly into Junction City and load at the civilian depot and siding there. Their purpose was to show the flag. Townspeople had lined the streets, still wiping the last of breakfast from their lips. They looked expectantly toward the Republican River bridge where they would first see the flutter of red-and-white guidons, hear the first tramp of steel-shod hooves.

The band had come into town ahead of the others, in a wagon — much to their disgust and humiliation. But there were not enough horses to go around, and these men would be shanks' mare until the regiment reached Nebraska, where additional horses would be bought. So they rode a wagon, grumbling.

"Play one for old Custer," someone had shouted. Everyone knew that when the band took its station at the loading platform, the first tune would be "Garry Owen," the regiment's marching song since Custer had commanded. There was laughter and shouting and small flags waving. Not a few men showed signs of early tippling.

Many of those bystanders had visited Fort Riley the day before, when the regiment conducted the final parade and review traditional for armies preparing to march off to war. Some had been invited to the officers' ball afterward, traditional, too, for departing hopefuls and heroes.

It had been a long time since the Seventh Cavalry had marched out to a possible engagement with hostile tribesmen. Always before, they had marched out from some other place. It had been the Indian-fighting Seventh, organized specifically for duty on the Great Plains. It had been involved many times in actions brought to pacify the wild tribes. The Kiowa and Comanche, the Nez Percé, and the Cheyenne. And, of course, the Sioux. And of these last, the most troublesome since the war had been the westernmost tribes, called the Lakota. As the great buffalo herds disappeared and the railroads and wire fences and cattle ranchers came, slowly the resisting tribesmen had been forced onto reservations. Some had gone peacefully. Some had not. It had been the job of the frontier army — the Seventh Cavalry among them — to ensure that the Manifest Destiny of the United States was fulfilled and the red man placed on reserves like cattle, to be taught the ways of civilization by an Indian Bureau man, an agent, and his employees. The purpose was to teach the Indian men how to fit their hands to a plow and forget the ways of lance and bow.

But those days had been gone a long time. The great wars of the plains were finished. For over a decade there had been the tribal reservations, where the teaching and missionary work could go on, enclaves of a vanished wilderness in a sea of rapidly advancing technology. But now the Seventh was marching out again because it was reported that some of the Lakota Sioux might attempt to break out of the reservations and try once more to refute Manifest Destiny.

The people of Junction City were exhilarated because it was their regiment going to do battle or whatever else might be required in Nebraska, where the trains would take them, or at Pine Ridge Indian reservation, their final destination. When the small boys who lined the streets and shouted at the band had grown old, they would tell the story again and again to their grandchildren. A few — the doctors, lawyers, and politicians — would speak before hushed and expectant audiences of later generations about the day they had watched the old Seventh Cavalry march out to Wounded Knee.

As they waited, none had ever heard of that small creek in South Dakota. Nor had the soldiers who were headed there.

Back at the post headquarters, the regimental staff had assembled, each riding a large bay. Col. James Forsyth, his adjutant, the quartermaster, a surgeon, a veterinary surgeon, and a number of enlisted men with the sergeant major and drawing up before them, the regiment.

A bugler had taken the cue from the adjutant and sounded "Boots and Saddles," the clear notes trilling across the parade ground and beyond to Soapsuds Row where the wives of non-coms and their children watched. The troopers mounted and brought their horses into line. Behind the post headquarters, across the Junction City–to–Manhattan coach road, stood the officers' wives, on the porches along Officers' Row. Leaning against the railings, they held white handkerchiefs to wave when the troops marched off.

In his living room, Capt. George D. Wallace had adjusted his plumed helmet before a mantel mirror. His command was K Troop, one of the two units that would march through Junction City. He and his men would parade in dress uniform with saber, showing off the Army spit and polish to best advantage. He tilted his head, and the light gleamed on the brass spread eagle at the front of his helmet and the yellow plume danced down to the level of his shoulders. He turned to his wife, who stood watching, and extended his arms like an actor accepting applause.

"Is this grand enough for wild Indians?"

From her sudden pained expression, he had known it was the wrong thing to say. He moved quickly to embrace her, speaking softly yet urgently into her ear.

"There's to be no worry here, and no frowning." And he promised to be home by Christmas just as all soldiers have promised since there have been soldiers. He moved back then, smiling, holding her slight shoulders in his hands. "I'll say good-bye to Otis."

She followed him into the bedroom, her eyes going to his saber chain clanking against the cased weapon, and she shuddered. Eleven years his junior, she looked much younger. Married eight years, they had taken their vows before her own Episcopal minister in St. Paul's Christ Church, and this would be the first time she had watched him ride off to possible combat. All the earlier campaigns had been finished before they met.

As Wallace leaned down to the playpen to lift his son, he was aware of his wife's anguish but knew of nothing he could do about it. His own excitement at the prospect of field duty had been impossible to hide, and he knew, too, that his eagerness had hurt her. He held the boy close. The quick fourteen-month-old hands went first to the shimmering plume and then to the chin strap. The child Otis looked at his father with eyes that were a reflection of the captain's own, cold blue. Man and boy made moist and unintelligible sounds, and the boy laughed. Wallace put the baby back into the playpen, and Otis sat down hard but scrambled up again, holding to the sides of the wooden contraption his mother had ordered from the Sears & Roebuck Company in Kansas City. He rattled it like a monkey in a cage and laughed again.

Back in the living room Wallace drew on his gauntlets, avoiding his wife's eyes.

"Remember when the cold comes, put newspaper under the door sills and keep a fire banked in the kitchen all the time," he said. "I suspect this whole thing is a tempest in a teapot, no matter what the newspapers are saying, and you're not to worry. Keep warm when you go outdoors . . ."

Then he looked at her face and reached to take her in his arms. He knew that the dress uniform buttons pressed hard against her breasts, but he held her tightly for a moment anyway. His saber hilt gouged her hip. He felt the wetness on her cheek when he kissed her. She had said almost nothing since his return to quarters half an hour ago to dress, and in fact very little during the last evening as they had packed his duffel after dancing at the officers' mess. Nor later in bed, when they were close, merely lying there and staring into the darkness and holding one another. She seemed somehow stunned at the thought that with the passing of the night he would be gone. Her shock transferred to him. There beside her in the dark, feeling her warmth and softness, he had for a few moments wanted desperately not

25

to be going with the regiment. But he had said nothing, because he could not trust himself to speak. Nor had she spoken. Now . . .

"Carrie, Carrie," he whispered. "My dear old Carrie."

Then he was away from her suddenly, not looking at her face because crying was not so common that he felt confident in handling it. He bounded across the veranda and down the steps, where his orderly waited, holding two grays. Not looking back at the window where he knew she was standing just visible behind the white lace curtains, he wheeled the horse and broke into a run across the road.

As he came around the post headquarters and onto the wide parade field, he saw the horses, men, and wagons coming into marching order, their lines extending for over half a mile across the flat ground. With the sight of the regiment, the familiar feel of the horse's movement beneath him, and the sounds of commands being shouted up and down the line, he could hardly restrain a shout of joy. He was swept up in the spirit of campaign and camaraderie.

Wallace pulled up near the regimental staff, everyone exchanging salutes. He could see his unit — K Troop — ready to move, drawn up in line and partly obscured by dust kicked up beneath the hooves of impatient horses. The anticipation had been electric, affecting mounts as well as men.

"Well, George," Colonel Forsyth had said, "I

don't know what the future might bring, but if we see real trouble, some of these people will bear watching."

"I know," Wallace said. "I've got only seven noncoms who've ever been under fire. A third of the rest are recruits." His voice had been sharp-edged, but the soft South Carolina drawl was still pronounced. "But don't worry, sir. They'll handle themselves smartly, you'll see."

His optimism had long been a fixture of the officers' mess. That and his even disposition. A sweet-tempered man, some called him, almost too gentle to be a soldier. Yet he had been mentioned in official reports for his valor in many fights. As he watched his troops, waiting for them to march past so he could join them, he was an imposing figure, almost six feet tall and slender as a lad only half his forty-one years.

"Do you really expect this thing will turn into a shootin'?" Wallace had asked.

"It's 1890 and the Indian wars are supposed to be over, I'll admit," Colonel Forsyth said. "But by God, when they send for the Seventh Cavalry, there's a fight brewing someplace."

"Just a show of force, perhaps . . ."

Gravel flying, one of the officers rode away from the staff and along the line of troops. At once shouted commands ran down the line, and guidon bearers reined their mounts into position. The troops started forward at a walk, in a ragged line that quickly adjusted itself, then wheeled into columns of four and came directly toward the waiting officers. Ahead of the troops, the regimental staff moved onto the road, going west toward Junction City, the colonel in the lead. He had a defiant air. This would be the first time he had ever commanded any unit taking the field against Indians. A few paces to the rear came the staff, and behind them, the colors. Then B and K troops, guidons popping. At the rear, the wagons pulled into position, drivers shouted, and lines snapped across horses' rumps.

There had been a final flurry of waving from the women along Officers' Row, and then they had stood immobile with hands raised, their faces wooden. The only sound was from the passing column, the beat of hooves, the squeak of leather, the rattle of chains. To those being left behind — the women — there were memories long put aside that now came flooding back, of other days and other farewells. To these women the issue had been a simple one: will my man be in the ranks when the regiment marches home again?

No such thought clouded the excitement of the townspeople. The horses made a great hollow clatter as they crossed the bridge, alerting the crowds ahead, who set up a shout and a cheer. The first riders came into view, plumes bobbing, saber cases flashing in the sun.

The cavalcade entered Main Street and was met with a rushing mob of small boys and yapping dogs. The horses' ears went back and their teeth showed, but they were held firm by each rider. Ladies began to flutter their flags and handkerchiefs, men waved their hats. At the depot, the band struck up "Garry Owen," and hearing the familiar notes the crowd cheered again. Standing in the street was the town constable, his badge of office gleaming from recent polish. As the regimental commander passed, the lawman raised his hand in salute, his face properly impassive and dignified.

Someone set off a string of firecrackers and the ladies screamed. Not to be outdone, the Kansas Pacific engineer blew his locomotive whistle in short blasts. Near the depot, after the column had turned off Main Street, was a group of ladies, demurely dressed yet with faces somehow pinker, lips somehow redder, than all the others along the way. They leaped and shouted and waved frantically once the regimental staff had ridden past and the soldiers were trooping by. A few of the soldiers winked, made faces, licked their lips elaborately, and wiggled their fingers on saddle pommels.

"Keep your eyes front, you slab-sided shit kickers," the K Troop first sergeant hissed from his position at the rear of the troop. "I'll have you bastards peelin' every potato between here and South Dakota if I catch you dustin' off them women from the pig ranch again."

One of the ladies in question pointed and screeched, waving a small ruffled parasol.

"It's First Sergeant Fitzpatrick. It's First Sergeant Fitzpatrick his own self."

The troopers struggled to keep their faces

29

straight, looking ahead as they heard Fitzpatrick behind them muttering curses around the massive bulge of chewing tobacco in his cheek. All the women in the little group were calling Fitzpatrick's name.

"Yoo-hoo. Oh Fitzie, we see you."

"Hello, first sergeant, you cute thing."

"Hey Fitz, when are you gonna come see us again?"

Then the constable started toward them, and they were quickly silent as they moved back from the street, grinning still.

Along the railroad siding the troop train was waiting. Immediately behind the engine were cattle cars where the horses would be loaded, ramps leading to each door. Then the flatcars for the wagons. Next, five passenger coaches for the soldiers, paint peeling from the sides. After that, a boxcar converted into a rolling kitchen with doors cut into either end. And, finally, a sleeping car for officers and a caboose.

As the column broke down and loading started, it was apparent pandemonium, yet horses began to disappear quickly up the ramps and the wagons were run onto the flats, nailed down, and the teams led off the loading dock to take their place in the cattle cars. Dismounted troops moved well back from the right-of-way after their horses were loaded, and noncommissioned officers marched them in platoons to waiting coaches. Once inside they threw off sidearms and heavy helmets. The sabers and plumed hats

country of the Ghost Dance people. It had been a journey of three days, first across Kansas to the switchyards of Atchison, north to Council Bluffs and across the Missouri, and on to Rushville, Nebraska. From there they had taken horse into South Dakota and to the Pine Ridge agency on the reservation of the Oglala Sioux, one of the bands of the Lakota.

Now 1st Sgt. Sean Fitzpatrick of K Troop wonders why it has not seemed a homecoming to him. He remembers with some fondness his service with the regiment when it was quartered at old Fort Lincoln, Dakota Territory, back in seventy-six. He had enjoyed the campaigning then, too, even the march out to Montana and the fight on Little Bighorn when he'd been assigned baggage train duty and thus had not been with his messmates when they all died on Custer Hill.

Of course, he thinks, Pine Ridge is a long way from Fort Lincoln, but this is still Dakota, still Sioux country. The only kind of Indian country there is left, even if it is only a few miles from the railroad. I saw a lot of duty in these high plains, scouting and patrolling.

But there is no sense of coming back to a place well remembered. There is only the feeling of something out of tune, something from a former time now out of place. Something dangerous because it is unknown.

3

CHICAGO INTER-OCEAN — An Indian scout at Pine Ridge named Buckskin Jack Russell has written a poem which he handed recently to our correspondent at the scene and we print it here for our readers:

I have tramped the Bad Lands o'er and o'er
    and camped on Wounded Knee;
But my heart grows faint at the warriors'
    paint,
And the lurid hue of the savage Sioux,
As they charge — in the *Omaha Bee*!

There are old buildings that were homes once, clustered together in slowly shrinking islands of resistance before the advance of a newer age, with walls close against each other as though taking comfort in being near their own kind. They have the look of defeat about them, yet there is a shabby defiance as well. Some were standing when the town was a dusty crossroads for cattle drovers and westering immigrants. Others were built during the railroad boom following the war, when the Union Pacific was laying track across the prairie toward the mountains. Then the packing plants and smelters and rolling mills began to stack up like slag heaps along the river, and the old homes were swallowed by the growing city.

There had been a certain splendor once in the two- and three-storied frame houses, glassed doors and sash-weight windows looking down through lattice porch railings to the street. In back, a stoop and usually a well curbing and some small buildings for chickens and perhaps a cow. Now the outbuildings are falling into ruin and the privies, too, though they are still used. Modern water closets have been installed in very few of these old houses. The houses stand in square simplicity, once-homes beside streets paved now with brick, and the paint peels off their sides and the rains running through their rusting screens etch brown watermarks beneath each window.

In the predawn, a boy approaches one of these old Omaha buildings, half-trotting along the cobbled roadway where the beer wagons and bread carts will soon be making their clatter. He runs onto the porch and pushes through a door bordered in stained glass. Like so many others, this house has been ruthlessly gutted inside, then patched and partitioned and hammered into as many separate apartments as a landlord living in Papillion or Bellevue or Council Bluffs could squeeze into it. But the entry hall and staircase are intact, and the boy starts up to the second floor, leaping and pulling himself up by the ban-

35

ister, taking two steps at a time.

In a room on the second floor, a man sits up in bed as the first footsteps send a thumping vibration up the stairwell. Wild-eyed and more sleeping than awake, he throws back the cover and leaps across the room, groping for the shiny Smith and Wesson pistol on the dry sink. From the floor he snatches trousers, the suspenders getting caught under one foot. He swears. Trying to pull on the trousers, he kicks over a half-empty whisky bottle left on the floor uncorked, and it skates across the polished hardwood leaving a slick of wetness and the smell of sour mash. Behind him, the woman in the bed sighs and rolls toward the wall, the blanket that covers her to the waist drawn tight across her massive hips.

The footsteps are in the hall now, at the door of the adjoining room. He is scrambling for his boots under the bed, the pistol still in one hand. There is a quick succession of knocks on the parlor door.

"Mr. Tapp? Mr. Quinton Tapp?"

The man straightens beside the bed and the boy calls again, his voice soft but sounding loud in the hall outside the parlor door. The woman moans and Quinton Tapp looks at her naked back, pale in the glow from the silica windows of the kerosene stove. Once more the boy calls his name, louder now, and he rises, drops the gun on the dry sink, and hurries to the parlor. He is still adjusting his twisted suspenders.

"Yeah? What is it?"

"Mr. Tapp?"

"Yeah, what the hell is it you want?"

"Mr. Goodall wants you right away," the boy says through the closed door. Quinton Tapp knows now it is a copyboy from the editorial staff of the *Omaha Bee*. "He seemed like he was in an awful rush."

Tapp unlocks the door and opens it a crack. The boy has a cap pulled down over his ears and a long muffler hanging from his neck. When he sees the man peering out into the dimly lighted hall, eyes puffy with sleep and sparse hair rumpled, the boy grins.

"Good mornin', Mr. Tapp."

"How'd you know where I was?"

"Mr. Goodall said you might be here if you wasn't at your own room," the boy says, and his grin grows broader.

"What's the matter? Is the town on fire?"

"No, sir. I think Mr. Goodall wants to send you to South Dakota."

"Where?"

"South Dakota. Where the Indian war is at. Where the Sioux are doin' all them dances and hootin' around."

"Damn! What time is it anyway?"

"About five, I reckon."

Quinton Tapp slams the door, leaving the boy grinning in the hall. He goes back to the bedroom, unhurried now. He looks at the woman who still lies facing the wall. He considers getting

37

back under the covers with her. She is fat and warm-looking. Like one of those lard grade sows at the stockyards, he thinks. Milk- and cornfed, as the saying goes, and all turned to white blubber. His own middle bulges a little, but he doesn't care. So long as there is no need to move too quickly, some fat is good. Besides, the ladies seem to enjoy well-fleshed men.

He lights a lamp and peers into the mirror over the dry sink, rubbing his chin with his fingertips. He has a full moustache but no beard. There is a porcelain pitcher and washbasin, and the water he pours for shaving is only moderately cold. In the dry sink drawer he finds brush, soap cup, and straight razor. As he whips the brush around in the cup, he is aware that the woman is awake now, turned facing him, the covers pulled up under her chin. He ignores her.

"Do you want me to fix your breakfast?" the woman says.

"No." The razor makes a scraping sound.

On the dry sink beside the washbasin are a glass bead necklace, a pair of matching earbobs, and a thick golden wedding band. Behind Tapp, across the room, is a wardrobe where he knows hang neatly pressed work clothes and one serge suit. Near the mirror, tacked to the wall, is a Union Pacific brakeman's schedule. All the names on the timetable are familiar to him — Omaha to Kearney to North Platte to Scott's Bluff to Cheyenne to Laramie. He thinks of the tracks, going across the Medicine Bow Mountains and down into Sweetwater Basin, to Rawlins and Bitter Creek. That's where the construction crews had been when he'd hired on the railroad twenty-two years before, a mere lad but a veteran of the battle of Pea Ridge where he'd been wounded and discharged before he'd ever touched a razor to his face. The Yankee Army had taught him horseshoeing, and he'd joined the UP as a blacksmith. People don't know how many horses and mules it takes to make a railroad run, he'd been told. He'd kept UP stock well shod until the road was finished in Utah in May of 1869 and a few years more besides.

Finished, he cleans the brush and razor but leaves the soapy water in the basin. The woman watches him pull on his shirt and coat. He crosses the room to the whisky bottle lying on its side against the wall and holds it up to the light, then quickly empties it, gasping with the harsh burn of the liquor. She says nothing nor does he, but he drops the bottle in a chair, blows out the lamp, and walks through the darkness to the parlor. As he and the boy start downstairs, the woman locks the door behind him and he hears her speak softly.

"You son of a bitch."

It has been a mild autumn in Nebraska, but the air has a bite and Quinton Tapp pulls his coat collar up around his ears. Ahead, they can hear cargo banging the decks of steamboats being readied for a run upriver to Sioux Falls or down to Kansas City. Switch engines in the Union

39

Pacific yards make their usual coughing racket, and there is a freight train going west, the whistle distant and mournful. They walk without speaking, aware of the city's wakening noises. They pass under hissing gaslights, for even though it is nearing the end of 1890 and there has been electricity in Omaha for some time, the old street lamps remain.

At the corner of Farnum and Seventh streets is the *Omaha Bee* building. Less than two years old, it stands high above the street. Windows from all seven stories blaze with light as they near it, and the boy looks up with delight.

"Ain't she a beauty?" he says. "They say she's the biggest newspaper building in the world."

Quinton Tapp grunts. I suspect you could get an argument on that in Chicago or New York, he thinks.

They can feel the ground trembling from the big Hoe rotary presses on the first floor. The sound the presses make is a high-pitched roar. The morning press run is almost finished. The first edition has been on the street for two hours. There is a newsboy in front of the *Bee* building shouting his usual spiel of violence and disaster and bloodshed, although mostly he shouts to an empty street. The home edition is being dropped on front steps across the city, and the mail edition is already loaded on railroad cars that will leave Omaha throughout the morning. Now the second street edition is coming off and will go into the library as the newspaper of record for this date, to a few select offices and banks, and into the streets in time for early crowds going to work, or travelers having breakfast at Harvey's near Union Station, or the night shifts coming from the smelters and UP work sheds, who stop for a bucket of beer and some hard pretzels in one of the German saloons along First Street. After that, the presses will be silent until noon, when the evening paper will start the cycle all over again.

"Mornin', Mr. Tapp," the *Bee* newsboy says, but Quinton Tapp pays no attention. He is looking at an old man in an ankle-length coat standing under a street lamp, a pile of newspapers at his feet. Tapp fishes two pennies from his pocket and hands them to the boy.

"Go buy one of those newspapers," he says.

The old man across the street makes a short bow and lifts his battered plug hat. He has been selling the *World-Herald* on the same corner for as long as Quinton Tapp has been in Omaha — eight years. When the massive structure of the *Bee* reared itself before him, he had not been intimidated but stood his ground, facing not only the hostility of brick and glass and stone each morning but the abuse of *Bee* newsboys as well.

Tapp knows it galls the editor of the *Bee*, Mr. Harold Goodall, to think that this old man selling competing newspapers is more an institution at the corner of Farnum and Seventh than is the *Bee* itself.

With the boy again, and his copy of the *World-Herald*, Tapp turns into the building. There is paper everywhere. In stacks and wadded clumps, in long streamers from the ticker-tape machine, in sheafs and reams and torn bits, on every level surface including the floor. The place is a blizzard of paper. With a wave, the boy disappears into the maze of cluttered desks, file cabinets, wastebaskets.

Across the far side of the large press room is a partition with three doors, one marked *Managing Editor*. Tapp pauses before it, removing his hat and brushing down his hair with one hand before knocking. As he waits, he thinks idly that the clattering of the typing machines is like Gatling guns heard a mile off. He had listened many times when he had been a blacksmith in Bismarck and the troops at nearby Fort Lincoln had practiced with the big machine guns. A good time, the Bismarck days, after he'd left the Union Pacific and after he'd bummed around the plains for a while, doing nothing. He had been in Bismarck when the old Seventh Cavalry — Custer's regiment — had marched out toward the Yellowstone country and the Little Bighorn . . .

"Come in," a voice calls, and he pushes open the door and walks into Harold Goodall's office.

"You want a chance to make something of yourself?" Goodall asks.

"I hadn't thought much about it."

"Sit down and think about it," the editor says.

The contrast between the two men is marked. Even slouched in the chair facing the editor's desk, Tapp appears massive. He is not tall, but thick, and as he slips off his overcoat, the size of his forearms and the slope of his shoulders testify to the muscle developed there from many years of smithing. His neck is thick and his jaw square, Sagging a little now under the ears. He is going bald, and the light shines across the top of his head, making the scalp gleam through thin strands of blond hair. What there is of the hair is straight and fine, almost like a woman's in texture. There is nothing else about him that is feminine. His face is like a slab of deeply lined sandstone, except that the lips under his sandy moustache are sensuous and full. His eyes are hazel and sometimes appear almost yellow.

Everything about Goodall is small, even pinched. The fat cigar clamped between his teeth looks as though it might tip him over onto his face at any moment, by its very weight. He has a fierce shock of black hair and a beard to match. He stalks back and forth behind his desk, pausing now and then at the big double window to stare out into Farnum Street, cursing the *World-Herald* and the old man who sells it below. On his walls are etchings of President Benjamin Harrison in profile, mostly from the pages of *Harper's Weekly*. There is also a large Union Pacific calendar, with a color print of an elk watching a passing loco-motive.

"Those Democrat bastards are claiming they've caught up to us," he is saying, the cigar smoke boiling out behind as he stalks back and forth. He expects no reply. "Caught us, by God.

The *World-Herald* will never sell as many papers as we do, and those bastards know it. And now, you're going to help us be sure of that."

Tapp knows that what the copyboy has told him is true. Goodall is sending him to South Dakota, to the Oglala Sioux reservation of Pine Ridge, or more correctly to the agency, that miserable little reservation town established by the Indian Bureau to house the agent and all the others who are supposed to civilize these savages. Pine Ridge. That's where the blood and thunder is — or may be. The stories from there give the *Bee* newsboys something to shout about on the street corners. It could be an uncomfortable assignment, he thinks. Could be dangerous, too. But it suits him fine. He's ready to get away, to get free of the city, away from the little man strutting before him. And away from a fat woman whose husband is out on the UP line four out of five nights a week. And the shabby little room he rents on Second Street, near the rail yards, and all those grimy people smelling of soot from the locomotives.

The little man pacing before him is responsible for his becoming a newspaper reporter. He had come to Omaha to get away from those dismal Dakota winters, and after a time in the smelters along the river, where the furnace heat had finally thawed him out, he had hired on as *Omaha Bee* smithy, keeping the horses and the heavy paper wagons in trim for hauling the huge rolls of newsprint up from the docks.

Then Goodall had offered him a composing room job, where he had done little more than empty the trays of type into the lead pot. Finally, he'd been brought into the city room and called a reporter. What he'd actually been was a body-guard for Goodall. Threats of bodily harm are a part of newspapering, and he had heen a hedge against such things. But now Goodall can no longer stand seeing a man doing so little to earn *Bee* money, so he is turning Quinton Tapp into a war correspondent. It has been twenty years since there was any war to correspond about, Tapp knows. But they're going to start calling me a war correspondent anyway, he thinks, along with Wilmot Cleaborn, the other *Bee* reporter already covering the Pine Ridge situation.

"Have you had breakfast?" Goodall asks.

"A swallow of sour mash whisky."

"Come on. We'll go out the back way. In my mood, if I had to walk past that old bastard across the street, I might murder him."

The Harvey's railroad restaurant is three blocks away, and as they walk along quickly in the growing light, Goodall explains what every-one knows by now is his position: that the Indian agent at Pine Ridge reservation, a man named Royer, is a fine Republican and much misunder-stood.

The only misunderstanding, Tapp thinks, is how little Royer knows about the Sioux or how to administer them. He is a man given the job of working with the red heathen because he has

45

been helpful in elections. Shaking out the Republican vote. But Tapp says none of this.

At Harvey's, Goodall pauses to speak with a number of friends, and Quinton Tapp finds a table and watches the Harvey girls in their black dresses with white aprons and high lace collars. The place is crowded and steamy, and it smells of frying ham and cinders from the locomotives that pass constantly only a few yards away. Only recently has there been talk of dining car service, but for now travelers eat only when passenger trains stop.

These Harvey girls have become a fixture all along the railroad line, and looking at them Tapp thinks they look much the same as the night women who appear at dusk each day in the riverfront saloons. Same dark dresses, same small waists, same lacy cuffs and long sleeves. Yet something about them speaks a different language to a man. Maybe it's the smell, he thinks. The Harvey girls are always soap-scented; the riverfront ladies smell of lilac water and London gin. He knows a great deal about that smell.

Goodall arrives at the table with the breakfast, puffing a new cigar and declining anything but black coffee. Quinton Tapp fills his plate with fried eggs, pork chops, biscuits, and gravy. He opens two biscuits and sets a chunk of butter between the halves. Harvey butter is never molded but placed on the tables fresh from the churn in great golden chunks with tiny beads of moisture still clinging to it.

"It always helps to know about the people and the things you are writing about," Goodall says. "In Pine Ridge you'll have a great advantage because you've been in the Army yourself."

"One helluva long time ago," Tapp says. Goodall continues as though there has been no interruption.

"You've been in the Dakotas. You've been around these damned Indians and learned some of their lingo."

"Not enough you could tell it," Tapp says, becoming more irritated as Goodall continues.

"A good reporter uses these advantages. He takes what he sees and adds what he knows, then uses his intuition to finish his story."

"You mean imagination, don't you, Mr. Goodall?"

The editor reaches across the table and touches Tapp's arm.

"So be it. Imagination, intuition, whatever. The good reporter knows how to . . ." Goodall pauses and looks down at the food left on Tapp's platter. ". . . salt and pepper the facts to make them alive. Do you understand, Quinton? To make them *alive*."

Tapp chews for a long time, looking into the little man's eyes. That's the only time I remember he's called me by my first name, he thinks.

"Our readers want to know what's behind the facts, and we'll give it to them. And forget all that swill about our agent at Pine Ridge, all that swill the *World-Herald* prints."

Here we go with "our agent" at Pine Ridge again, Tapp thinks. But Goodall's loyalty is steadfast to the agent who screamed for the Army at the first sign of trouble among his Sioux wards. A good man with Indians could have avoided calling for troops. Still, you can't be sure how much of it is "our agent's" fault. Even a good man can be ruined in the agent business because you can't ever tell what an Indian might do next. They don't think in any sensible way. Especially a Lakota Sioux.

"Wilmot Cleaborn's doing fine," Goodall says. "Been at Pine Ridge a few weeks now and doing fine. But we need two men there."

Wilmot Cleaborn is a tall, gaunt young man who had had even less reporting experience than Tapp when they sent him north. Now, Tapp thinks, he writes all that bullshit and sends it to us, and we put it in the *Bee* and send it all over the country on the Associated Press wire. Cleaborn's predictions of violence and death are printed as far away as New York. The skinny little bastard stutters so bad you can't understand a word he's saying half the time. And they're paying him twenty-five dollars a week!

It startles him when he realizes Goodall is talking about pay, and for a moment he thinks he might have spoken his thoughts aloud.

"You'll get a good raise. Top wages from now on. All expenses, of course, plus eighteen dollars a week."

Tapp scowls, but the editor is opening his railroad Waltham and rising. The pork chops were tough, and the conversation on top of that has given Tapp a bad case of indigestion. I hate that little bastard talking to me like I was a wet-faced kid, he thinks, and me about to give him a dozen good years.

Outside, they pause to pull their coats about their necks in the freshening morning wind. It is full daylight, clear and sunny. Goodall smiles as he sees a *Bee* newsboy nearby, shouting his headlines. Then he turns to Quinton Tapp and says the most important thing he has said all morning.

"One thing you've got to remember. Don't ever let the *World-Herald* get anything first or guess anything first."

All right, Tapp thinks, but it will cost you more than eighteen dollars a week salary! I may need a horse. Two blankets, woolen socks, red underwear, some tin mess gear. A heavy coat with split tail and a Russian hat with ear flaps. And a heavy pistol. The little Smith and Wesson is all right for whoring around, but for a painted buck with a hatchet in his hand, you need a big Colt. God, that mob of reporters on the reservations have got me thinking there's really a war going on. I may have more imagination than Old Man Goodall suspects. On the other hand, a man caught without a gun when he needs one is buried a fool, as the saying goes.

4

CHICAGO DAILY TRIBUNE — There are many things to show that empty stomachs as well as the Messiah craze have had something to do with the present Indian troubles. Is it not about time for the government to modify its Indian policy?

It is not yet winter cold, but the old man coughs and shivers, pulling the blanket tighter about his stooped shoulders. He has a face deeply lined and wrinkled, and the hands holding the blanket below a turkey-wattle neck are large-veined, the bones of the joints and wrists swollen and knobby under parchment skin. His hair is thinning and gray, parted in the middle and drawn down into rattail braids on either side. Although he is tall, he looks frail. He rides on the seat of the wagon awkwardly, his long body swaying as the wheels roll over the uneven road. Everything about him is old, except his eyes.

Beside him, a young man drives the team, his hands holding the lines loosely. He whispers constantly to the mules in a language known only to animals and those who talk with them. His name is Man Talks With Horses, but the People call him Talks. He is a handsome young man, his hair falling black and free across his shoulders, then down along the back of the white man's coat he wears. Sometimes the east wind blows the hair out before his face because they are traveling west along the Cheyenne River road and the sharp gusts since dawn have been coming from their backs. The old man looks at the young man and smiles. He recalls the days when the men had gone out to hunt and the wind blew the hair into their faces and it had felt good. But soon his smile leaves, swallowed by a frown. For now this fine young man in white man's clothes drives a white man's wagon along a white man's road, on the way to see a chief of the white man's soldiers. And the buffalo have been gone a long time.

"Are you cold, father?" the young man asks.

"Yes. *Lila osní.* Very cold," he says. "But it doesn't matter. Are the People coming?"

The young man looks back along the road, and there are the People, the Miniconjou, coming in wagons and on horses, and a few walking beside the wagons with the dogs. Directly behind the old man's wagon are three young men, with hard faces painted and with rifles, riding fine horses decorated with feathers. They are the bodyguard of this old man, who is a leader among his people and in these troubled times requires young men to protect him. At the head of the bodyguard is the man called Black Coyote. He is smoking a large cigarette, tobacco rolled in a piece of newspaper. He has trouble keeping it lit in the wind and must use the long, wooden white man's matches many times. Often they do not come to flame but make a blue smoke and smell bad. Because of this, Black Coyote has an unpleasant look on his face.

"The People are all coming behind, *até*," Talks says, calling the old man "father" as do most of the People.

Close behind the wagon is the daughter of the old man, on her spotted pony. She is a young woman much in Talks's thinking and he can still see her in his mind even after he has turned his eyes back to the mules. She rides straight and fine, a blanket hooded over her head. Her eyes are large and black, like a fawn's, yet bold as well. But now, Talks has other things to do than think of her with the budding breasts and full lips and a walk that reminds him of water flowing gently over the soft curves of rocks in a clear stream.

The old man is Big Foot and he is Miniconjou. Sometimes he is called Peacemaker among the other bands of the Sioux because he has shown himself to be a great speaker and a man of reason. He can make others understand the proper road to follow, even when there is anger and other leaders shout and would move blindly no matter how hurtful to the tribe. And sad as it is to admit, Big Foot knows there are many such chiefs.

His peacemaking role is one of the many things that bother him as they travel the Cheyenne River road toward a meeting with a soldier chief he has never seen before. A soldier chief named Sumner, one of those recently sent into the area because of the dancing. Sumner's messenger had come to Big Foot days before, explaining to Big Foot that he must bring the Miniconjou in for a talk, for a meeting. In one way, Big Foot thinks, it is an honor to have our own soldier chief sent to watch over us, especially sent with his own troops that were not here before the dance. But in another way, it is no honor at all. It means maybe the white chiefs far to the east do not trust the Miniconjou or their leader. It does not disturb him so very much that soldiers have arrived at the Brulé and Oglala reservations to the south. But they have been sent here as well, to Cheyenne River. To watch us as though we were children, he thinks. That is not much of an honor.

Big Foot has been a chief for a long time, and it makes him proud to think of it. These Sioux will not follow a man they do not trust. They are a very critical people. Yet, even with all the recent disagreement and dissension about what should be done, he still leads. Perhaps as many as four hundred follow him, counting children. Most of these people take his wisdom without question. But there are those who are young, with blood running in them hot as a rutting bull elk, and these are hard to control. They are too young to remember the terrible thing war can be against Blue Coats who fight even in winter when the ground is heavy with snow. They think it is brave to act arrogant at the mouths of cannons when any man of reason knows such things are not brave but foolish. They are his special burden, these young men of hot blood. But then, he thinks, it is the way of young men. They have forever been the burden of the old and wise, but the greatest treasure as well.

Big Foot is concerned that wisdom sometimes makes only some of the answers clear. When the messengers began coming with the news that a Messiah would appear if the People would follow His teachings and dance His dance, Big Foot had led his people into it. He had become a big dancer, a fanatic dancer. Then it became clear to him that the dancing made the white men nervous. Big Foot told his people.

"Be careful. Do not be arrogant. Do not give any appearance of violence or hatred; do not fire your guns or wave your knives as some of the brothers on reservations south of here have done."

Most of the People had done what he suggested. He had allowed them to continue dancing and continue believing the Messiah would come. But some of the young ones still kept their guns close by. What was worse, his old friend Hump, another chief of the Miniconjou, had turned coat. At first Hump had danced, too. But when the white soldier chief told him to stop, he not only stopped but went to Fort Bennett and became a Blue Coat scout, as he had been over a dozen summers ago when he worked with the Army in the high country beyond the Big Muddy, against the Nez Percé. Big Foot was sorry for the disunity such things caused. But he allowed his people to dance. He doubted he could stop them anyway. Because the white men were nervous and perhaps afraid, he even said it might be good to store up ammunition for the rifles.

"You can never tell," he had said to his people many times. "You can never tell what white men will do, even when you believe they are your friends. They do not think in our way."

The Pine Ridge Oglalas had asked for Big Foot's help in deciding whether to dance or not. But it had been time to go to Fort Bennett for monthly rations. So he had put off the decision to ride south to Pine Ridge, instead going to Fort Bennett. On the way, a number of Hunkpapas had joined him, coming from Standing Rock reservation where they said old Sitting Bull had been killed by Indian policemen.

The Sitting Bull people were fed, but later a few of them slipped away, stealing some of the Miniconjou horses as they went. It didn't matter, Big Foot told his people. They would go on to Fort Bennett for their rations.

Then the bad news came. Hump, who had danced with them when the Messiah preaching first started, was making threats at Fort Bennett against all who still danced. Big Foot had a council and turned back from Fort Bennett, riding west along Cheyenne River, back toward the

Miniconjou village on Deep Creek. And then a messenger came from this new soldier chief who had his men camped up the Cheyenne River, and the soldier chief whose name was Sumner asked for a talk with Big Foot. The old man was anxious to talk with this new soldier chief who had come into the country only since the white man became frightened from the dancing.

Now, moving toward that meeting, Big Foot becomes impatient with the slowness of his mules.

"I am going to ride ahead," he says to Talks. The young man looks at him and shakes his head because he does not like having this old chief riding away from his people and his bodyguards.

"We will be there soon, *até*," he says.

"No," Big Foot says. "I will ride ahead. I want a horse. I will take two of the Hunkpapas who were Sitting Bull's people and are still with us and one of my own young men, and I will go ahead."

"Take all your young men, *até*."

"No. I will take the Sitting Bull people and one of my young men. I do not want to give this soldier chief the wrong impression."

Talks stops the wagon and the People come up, and when they hear what Big Foot is planning, they protest. But he makes them be silent with his soft talking. One of the bodyguards brings a horse with an Army saddle, and they help the old man up. He selects two of the sitting Bull people and one of his own bodyguards and they ride off, moving fast toward the west, soon leaving the others behind.

"Why is he doing this foolish thing?" Black Coyote asks.

"He wants to speak with the *akícita,* the soldier chief Sumner," Talks says.

"Another Hair Mouth chief!"

"I think he wants to get permission to go to Pine Ridge and there help our brothers back to harmony."

"The Hair Mouths will not let him go. And besides, why would we go to Pine Ridge? The Blue Coats of the yellow hair are there now."

"They are not Custer's Blue Coats. Custer is dead, and that was a long time ago," Talks says.

"The white man calls them Custer's Blue Coats."

"It is only a way the white man talks. A way of speaking. Custer is dead a long time ago."

"We should go to Fort Bennett and get the annuities," Black Coyote says. "And if Hump wants to fight, we will give him all he wants."

Talks looks disdainfully at the young body-guard who rides proudly, his back stiff and his Winchester held boldly in the crook of his arm.

"And what of the women and children? Would you have them fight Hump's Army scouts, too?"

"There is too much talk of women and children and not enough of courage and taking what is ours. In the old warrior days —"

"In the old warrior days," Talks cuts in, "there

were chiefs who thought of the safety of women and children, else you would have been eaten by the wolves before you were big enough to smear that white man's stove polish on your face."

For an instant the young bodyguard's eyes flash, and he glares at Talks as though he were looking at a foreign thing. Then, spitting, he wheels his pony away from the wagon and rides back along the line of following people, making a small barking sound as he goes.

The young woman, close up beside the wagon now, watches. For a heartbeat, Talks looks into her face and feels his breath catch because of the beauty the hooded blanket cannot hide. She looks at him boldly, yet with the innocence of a girl, and his chest swells, making it difficult for him to speak.

"Your father is good, and no harm will come to him."

Her face does not change but he sees a smiling come into her eyes, a warmth that makes him forget the wind against his back. When she speaks to him, her words are like the notes from a cedar flute, soft but clear and unmistakable.

"I will ride near the wagon if you will allow it," she says. He makes no reply but whips the mules forward.

Talks thinks of the old man up ahead, looking for the white soldier chief. He wishes he were there. He does not know, nor do any of the People know, that already an order has been sent out to arrest Big Foot because it is thought he is dangerous and a menace to the peace, having been a leader of the dance among the Miniconjou when it first began in the season of leaves falling.

5

OMAHA BEE — A telegram has just reached our train stating that an engagement has been fought and 60 soldiers and Indians have been killed. There is apprehension of serious trouble in this part of the state. On making an inspection of the passengers on this train, it was found that 9 out of 10 have not one but two pistols of extra caliber.

Quinton Tapp stands at the Western Union cage in the Fremont, Elkhorn, and Missouri Railroad depot in Rushville, and he is very tired. In his mouth is the taste of brass. He credits this to lack of sleep, the night spent in a railroad coach car filled with kerosene smoke and cinders, and to a lesser degree to the generous swallows of sour mash whisky taken at frequent intervals as he rode across northern Nebraska. Waiting for the operator to finish taking an incoming message, he stares sullenly at the east windows. They are translucent, covered with many years' accumulation of dust and sticky coal smoke. The first rays of the sun on this cloudless and warm day make them glow.

He has already informed the man in the cage

who wears a green-visored cap that he represents the *Omaha Bee* and the Associated Press. The AP is the news service whose beginnings go back to pre–Civil War New York. Now a competitor, the United Press, has appeared. It has made a cutthroat business out of the whole thing, Tapp thinks, but it amuses him to think of Old Man Goodall squirming under the pressure.

"Sorry to keep you waiting, Mr. Tapp," the man in the green cap says. "This time of day, none of the other operators are in yet."

"I can see that."

"All this Indian trouble, Western Union's hired six extra men just to get the copy out for you newspaper folks."

"Yeah. Well, I got something here for Omaha. For the *Bee*."

"You bet. Mr. Cleaborn sends copy almost every day. He sends more than anybody else, I suppose. We sure know the *Bee*'s code by now." The operator laughs and shakes his head, and Tapp stares at him.

"Yeah. Well, write this down."

From a crumpled slip of paper he starts to read.

"Arrived Rushville 2:00 A.M. this morning and found the report set afloat last night that I sent by wire from Valentine in regard to a battle in which sixty soldiers and Indians were killed is false. The rumor was practically not worth a second thought. But trouble is expected any minute."

Tapp wads the paper and flings it toward a cuspidor. It bounds across the floor like a ball with flat sides and comes to rest among the moist splotches of tobacco juice and chewed cigar butts. As Tapp starts for the door, the operator calls after him.

"Mr. Tapp, did you hear that part about trouble from the Army?"

"Just send the goddamned thing," he mutters. Maybe now Old Man Goodall will understand that Quinton Tapp will not be beat by the *World-Herald* on anything, not even rumors.

As he steps onto the platform, he almost collides with a large black soldier. Two yellow stripes are on the soldier's sleeve, and in his forage cap he wears a blue jay's feather. Tapp steps back quickly and starts to say something but does not as the black man's eyes meet his squarely. They pass around each other without a word or even a sign of recognition that the other exists.

"Son of a bitch," Tapp mutters. He moves along the platform until the sun is full on him and takes off his hat. He stands with eyes closed, rubbing his head with one hand, rumpling the fine hair. He thinks about what the telegraph operator had said. "Did you hear that part about trouble from the Army?" Hell, he thinks. My first contact with that bunch is a big nigger almost runs over me and never says kiss my mule.

Well, the world is full of injustice, and nothing to be done about it, he thinks. Taking out his watch, he drops a business card onto the platform. He picks it up and reads it again for the tenth time, and he smiles. "Thelma Hanson Duncan, the *Chicago Herald*." Lady reporters! He'd met her on the train and she'd given him the card. She wants to write about the red heathen, but all she knows so far is what she's seen on the cover of *Wild West Weekly* dime novels. She signs her stories "The Widow" because her husband died two years ago, drowned trying to operate a two-man submarine in Lake Michigan. She's a good looker, he thinks, not one of these fluffy little birds, all feathers and fuss. Some heft on her. And a few years of experience.

I could never get anywhere with such a woman, he thinks. She was going to Rapid City to see General Miles before coming on to Pine Ridge. In tall cotton already just because she's a woman. The Army has accredited her as a correspondent on the reservation and found her accommodations at the agency boarding school. The damned Army, he thinks. They sure as hell haven't made any advance arrangements for me . . .

By the time he had lifted his hat to her as the train pulled into Rushville, he had been a little drunk. Throughout the trip he had moved back and forth from his seat to the water cooler at the end of the car, where he could sip from one of the bottles of sour mash he'd brought along from Omaha. Then on the station platform, he tipped his hat again in grand style and somewhat wobbly farewell as the train pulled out, the Widow watching him from the window. He'd almost fallen under the wheels bowing and scraping, and he'd seen she was laughing as the train pulled off. A woman of character, he'd thought at the time, and plenty of good solid heft.

She had boarded the train at Fremont, transferring from another line out of Chicago. Her handbag had a press ribbon on it, and he allowed her time to get settled in her seat before he introduced himself as a reporter, too. She told him she had been sent to cover the Pine Ridge affair for the *Chicago Herald*, although the paper already had two men doing the job.

"I had no idea they were sending ladies to cover wars," he'd said.

"I may be the very first," she had said, smiling and showing a fine set of teeth. She was wearing a brown suit with a long, full skirt and waist-length, high-lapel jacket open down the front to show a ruffled shirtwaist. There was a flare of lace at her throat. Her hat was a round, fur box with one large, curling feather at the top, arching along her back. She wore a cape, fur-lined and open. From the first, Quinton Tapp had been impressed with her bosom, which was of considerable size and pleasant proportion.

"I suppose you're another Nellie Bly."

"No, I have no intention of going 'round the world."

"Then you're just a war correspondent, like the rest of us?"

"Yes, but I wouldn't call it a war, would you?"

"No, but if your editor is like mine, it had better look like a war in your copy."

For a while they had made conversation about the weather and the country through which they were passing — but couldn't see in the darkness. He was telling her about Nebraska and the Dakotas when the conductor ran through the cars waving a note he'd just picked up from a way station as they passed. He was yelling about a big Indian fight, and Tapp cornered him in the vestibule long enough to read what was written on the paper. Back in his seat beside the lady reporter, he had taken out his pocket pad and a pencil and scribbled some notes for a dispatch to the *Bee* when they reached Valentine. She asked if she might see what he had written, and he was glad to show her. Besides, it was time for another trip to the water cooler.

When he returned, still feeling the heat of the sour mash along his gullet, she seemed a little upset about what he had written.

"Do you really intend sending this to be printed all over the country?"

"You heard the conductor."

"Oh, but surely you can't believe such a wild story. At least, shouldn't you wait and verify it from . . . well, some other source?"

"I'm here to write about what's takin' place, and what took place here was the conductor came along with a story about a big fight. I doubt there was any fight, but in case it's true, I'm not goin' to wait 'til mornin' and have somebody else write the story first."

She had looked at him a long time, then suddenly laughed.

"That's outrageous. The most outrageous thing I think I ever heard," she said. "I don't know whether to take you seriously or not."

"Well, ma'am, I think you've noticed by now, I'm not some young sprout come here to make practical jokes."

"And I suppose you've had wide experience with corresponding."

"More than most of these people they've sent out here." He bent toward her and smiled. "Present company not included, as the sayin' goes."

She seemed not to mind his whisky breath or the fact that he stared quite obviously at her bosom as he spoke. He had been encouraged to tell her of his experiences — at least a few of them acceptable to a lady — with the Union Pacific and later as a smithy in Bismarck. She was most interested in the interval, when he had been bumming around the high plains learning something about Indians.

"You seem to know something about these people," she had said. "Do you think they're about to break out of the reservations and start slaughtering everyone?"

"Ma'am, you can't ever tell what a Sioux will do. But I doubt it. They aren't goin' to leave regular rations, even if they do claim there isn't enough of it."

"Then why all this business about burning and

killing that will erupt at any moment?"

"Why, it's a little politics and a little business and a little excitement for the locals who think they might get scalped. It's a little game we're playin'. Pretty soon now all the Indians will come into the agencies calm and peaceful to get their meat and corn, and the whole thing will be forgotten."

"You really believe that?"

"Maybe a young buck or two would cause some trouble if you left him alone. Maybe some crazy old man, like they say Sitting Bull was, could stir it up. Of course, Sioux policemen killed him the other day. But even if you let 'em all alone, they'd steal a few cows maybe, burn a few haystacks, mostly their own people's. The old chiefs don't want any trouble. They remember how bad it is, fightin' the Army. Old chiefs have one helluva time controllin' their young bucks, though."

"Then it is serious?"

"It's mostly a big fake."

"If that's so, why doesn't the Army go away from here?"

"The farmers and ranchers would have their congressman's hide . . ."

"But why?"

"They're scared maybe it *might* be dangerous. If you figure it might be dangerous, you don't take any chances. You holler for help. Now take the Army. The brass and the troops too are more than willin' to do a little Indian war work. That's the reason they exist after all. Besides, with a few months in a peacetime barracks, a man would do most anything to get out — to find a change."

"Surely there's more to it than that . . ."

"And the politicians and the businessmen. They can see a lot of profit in having the troops around to buy stuff. There's a barrel of good federal money in Nebraska now from all this mobilizin' of forces. Those politicians and businessmen aren't goin' to make too much complaint about that. In fact, they'll encourage it."

"You make it all sound like selling bolt cloth," she'd said.

"That's a big part of it. The money comin' in. Wait 'til you see Rushville. Why, you can't buy a decent eighty-dollar horse for anything less than a hundred and sixty-five. If you're goin' to be a war correspondent, you got to learn that wars are a time for some people to feather their own nest, as the sayin' goes."

"So you make it look like a war, even when it isn't?"

"We do our share." He had laughed then. "It's the little game. Nothin' will come of it, except some of the locals will make a few dollars."

After that she had sat a long time, looking out into the dark, saying nothing.

She tried to come back to it a few times as they rode across Nebraska, but he was tired of it and turned the conversation away. He learned that she was from Wisconsin and had started writing ladies' news and cooking hints in a Milwaukee newspaper. Then she had gone to Chicago after her husband died. Tapp didn't exactly resent her as a reporter, yet he had an uneasy feeling about it.

After Valentine, where he had sent off his story of the big fight, she had opened her bag and showed him some of her clips. Her writing on Indians was mostly a mishmash of inaccurate information about traditions and customs of high plains tribes, probably gained mostly from lectures given by missionaries' wives returned to the city from the Wild West, where they had assisted husbands administering the Gospel according to whichever denomination they happened to represent. All he had said to the Widow was that he would have to teach her a great deal about Indians before she returned to Chicago.

"I shall take you seriously on that," she had said, but even as she said it, he seemed to sense that she would never ask him advice about anything.

And so they had arrived in Rushville, he dismounting with his duffel and making a spectacle of himself on the platform as she laughed from the window.

Now, with the sun well up and Rushville beginning to stir, Quinton Tapp has his business ahead. At the moment that involves getting accredited with the Army and buying what he thinks he needs for Pine Ridge. The first is easy enough. The horse and gun are a little harder. He browses along the railroad siding, where the

Army is buying horses. Troops are everywhere. A great many of them are black, and he sees their Ninth Cavalry insignia. Some of them are loading wagons with hay and sacks of grain, and off to one side he sees the white officer in charge and with him the black corporal who had run into him on the station platform. The man is riding a large, magnificent bay, and Tapp curses under his breath. "Goddamned nigger got a good horse."

Quinton Tapp finds a claybank mare that looks sturdy enough to carry his weight, and the livery man claims she's got a soft mouth. He pays $175, which doesn't include the saddle. He uses up a great deal of time getting his leather gear, then finds the biggest gunsmith shop in town.

"Folks been buyin' up handguns," the man says. "Handguns are their favorites. Easy to carry. Now for real shootin', one of these fine new repeatin' rifles is best."

"A handgun is accurate as I'll ever need," Tapp says. "I won't be shootin' at anyone unless he's close enough to smell. I'm not fixin' to haul around a long gun."

He finally decides on a good, used Smith and Wesson, a breakdown Russian model in .44 caliber. He buys a shoulder holster and a box of fifty rounds. He scratches the solid lead bullets with his fingernail. I'll gouge a hole in each one of these, he thinks, so if I ever do need to shoot anybody, they'll feel it.

There's a barber shop, and he waits in line for

one of the tubs in the clapboard shack in back. The water is carried by two Indian boys, down from the reservation on work permits. It is hot and soapy, and when he gets out of the tub and dries off, it is only moderately cold in the un-heated, wind-sprung building.

For a moment he recalls the monthly baths he had taken as a boy during those cold Missouri winters, staying in the tub of soap-slick water as long as possible because it was warmer than the air on the back stoop where such duties were performed. Usually, his baths were taken in water just used for laundering clothes, because they had to haul everything except drinking water from the creek two miles off. The drinking water came from a limestone cave spring and was so cold it hurt a boy's teeth to drink it, even in August. That cave spring water was sacred, and nobody ever thought of bathing in it, even if there had been enough of it. He had taken his first drink of hard liquor — some of his uncle's homemade lightning — behind the chicken coop when he was eleven years old and followed it with a swig of that cave spring water. The water had been so cold it almost killed the taste of the corn. Almost.

Quinton Tapp starts to pull on a pair of new wool socks when the door swings open and in walks 1st Sgt. Sean Fitzpatrick, face still cherry red from the barber's scalding towel. He stops and stares for a moment, his eyes popping.

"Dear God, is this who I think it is?" Fitz-patrick bellows.

"Well, I'm damned," Quinton Tapp says. He leaps up and extends his hand. The first sergeant laughs as he looks at the other man, standing naked.

"Dear God. Dear God. It's been a spell."

"I'm damned if it hasn't. A helluva spell."

Fitzpatrick observes that Quinton Tapp without clothes still looks more studhorse than man, and Tapp replies that the Irishman still looks like a beer keg painted red. They fall into familiar patterns quickly, these men who are of a feather and were friends at Bismarck years before. They are much alike physically. Tapp is the taller, but Fitzpatrick likely outweighs him by ten pounds. They banter and laugh as Fitzpatrick undresses for his bath. They begin to recall the times the young Irish corporal would come to the blacksmith shop, and they would get drunk on elderberry wine and beer and sleep it off in the horse stalls. The weekends of horse racing at Fort Lincoln. The noncommissioned officers' annual Christmas ball, when Tapp would almost get himself into a fight with every sergeant there who had a wife.

"You was always out for them Soapsuds Row lassies," Fitzpatrick yells, up to his neck in water.

"The Army's always afraid of losin' its own women."

Pulling on his coat, Quinton Tapp rushes out and within a few moments is back with cigars and a quart bottle of sour mash. They light up and start passing the bottle back and forth.

Fitzpatrick is sponging elaborately, almost lost in the suds.

"Remember the night we went to the pig ranch downriver from Fort Lincoln?"

"Squirrel Tooth Lola's?" Tapp asks.

"That's the one. You got into a fuss with them cotton goods drummers from St. Paul and kicked out the front of the piano."

"It wasn't near as bad as the time you hit that sergeant from D Troop in the face with a beef-steak in the Royal Café."

"Trouble was, half of D Troop was there too. They pert' near stomped us before we could get out that back door."

"Busted china cost me nearly sixty-five dollars. God, Fitz, there never has been times like that since."

They bring things up to date, and Fitzpatrick is astonished and then amused that Quinton Tapp is a bona fide newspaper reporter. He mentions his troop commander, and Tapp says he remembers Wallace well and always liked him, although the South Carolinian was a mite strait-laced. They recall other mutual acquaintances from the old Seventh. One dead in the Nez Percé war, another with neck broken when he fell off a train platform just outside of Grand Island, one dead from eating fried toadstools that he mistook for mushrooms.

"The last two," Fitzpatrick says, "would still be with us today exceptin' they was drunk at the time they made their mistake. I tell you, Quint, drinkin' has become a terrible plague in the Army."

He takes another long pull at the now half-empty bottle.

"Speakin' of plagues," Tapp says. "This place is swarmin' with nigger troops."

"The Ninth Cavalry? Oh, them's good sojurs. They got a helluva record against the red bellies. Don't undersell the Brunettes."

"Brunettes? Is that what you call 'em?"

"That's one name. They've been called others. Especially in such places as Texas and other southern states. Most of the tribes call 'em buffalo soldiers. And sometimes the Sioux call 'em *Wasieum Sapa*. The black white man."

"Well, I never had any use for any of 'em."

By the time Fitzpatrick is finished with his bath, the first bottle is empty and a second well started. They are a little drunk. Tapp tells about his meeting with the Widow. Fitzpatrick encourages him to elaborate on the structure of the female correspondent, something he has never seen before. Somehow the mistaken notion takes hold that she will be back soon at the railroad station, waiting for transportation to the agency.

"I got myself assigned to this ration detail because I wanted to come in here to town and find some fresh fruit for the boys," Fitzpatrick says. "But this town's picked clean as a tooth. But listen, listen now, Quint, we can sure as hell give this nice Widow of your'n a pleasant ride back to the agency in a ration wagon, and a damn fine escort of sojurs to protect her from the savages."

On the way to the station, they stop in the first saloon. There is a pool table in the rear, and they shoot a game of eight-ball, making a lot of noise and attracting a crowd of onlookers. Fitzpatrick wins when Tapp scratches on an eight-ball shot.

"I couldn't find no fresh fruit," Fitzpatrick is saying as they go down the sidewalk, staggering a little now. "So I bought two small kegs of brandy. A little thimbleful of that each day after patrol will perk the boys right up."

"Perk 'em right up. It'll perk 'em right up."

"Here's a saloon, by God, let's have a little drink first."

In this bar, Tapp shows the first sergeant his new pistol. Fitzpatrick aims it at a backbar row of glasses and snaps the trigger. Luckily, Tapp has forgotten to load it.

"I wouldn't give a goddamn for a Smith," Fitzpatrick says. "The balance is about as good as a claw hammer."

"Hell you say, hell you say. It's double action, and it loads faster than your Colt."

The bartender has seen the long-barreled gun and comes quickly, holding out his hands.

"Now men, don't do that, put that thing away."

"It ain't loaded," Tapp says, but he takes the pistol and slips it back under his arm into the shoulder holster. "And the trigger pull is sweet . . ."

"Hell, this here is the sidearm for you,"

Fitzpatrick says, yanking out his seven-and-a-half-inch-barrel, cavalry-model Colt. Looking into the cylinders, the bartender can see the brutal snouts of lead slugs.

"Now sergeant," he yells, "I'll have to call the law. That thing's loaded, I can see it's loaded."

For a moment Fitzpatrick glares at the barman, then holsters his pistol.

"You're a damned fussbudget, mister. I'm surprised you got any business at all."

They move on, wobbling visibly. Fitzpatrick tries to hold his arm across the taller man's shoulders and has trouble doing it. It keeps him off balance, and he looks like a river skiff with a list.

"Tell me about that white ruffled blouse again, Quint," he giggles. Each time he tells it, Tapp makes the Widow better-looking. By now she is in their minds as beautiful as Lillian Russell. The day is drawing to a close, and already the covered sidewalks are turning dark as they go into a domino parlor and bar. It is there that four soldiers from the ration detail find them almost two hours later. It takes a great deal of effort to get the two of them outside and onto one of the ration wagons. Soldiers, along with a number of Rushville citizens, stand around grinning.

Quinton Tapp somehow makes them understand that his horse and gear are still at the barber shop, and one of the soldiers goes for them. The two big men wallow around on a tarpaulin that covers a load of beef carcasses. Fitzpatrick is trying to sing, but Quinton Tapp is talking about the Widow again.

"We gotta go get the Widow, we gotta go get the Widow," he says.

Well out on the agency road north of Rushville, the wagons lurching along in the dark, Fitzpatrick demands to know where his brandy is hidden.

"Right there under the tarp," a soldier on the seat tells him.

After considerable thrashing about, the first sergeant has one of the small kegs between his legs. Using his heavy Colt pistol like a hammer, he smashes in the head of the keg, splashing brandy down his front. From an inside pocket he takes a tin collapsing cup and fumbles it open. Quinton Tapp sits up beside him, trying to see what's happening.

"You got a drink there, sergeant?" he mumbles. "You got a drink there?"

Fitzpatrick hands him the cup. The soldiers on the seat smell the liquor and whisper among themselves for a moment.

"Hey, sergeant, could we have a sip of that?"

"Hell yes, can't let the troops go dry, hell yes, hell yes."

It is almost dawn when they arrive at the agency. Tapp and the first sergeant are sleeping, each wedged between a bare half of beef, the covering tarp long since lost along the way. The horses have pulled the wagons home mostly on their own initiative. Before it was finished, the first keg had fallen off the wagon into the road, and the second had been bashed open. Now the empty barrel rolls gently back and forth under one of the driver's seats. All the soldiers are drunk, and two are singing an Old South tune they have picked up from the Ninth Cavalry.

> When I get to heaven, first thing I'll do,
> Grab me a horn and blow for Ole Blue.
> Then when I hear my houn' dog bark,
> I'll know he's treed a possum in Noah's
>   Ark.
> Go on Blue, go on Ole Blue . . .

None of them seems aware of the many fires burning along the northern horizon, fires set ablaze by parties unknown, destroying haystacks and cabins of reservation Sioux who have come into the agency. The light from them shows through the predawn darkness like flickers of red lightning beyond the ridges. As the singing soldiers drive past the gun positions along the agency perimeter, they fail to perceive, too, that the Gatling and Hotchkiss cannons are fully manned by artillery troops who watch the fires in the north. And none of them smiles as the ration detail passes along its noisy way.

PART TWO
THE AGENCY

6

OMAHA BEE — A report from Mandan says a man who knows Indians and speaks their language has said that every Indian on the Sioux reservations will soon be on the warpath. They have guns from Custer's troops which were never recovered by the government after the battle of the Little Big Horn in 1876.

The late afternoon sun slants across the hogbacks around Pine Ridge agency, creating an orange glow above the huge Indian encampment lying across the pine-dotted slopes that stretch away to the west and south. The tipis are not arranged in any formal way, as they once would have been, but are set down haphazardly in clusters and bunches, scattered like a fistful of peach stones cast in the sand. They are made of canvas, not hides, and are smoke-blackened at the tops, the stain leaking down into grays and yellows and dirty pinks along the sides.

"They look like old meerschaum pipes," says Capt. George Wallace, squinting his eyes against the sun as he looks out at the great camp. The nearest of the tipis stand within a few hundred yards of the agency buildings and are separated from them only by the tents of the Army. The farthest of them are below the ridgeline; all that can be seen are the splayed lodgepoles at the top, like rigid growths of Spanish bayonet.

It is the end of another mild December day, sunny and cloudless. The Signal Service weather station at Fort Sully, northeast of the agency on the Missouri River, will report that the maximum temperature has been sixty-two degrees. It is not that any longer, and the mercury is falling rapidly. Before midnight it will be freezing, but only enough to put a fine skim of ice on still water. There is a breeze out of the east.

Wallace and 1st Sgt. Sean Fitzpatrick ride along the outpost line as they do at this time every day while the rest of the soldiers in K Troop are grooming horses and cleaning equipment after another day of patrolling. The routine had begun in the first days after the Seventh Cavalry arrived at Pine Ridge over a week ago, after almost four days on the train from Kansas. Toward evening a staff meeting is always held for those officers not in the field with troops. Operational and logistical matters are discussed, as well as new developments in the problem of the Indian Ghost Dancers. During these meetings, held in a large Sibley tent being used as a regimental headquarters, Fitzpatrick readies two horses. By the time the officers are finished, he waits with the saddled mounts. Then with Wallace he makes a circuit of the agency, and each uses this time to inform or instruct the other. Neither is sure which is which, nor does it matter to either of them. They have been together a long time and have formed the best kind of officer-noncom relationship, comfortable and candid, but with considerable formality and mutual respect. It is like the affinity between a gentleman's gentleman and his employer, warmth and even affection, yet with each understanding full well his exact boundaries and limitations.

On this day there is a reserve between them, the consequence of harsh words leveled at the first sergeant after the drunken arrival from Rushville with the ration wagons. As they pause in their ride to look into part of the Indian encampment, Wallace is telling his first sergeant everything he needs to know for the next day's activities.

"I will be patrolling tomorrow," he says. "For detail, five men at ration breakdown in the morning at the agency commissary. At four A.M. No mounts but have them carry sidearms. Have Cookie at the commissary by mid-afternoon to claim our share of the fresh meat."

They ride on slowly, reining their horses close together. Wallace continues his instructions.

"Warn the men to stay in our camp at night. The Sioux policemen are spooky about soldiers wandering around that Indian school and the villages."

"There are a lot of young girls at that school, so I guess the police ought to be spooky about sojurs."

"They arrested half a dozen men from the infantry units last night poking around that place, and it made the agent and the general unhappy. Keep the men in camp unless they want to go to the trader's store. Then they go in threes and with an NCO."

"That's what we been doin', cap'n. I tell 'em every day, stay away from these Indian women. Even if some buck tries to sell you a good piece of a squaw, stay away."

Wallace stops and looks at Fitzpatrick, frowning.

"Has somebody tried to do that?"

"No, but just in case they do."

They pass slowly along the line of infantry pickets and the positions where Gatling and Hotchkiss guns are trained on the camps. Wallace has heard that some of the old chiefs have complained about the guns being pointed at their people, and he can understand their concern. Still, General Brooke has to cover the approaches to the agency in case things turn wicked. As they ride by, each sentry and gunner stands to attention and salutes. Wallace speaks to each one.

"Evenin', soldier."

And they generally smile and respond with his name because he has already become known to these men of the infantry and artillery who had never seen him before coming to Pine Ridge. Wallace takes such a thing for granted, but Fitzpatrick is proud that his Old Man is well known among these gravel kickers and ball polishers.

With the day's end, there is considerable movement in the Indian camps. The women are out of the tipis, making the evening meal. They wear long dresses cut and sewn in the old way but made from blanket cloth or trade store cotton. They bend over cook pots suspended above small fires from lodgepole frames.

There are dogs in the camp but not so many as Wallace has seen before. They sit motionless near the fires, their eyes following each bit of food lifted by the women. They make no commotion, he thinks, because somehow they are aware that only by remaining unnoticed do they increase their own chance of staying out of the cook pot.

With the dogs are the children, in their ill-fitting, cast-off clothing. They are motionless, too, watching the women. When food is not cooking, Wallace has seen them running and playing, sometimes in the streets of the agency, all unaware of the tension of the older ones, with whites around them and Hotchkiss cannons pointing at their tipis.

"Remember that day on the Little Bighorn, cap'n," Fitzpatrick is saying, "when the red bastards started to move their village? There wasn't nary a wagon amongst 'em. Now it looks like a rig for every squaw."

"And their horses are mostly old nags," Wallace says. In those days, he thinks, a man was measured in the fine hunters and war ponies he owned. How is he measured now? All the horses he can see are head down, listless-looking, nuzzling the barren ground where the last sprig of grass has long since disappeared.

He sees only a few men but watches them closely. They appear at the tipi entrances and hesitate to come out, looking about as though half expecting to see some mounted enemy bearing down on the camp. They move cautiously and stand in little groups talking with heads close together. They wear white man's clothes but no longer cut out the seat of the pants as they once did. Wallace wonders if that is a sign of civilization or simply resignation. Standing in the wind, they look like crumpled newspapers.

They are almost a different people now, he thinks, from those we fought in the seventies. There is little here to admire. Once they were fierce and proud, feathers in their hair and paint on their faces, shouting their defiance. He had seen them. At the Little Bighorn and afterward. He had admired them for their dash and courage and was always glad for the sake of his troopers that they had not even a rudimentary knowledge of organization and discipline. And often, it was a mutual thing, the admiration between these people and some of the old soldiers of his and other regiments. The respect that one fighting man always gives another, though sometimes grudgingly.

Watching them now in the paper-wrinkled

trousers that are not cut out at the seat moves him in a strange way. It somehow hurts him that these old warriors are like foxes caught in a wire cage, furtive and nervous.

Yet at the edge of his compassion stands the duty he must and will perform if an issue is forced by either side. If a mistake is made, he thinks, or a movement misinterpreted that could cause these paper-wrinkled people to boil up in fury, I would not hesitate to lay waste their men and horses.

He pushes that phrase around inside his head. Lay waste. To lay waste. Is that biblical, or Roman? Perhaps Tartar. It keeps popping into his mind. To lay waste. It makes him shudder.

"They look peaceful enough now, don't they, cap'n?" Fitzpatrick says, seeming to sense his commander's mood.

"If they stay that way until the others come in from the Stronghold . . ."

"When I heard about old Sitting Bull getting shot dead up north, I figured it might set things off here."

"Maybe it was too far away," Wallace says. "Maybe it has something to do with the fact that Sitting Bull was killed by Sioux policemen instead of white men. I don't know why they took it so calmly. But maybe these people have so much trouble of their own, they can't be bothered with somebody else's."

"Just so long as they don't bust out and slaughter us with our own rifles the newspapers are sayin' they picked up at Little Bighorn."

They both laugh. It is a joke among the veterans of the Seventh, this talk of weapons salvaged by the Sioux in 1876. They all hope that if trouble comes, it is true. What worries them are not the old single-shot Springfields the Seventh used that day in Montana, but the repeating rifles they have seen in the Indian camps — the Winchesters and Marlins. The joke has little humor in it because the Seventh is still armed with single-shot Springfield rifles.

"About the Stronghold," Wallace says, "we're told that General Brooke thinks the dancers may come in soon, that they're discouraged and bickering amongst themselves. Pass the word. We may be seeing a great many of them shortly, and we don't want one of our fresh young men to start shootin'."

"Yes, sir, I been cautionin' these new recruits ever' day pert' near, and some of 'em are comin' along good. But most are still just recruits, and nothin' short of ten years' active service is gonna change it."

The Stronghold is in the Badlands to the north of the agency, beyond White River and not far from the mouth of Wounded Knee Creek. It is there the fanatics of the southern Sioux reservations have gathered to dance. Brig. Gen. John Brooke, who commands the field forces at Pine Ridge, has been sending friendly Sioux and mixed bloods to persuade the dancers to come in and forget their rituals and be fed on good

88

Army beef. The orders from Gen. Nelson Miles's headquarters have been passed along to the lowest rank: there is to be no provocation by troops, and there will be no campaign of assault into the Stronghold.

"All them newspapers are bellyachin' about the Army sittin' on its arse and not chargin' into the Badlands after the red devils," Fitzpatrick says. "And some of the troops are beginnin' to grumble, too. Them as can read especially. I never liked troopers who could read."

"No matter what the newspapers say," Wallace says, "you tell the men we're here to keep everything in place as well as we can. If we can just keep any more wild-eyed ones out of the Stronghold, and keep the ones in there arguing amongst themselves until they get hungry enough, we may get out of this place without having to kill a mess of these poor devils. You tell 'em that."

"I'll tell 'em, sir. But it'd do me good to put a few shots into some of these smart-aleck young bucks."

"If it's Sioux blood you want, some of it was spilled this afternoon in that camp down there." Wallace points toward the southern group of tipis. "One of the big Ghost Dance medicine men got an urge to prove his power. Put on his Ghost Shirt . . ."

"That's agin the law."

"I know that. But he put it on just the same, so he could be admired by his followers; then he proceeds to show how effective it is. Took a

Colt's pistol and shot at himself. Almost blew one leg off, and the muzzle blast set fire to the shirt."

Fitzpatrick sways back in the saddle, laughing so hard he has to grab the pommel to keep from falling. The people in the southernmost camp are the ones who came in only recently. They are still Ghost Dancers, but they are afraid of the soldiers. Brooke has given instructions that they must be carefully watched.

"Them stupid, dumb heathens," Fitzpatrick gasps. "How the hell did such a people ever learn to be so good with horses and weapons?"

They ride on, coming abreast of Red Cloud's house, a two-story frame building the government has built for the old chief. During warm weather he stays in a tipi in the front yard. All the friendly Indians who have come into the agency are camped from Red Cloud's house back toward the western horizon.

"There's the old politician himself," Wallace says. "Red Cloud."

"Yes, sir. I seen him goin' into the Episcopal church with some of General Brooke's staff officers Sunday. I thought he was supposed to be a Catholic."

"He is. They say he keeps a picture of the Virgin on the wall above his bed."

"Damned red heathen is what he is," Fitzpatrick says.

The chief of the Oglalas is sitting on the steps of his house, and there is a smile on his face. His old eyes, puffy and almost closed, have an Asiatic slant. Looking at him, Wallace is somehow reminded of drawings he has seen of the Mongol horsemen of Genghis Khan. He wears a white cotton shirt and a vest open down the front, white man's trousers, and Sioux moccasins. Behind him stand four young braves, with beaded jackets, feathers in their hair, and quill decorations on their leggings. There are good trade store blankets around their waists, which hide weapons. They are the old man's bodyguard, and nobody has made any fuss over the weapons because Red Cloud is considered a force for peace.

"Look at those dude bastards," Fitzpatrick says. "I'll wager they got more firepower under them blankets than a section of Gatlin' guns."

"So long as they keep it under the blankets," Wallace says.

Red Cloud is engaged in conversation with a number of white men standing before him. One, taller than the rest and wearing a squirrel-skin long coat and a Scotch Glengarry cap, speaks with great animation, leaning close to the old chief's face. He has a black box in his hand, a Kodak camera.

"That's the *Bee* man," Wallace says. "Cleaborn."

"Yeah, the skinny bastard," Fitzpatrick says. "He's one of the ones been hangin' around the telegraph shack, listenin' to our messages."

"If he does that, he's not alone," Wallace says.

91

"They've already run one reporter off the reservation who was always listening in. And he said some pretty harsh things about the agent, too."

"From what I've seen of Indian agents, they mostly need bad things said about 'em," Fitzpatrick says. Like all the Old Army people, the first sergeant is suspicious of anything civilian, most especially anything concerning the Indian Bureau and its employees, who in normal times are charged with the administration of Indian affairs. Wallace concedes in the case of the Pine Ridge agent that Fitzpatrick is right.

"They had a telephone here before we came," Wallace says. "But the thing never worked too well and you had to shout into it, so they changed to a key. Now, at least, if anyone wants to eavesdrop, he's got to know Morse."

"A telephone is it? God, these new doodads they come up with, and none of 'em worth a lively shit."

From the Army encampment to their backs, a bugle begins to blow "Beans." They turn their horses toward the Seventh Cavalry area, where the horse picket lines and the troop tents are aligned in even rows, guidons marking each troop. At the ends of the rows are the cook tents and tent flies.

"Let's see what wonders old Cookie has done for us tonight," Fitzpatrick says.

Directly to the east of their own tents are the buildings of the agency, the last of the sun now making the roofs pink with light. Above the large buildings that house the commissary and the boarding school and the police barracks rise the steeples of two churches — Episcopal and Presbyterian — and the water tank.

As they draw up to the troop mess, Wallace remains mounted as his troops form the chow line. Some nod to him as they hold their tin mess gear, and a few smile at the famous Wallace profile. His soldiers say he has the most glorious nose in the Army. It thrusts out between wide-set eyes above a modest moustache that is sandy like his short hair. His chin recedes sharply from a large mouth, and his neck is long and slender. This often gives him the appearance of a turkey gobbler as he sits motionless in the saddle, only his head moving with the great beak and the long neck. But if he is not beautiful, he is at least admired by fellow officers and nearly worshipped by his men. They say he can crack the whip but that he is fair. And with Indians he has always seemed to have a special understanding.

A letter this day has informed him that little Otis has chicken pox, and he finds himself wishing he were back at Fort Riley. The daily routine at Pine Ridge has been insufferable. The exhilaration of field duty had worn off before fairly begun.

He isn't sure he wants to wait eight years for retirement. The future looks to be a long series of cloistered military posts where peacetime troops must be drilled and drilled and drilled because there is nothing else to do with them. If they could find a town with a good position . . .

Certainly it would be unlikely in his native South Carolina. When he had been posted to the Seventh Cavalry in 1872, the regiment had been on occupation duty in the South. His own unit was in South Carolina. The United States attorney general said it was there to protect civil servants in the discharge of their duties. The local people had other words for it.

He knew how it felt to be called Blue Belly, and by his own people in the streets of Columbia. The Palmetto State was the land of proud people, and they were quick to point out that she had been among the original thirteen. Her sons had fought and died in the Revolution, some on native soil. Quick to point out as well that South Carolina had been the first to defy northern manufacturers and politicians in the day of old Andy Jackson to bring on the nullification crisis of 1832. And first again in leaving the Union.

Then Blue Belly bayonets in their streets, an army of occupation that stayed for a dozen years to strip them of every bit of liberty and freedom the abolitionists had been preaching about for so long.

The bitterness that dies so hard in South Carolina has washed over him. He loves his uniform and is loyal to all its causes. Yet he knows, too, that those people of Carolina can say with some justification that loyalty belongs to the elder sovereignty. And there had been a Carolina since King Charles I had so named it over a century and a half before the United States was born.

More and more as he grows older, he thinks of the mountains of the South Carolina border country where he lived as a boy. Of York County, where King's Mountain was fought, and not far from Cowpens. Sometimes his family would visit Charlotte, just across the line in the Old North State, or sometimes they would send him to relatives who lived in the Tidewater country along that wonderful coast north of where the Pee Dee River came down to the sea, the long golden beaches and the gulls sweeping low.

It is all long past now, but still the faces and voices of that pineywoods country come to his mind.

"Feedin' all complete, cap'n," Fitzpatrick says, standing at his stirrup. "Any further instructions for the night, sir?"

"Fitz, have you ever tasted thick black coffee sweetened with a lump of good Swiss chocolate?" Wallace asks.

Fitzpatrick stares at him a moment, his jaw stilled on the cud of tobacco in his cheek.

"No, sir, I ain't. You wasn't expectin' anything like that in a troop mess, was you?"

"I was just thinking. My grandmother used to make coffee like that." Wallace yanks at his hat and starts to pull his mount around toward the horse picket lines. His face sets in hard lines as his mind comes back to Pine Ridge and the moment. "No. There's nothing more, sergeant. Nothing more."

7

THE ROCKY MOUNTAIN NEWS — Our courier from along the Cheyenne River rode into Rapid City with the story that there has been a clash and two officers with 50 soldiers have been killed but the copper faces were routed. The report is credited. (The editors include for the benefit of our readers a sketch of the RMN correspondent riding for his life with this report, redskin bullets flying all around him.)

Some of the old men in the cabin are unhappy and resentful when Talks stands up to speak. They are like old men everywhere. They do not enjoy having a young man speak to them as an equal. But they say nothing. They know Talks is powerful. Big Foot loves this young man like a son, and he has been to the white man's school yet has somehow not become a white man. They sit silently, and only their eyes tell of displeasure when Talks speaks and looks at them with level gaze.

The council is in the cabin of Big Foot, who lies on a pallet in one corner. He has a coughing sickness and holds a blanket up high over his thin body. He had talked with soldier chief Sumner on the river road as the Miniconjous came up. Big Foot had agreed to take his people on to Camp Cheyenne. Many of Sumner's soldiers had been there as they talked, and when the Miniconjous rode up, it was a dangerous time. The young men of Big Foot acted angry and made no effort to hide their weapons. The soldiers were nervous. But with Sumner and Big Foot talking softly, the entire party started on west along the river, toward Camp Cheyenne, the soldiers riding alongside the People.

Then the People made a thing happen. They had stopped at their old camp on Deep Creek, the place they had started from toward Fort Bennett a few days earlier. There had been another conference, and Big Foot had promised to bring his people on to Camp Cheyenne later. Sumner and his soldiers had gone on, and the People had stayed at Deep Creek. But this defiance of the Blue Coats is not enough for the old medicine man Yellow Bird, the biggest Ghost Dancer of them all, and he has asked for a talk among the leaders of the People. To convince Big Foot that the People should slip completely away from Cheyenne River and go south. To the Stronghold, where the Miniconjous can join the Brulés and the Oglalas who dance there, awaiting the coming of the Messiah.

"Some of you have forgotten what has happened," Talks begins. His voice is strong, and he looks directly at Yellow Bird. "The soldier chief

Sumner was told by his chief to take the People to Camp Cheyenne. And we agreed to go. We were riding there when we came to our village."

"This place is our home," Yellow Bird says. Talks is looking somewhere else now, and he continues as though he has not heard.

"You forgot there is no food here. You forgot there is little here to burn. You forgot that now with Hump at our agency at Fort Bennett and angry with us, we will not go there and cause trouble, and the only other place there is food to give our children is at the Blue Coats' camp at Camp Cheyenne."

"We were cold on that day, and these are our cabins," Yellow Bird says. He sits hunched over, his legs folded under him. Nobody in the band wears his Ghost Shirt as much as Yellow Bird, and he has it on now.

"Yes. It is our home," Talks says. "And this is what Big Foot told the soldier chief Sumner. And Big Foot said that we have done nothing wrong and have hurt no one. And so we should be allowed to stay here. The soldier chief Sumner could have been very angry. He could have turned his Blue Coats on us. But he did not. He saw the wisdom of what Big Foot said. He allowed our people to remain here at Deep Creek."

"Sumner is a Hair Mouth," Yellow Bird says, and others grunt in agreement. "You cannot change that. He is a Hair Mouth. And you cannot trust a Hair Mouth any more than you can trust the weather in the season of new leaves coming."

But Talks goes on, his voice soft but somehow strong, too.

"The soldier chief Sumner said the people of Sitting Bull who were still with us must return to the north. But Big Foot said they were hungry and needed shelter. The soldier chief Sumner saw the wisdom of this, too, and let them stay. Now, even though Big Foot has promised the soldier chief Sumner that he will come to Camp Cheyenne tomorrow and bring the Sitting Bull people with him, you say we must slip away and go to the Badlands. To the Stronghold. You say that our chief must break his word."

"Yes," a number of them say.

"Yes," says Yellow Bird. "And besides, how can Big Foot keep that promise anyway? Last night all of those Sitting Bull people disappeared."

Listening, Big Foot coughs from time to time, but he does not join in the discussion. His eyes, bright with the fever, dart back and forth from one man to the next, and as Talks speaks, the old man watches the young man closely.

"It is a part of the promise he cannot keep," Talks says. "But it is something those Sitting Bull people did. It is not something Big Foot has done."

"I say leave here, now, while the good weather lasts," Yellow Bird says. "I do not like sleeping so near the Blue Coats."

"The soldier chief Sumner has allowed us to stay here, even though his own chief has told him to bring us to Camp Cheyenne. He has his soldiers there, away from us, because Big Foot has promised to go in and talk with him. If he bore us ill will, why has he not come down on our camp in the night with his soldiers and wagon guns? Why has he not attacked us while we sleep? If he bore us ill will, why did he butcher those cattle the first night our people and his soldiers came together? Have you forgotten the feast of that night? Even our angry young men forgot their anger because there was food, good meat for the first time in many sleeps, and the children were not hungry. Have you forgotten that? You should not forget it. I saw some of you gnawing on rib bones far into the night."

Everyone laughs except Yellow Bird.

"If you trust a Hair Mouth, you are a fool," he says. "If you trust a Hair Mouth, you will die. I will never trust any of them. I will trust the Messiah and this." He slaps the front of his Ghost Shirt. A few murmur in agreement, but others are silent and look troubled. Finally, the chief rises on his pallet to speak. They all turn toward him and wait as he coughs, his body shaking. He pulls the blanket up around his face.

"Yes. I have promised to go in," he says, "and talk with the soldier chief Sumner. And I must do it. It is the honorable thing."

"What is there of honor left?" Yellow Bird says bitterly. "Since we have seen the Hair Mouths coming from the east, there has been no honor on either side. And besides, what does the white man know of the People's honor?"

"He may know nothing of it, but we know," Big Foot says, and smiles sadly. "Honor is what a man lives with inside himself, and it doesn't matter if others do not understand it. If we run away, the soldiers will be angry. It is better to have them watching us and giving us meat when we need it and patting our children on the head, than to have them coming after us with guns."

"I do not like them patting our children on the head, and I do not like them giving our children sweet candies."

"Yes, but you like their meat," Big Foot says softly.

"I want to be rid of them. And in the spring . . ." Yellow Bird stops, realizing that everyone is looking at him now and that he has perhaps offended Big Foot by speaking so harshly. "I am uneasy with the Hair Mouths so close to our camp," he mutters and then looks down at the floor as though searching there for the tracks of mice.

"We must not bring soldiers down on us, angry and with their guns up," Talks says.

"The soldier chief Sumner is good," Big Foot says. "He allowed us to stay —"

A fit of coughing brings it to a close, and the old chief sags down on his pallet like a limp rag.

"Many of our people have this sickness now," Talks says. "Even in this good weather, travel would be hard. And winter will come soon."

They continue to talk, except that Yellow Bird still studies the floor for the tracks of those mice, and he says nothing more, The cabin is a large one, largest in the settlement because it is the chief's. There is an iron stove, but Big Foot has refused a fire on this day to conserve precious wood. The sun is warm on the cabin roof and inside there is no chill. Big Foot is drowsy in the warmth. He listens to the talk around him with only a small part of his mind because he already knows now what everyone will say. Beside his pallet is a cup of honey the Army has given him, and he dips a peeled willow stick into it, then sucks on the stick.

It is not the kind of honey he remembers as a boy, when he could track bees to their den tree. Once, when the People were fighting the Crow for the Black Hills, he had almost been captured by a Crow war party just as he was about to climb a bee tree. That would have been expensive honey, he thinks. He had hidden and let the warriors pass. And got the honey after all. This white man's honey that soldier chief Sumner has given him is weak and very sweet, and good, too. But not so good as the old-time honey from trees in the Black Hills. That honey had a bitter kick to it, a wild taste, and the comb was waxy and good for chewing. This white man's honey has comb like paper, and it disappears inside his mouth like morning vapor even before he has a chance to chew it with the few good teeth he has left.

Why is there always trouble around me? he thinks. Why did I do things in my younger days that made the white man angry? Now I am old and have grave responsibilities, but the white man remembers what I did when I was young and distrusts me. If a man does a bad thing in the eyes of a white man, no matter how many good things he might do, it is always the bad things they remember. I am old now and will do as they ask. Except I will not wear a blue soldier suit and talk against my own people and threaten to shoot them, as Hump does. Well, he thinks, we have some strange men among us, too. But none so strange as the white man.

"And now, the council is finished," Talks is saying. "The old one is tired."

"The council is finished," Black Coyote says, and he stands at the door, waiting for the others to file out. Many of them grumble as they go, like women. But as they pass the old chief, they nod to him. Big Foot nods to each one in turn. Then everyone is gone except Black Coyote and Talks, and the young men squat beside the old man as the women come back into the cabin. They flutter around, one pulling the blanket up under Big Foot's chin, one tucking it around his ankles, one looking into his honey cup to see if it is empty. They all scold softly, as though the old man has done something childish, but he ignores them. He chews slowly on his honey stick.

Among the women is Big Foot's daughter, and her eyes go quickly to Talks. Big Foot smiles inside as he sees the young man trying to avoid her gaze, trying to pretend she is not there making his blood rise. It is a good sign, Big Foot thinks. It means the People will go on because men are still men, and women are still women. But there is more than that. Here is his daughter, coming to her womanhood, and the young man already like a son.

The women move away and Black Coyote leans closer to Big Foot.

"Father," he says, "I will do as you say always, but those soldiers being so close make me nervous."

"They stay in their camp. We stay in ours."

"I do not trust any of these Hair Mouths."

"It is not good to be watched," Big Foot says, and his voice is weak. "But perhaps it is good to have them close by to give us meat. The snow is not here yet, but our corn from the planting is already gone."

"Planting." Black Coyote spits. "White man's work, grubbing in the earth like a gopher."

"For the season of *waniyetu,* the time of snows falling, the only meat we will get is from the white man," Talks says. "One way or another, and the soldiers give us more than the agent does."

"I have killed more than one of the white man's cattle on Cherry Creek, near its source," Black Coyote says.

"Don't tell me of it," the old man says, raising

a hand from beneath the blanket. "That is white man's country, and you are always going there to kill cattle. Don't tell me of it!"

Black Coyote's mouth turns up. He squats there with the rifle cradled across his thighs, and his fingers stroke it as another man would stroke a woman.

"In the old days," Black Coyote says softly, "we would go to the Hair Mouth's camp when his eyes were still filled with sleep and drive him from our land."

"What do you know of old days?" Talks says. "You have been listening to dream words again."

"I was a warrior once," Big Foot says. "But my sons, those times are gone forever unless the Messiah comes."

"Will He come, father?" Black Coyote asks. For a long while the old man looks at the proud young man, but he says nothing. Talks, who has never believed the Messiah will come, says nothing either. Black Coyote finally rises and leaves, but for a few more moments Talks stays beside the old chief. Big Foot's eyes are closed.

"That is a fine young man," he says, his eyes still closed. "But a little hard to restrain. Like a good war pony. A will of his own and a mouth of iron. He is a real stallion, that boy."

"Yes, and he'll make trouble if he can," Talks says. "He is arrogant and bull-headed."

The old man's eyes open and he smiles.

"These are not bad qualities sometimes."

"If they are flavored with some good sense,

which is a thing Black Coyote does not have. He loves that rifle too much. Did you see him making love to it?"

"A man must have some relationship with his weapons. He must know what they are and what they can do."

"Yes. And this young man of yours, he thinks his weapon can do much more than it can ever do. It can only cause trouble."

"He is *sunk blóka!* A stallion," Big Foot says, smiling, and his eyes are closed again. Soon, with Talks still squatting there, he is asleep.

Talks rises from beside his sleeping chief. Going to the door he motions to the oldest of the women, the one most trusted by the chief, the wife longest in his lodge and bed. Outside the cabin, Talks turns to this woman.

"Does he truly trust the white soldier chief Sumner?"

Everyone knows that late at night, even now when they are both old, Big Foot lies with this woman and he tells her many things. He shows his heart to her, even though she is half Assiniboin.

"Does he trust that white man?"

"Yes," the woman says. "He told me the white soldier chief Sumner is a good man and will do nothing to harm us. That's what he told me."

Talks looks into her eyes a moment and then turns away. She is untroubled, yet in his belly is a stone of uneasiness. He knows the white man's way. Sumner may be a good man, but he has a chief, too, who tells him what to do. What about this chief of Sumner's? Is he good too? Even if he is, how does he know about the Cheyenne River people, the Miniconjou? He is probably far away. Who is to say what such a chief might tell Sumner to do? And once told, Sumner must do it.

Talks would be more troubled still except he does not know that the white chief Miles thinks Big Foot and his people are at this very moment the prisoners of Sumner. And in order to make that mistaken thought by his chief a reality, the good man Sumner will soon set his troops in motion toward the Big Foot camp.

And worst of all, despite the brave talk of honor, the old man lying in the cabin under the blanket knows he will not go in to talk with the soldier chief Sumner tomorrow. And perhaps this is honor, too, that will prevent it. But for whatever reason it will not happen, and Big Foot will never again look on the face of any white soldier chief except those who are far south of Cheyenne River on Pine Ridge reservation. The men of Custer's old regiment.

8

CHICAGO INTER-OCEAN — A fight seems imminent. The hostiles are at the Stronghold in the Bad Lands about 50 miles northwest of the Pine Ridge agency. General Brooke has excercised the greatest patience and seems determined to exhaust every peaceful means of settlement before the attack is made.

Quinton Tapp's first day at Pine Ridge agency is almost his last. His head aching and his stomach sour from the brandy, his is no temper to take with any sort of grace the bellowing Captain Wallace makes over the drunken arrival of the ration detail. It was just a nice little drunk, he thinks, but from the way that skinny bastard carries on, you'd think I'd tried to start a mutiny. Trying to find quarters at the crowded agency does nothing to sooth his disposition. He finally finds a place in the shed behind the Episcopal church, where two other correspondents are already bunking, sleeping on quilt pallets on the dirt floor.

From the start, he despises the pack of reporters who mill around trying to invent stories, trying to find some way to pass time until something really happens. Their antics and practical jokes do not amuse him. And these damned Sioux policemen, snooping around and glaring at him, as though they were afraid he might try to steal the agency hogs. It is all more than enough to make him decide to saddle the mare and ride back into Rushville and to hell with Goodall and the *Omaha Bee* and the whole silly Indian war that is no war at all.

He waits until dark, and rides past the Indian police sentinels and the Army line toward the south, grumbling to himself about the injustice and stupidity of asking a white man to go onto an agency where whisky is very nearly nonexistent and the prospect of a woman out of the question. Then in the growing darkness beside the road, he sees her.

At first, it is only a blur of color in the ditch. He reins in the mare and dismounts and finds her, sprawled limp and smelling of liquor, wearing a long, bright yellow dress and mumbling something about Valentine. He lifts her face and sees she is a young woman, and his feeling hands discover well-formed breasts and firm thighs.

"By God," he says. "Where'd you come from, honey?"

He pulls her to her feet and she hangs against him. She must be cold as hell in nothing but this thin dress, he thinks. She says Valentine again, and then for the first time seems aware that she is being held up.

"You take me?" she mumbles. "You take me Valentine?"

"Well, we'll see about that," Tapp says. He pulls her off the road and into a small stand of pine timber. She is limp in his arms and he lays her on the ground and pulls at the dress, "We'll just see about that, honey," he says, and lowers himself over her. She lies beneath him like a discarded saddle blanket, lifeless, as though unconscious. But Tapp can see her eyes open and staring at him as his face moves above hers.

Afterward, he takes the blanket roll from his saddle and spreads it over her and lies next to her, waiting for the throbbing to leave his head. It's always like that, he thinks. When you do it after a big drunk, it's always a head popper, but good just the same. Maybe the best. Later, he moves over her again. This time she responds to him, the way a woman is supposed to.

It's always better when the woman enjoys it, too, he thinks, or anyway makes a pretense of enjoying it. His head is better and it is warm under the blanket and he lies there with her, listening to the mare a few feet off pulling at the tough grass. Soon, he sleeps deeply and the woman slips from beneath the blanket and away into the darkness, leaving him alone.

Quinton Tapp dreams, as he has been doing for some time now, an irritating thing to him once awake because he is sure it is a sign of advancing age. Always now, his dreams are of things past, of his Union Pacific days, reliving the best memories again in his sleep. Tonight, after the satisfaction of the woman, he dreams of the buffalo hunts. Often, he would leave his forge and go with the professional hunters who went after meat for the construction gangs. They would shoot a dozen or more buffalo and before loading the skinned carcasses onto wagons would cut out the tongues of a few young cows and roast them over a low fire. Now, twenty years later, he dreams of it, then awakens, hungry and almost able to smell the Army bacon cooking in the Seventh Cavalry camps back at the agency.

But it is still dark, and he sleeps again, unaware or uncaring that the woman has slipped away. And he dreams again, of wintering with the Cheyenne, of spring in the Big Horn Mountains, where the high meadow water is so clear it looks black and fish in them easy to take with the bare hands.

Across the agency at the Seventh Cavalry camp Fitzpatrick lies listening to the wind and the solid tread of the sentry passing along the rows of tents. He is disturbed by the presentiment of trouble that began back in Fort Riley. It worries him even though he has never been a man to play hunches or to trust anyone who did.

Fitzpatrick is an old soldier, in terms of service and of years. Born to a large and destitute Irish family in 1841, at age eleven he had been shipped steerage to the United States in search of an uncle supposed to be a member of the Boston police force. Whom he never found. By the time

President Lincoln called for volunteers, Fitzpatrick had already been a private soldier of cavalry for two years. In a wartime Army he had learned to ride and fight, and to read and write as well. But by then he had forgotten any reason for communicating with his family in the Old Country, so he never had. His only loyalty became, and continues to be, to the Army and the colors of his regiment.

He has never married nor thought seriously about it. His friends are those who have soldiered with him or men closely associated with the Army, and there have been only a few of each. Like most good soldiers, he does not hate the enemies his country selects for him, but rather admires their combative qualities and fights them with considerable relish. Whether white rebel or red heathen. Like most good soldiers, too, he knows how to respect the weapons of his opponents while at the same time complaining bitterly about the quality of his own.

Chevrons on his arms have come and gone, his pugnacious nature remarkable enough in combat to elevate him, the same characteristic in barracks to reduce him again for fist fighting. But his has never been the sin of insubordination, and although he has served under officers he despised, his larger concern for the discipline of the organization has made him obedient. Of course he would never put such things into words himself.

Fitzpatrick is in fact the perfect soldier. He

enjoys discipline and the rigid structure of regulations and protocol. He is tough, resilient, adaptable, and possessed of a shrewd intelligence that makes him capable of accepting orders or giving them, both without passion and as the case demands. He is, in short, the kind of soldier that makes all successful armies successful. Half predator, half automaton. And he has that strange sentimentality of hardened veterans that brings tears to their eyes when the colors pass in review.

Fitzpatrick has felt the bite of lead. He has frozen and been blinded by sweat and dust. He has eaten horse and mule and a few things better left unmentioned. He has cursed stupid orders and officers. He has campaigned in boots that fell apart in the first rain. Always underpaid and sometimes not paid at all, he has served with weapons that would not fire, with horses that would not run. Yet he has known the warm comfort of the barracks room and felt the surge of pride and camaraderie in moments of deadly peril. He has never for a moment since he was seventeen years old suspected that anything in civil life could compare with the Army.

He is also soldier enough to know that when the opportunity for sleep presents itself, one must sleep. And so, before his mind is well started toward more worry about the future here on this Indian reservation, by force of will, he sleeps.

9

RAPID CITY BLACK HILLS UNION —
So far, the only lives lost in the campaign
are the two soldiers who failing to obtain
whiskey, drank alcohol with fatal results. If
Deadwood could only transplant a few of her
saloons into the Bad Lands proper, it might
prove more effective than the military.

———————————⟶»•«⟵———————————

There is a hotel on the Pine Ridge reservation.
The correspondents call it the Hotel de Finley
because it is operated by James Finley and his
wife. It is a one-story affair with three guest
rooms. Like all the rest of the lumber used in
the construction of the agency, the whitewashed
tongue-in-groove siding was hauled by wagons
from the railroad in Rushville. The only thing
pretentious about it is the picket fence around a
plot of ground in front where Finley has tried
during the warm weather to grow lawn grass, an
effort watched by the agency Indians with considerable amusement. Or perhaps contempt.

There is a wide front stoop where the newspaper reporters gather late in the afternoons when
the weather is warm enough. They loiter there,
exchanging rumors and making jokes until Mrs.

Finley lays down the evening meal of roast pork and sweet potatoes or a good Irish stew with biscuits. The front of the building is completely taken up with a combination lobby-parlor-dining room. Since the Indian troubles began in November and the Army moved in, there have been pallets from time to time for the overflow guests not fortunate enough to have obtained a space in one of the three beds. Guest rooms are toward the rear, one bed to each. There is a large kitchen and finally the Finley living quarters with its own back stoop. A storage shed has been converted for a family dining room, complete with Persian rug, sideboard, and Mrs. Finley's foot-pumped organ, shipped all the way from Boston and only slightly out of tune in the higher registers.

In this room the Finleys entertain. On what has become almost nightly occasions, four or five people are asked to dine, from among those overrunning the agency. The income of a hotel keeper in such a desolate and dreary place as a Sioux reservation could never support lavish goings-on. But now, for the first time, with newspapermen willing to pay double for the privilege of sharing a bed with a total stranger and for sitting at a table prepared by female hands, there is such an abundance of funds that Mrs. Finley can have all the guests she wants. And hire Indian girls to wait her personal table besides.

But though they provide the cash for these affairs, the correspondents are never the beneficiaries. The Finleys are aware that many of the reporters and certain Army officers who often are invited do not agree on how the story of the Ghost Dance and its subsequent problems should be told. So correspondents seldom see the rear rooms of the Hotel de Finley. "Besides," Mrs. Finley says, "they're like hogs at a trough. Even those who are obviously gentlemen at home, once here in this godforsaken place they're like hogs at the trough."

But there are exceptions, and on this cold evening a few days short of Christmas a correspondent has been invited. When she heard that a bona fide female reporter was on the way, Mrs. Finley had insisted that the newspaper lady's first meal at Pine Ridge be as civilized as possible and taken, obviously, at her own table at the Hotel de Finley. There hardly had been time for Mrs. Duncan to settle her things at the room in the boarding school before Mr. Finley himself appeared to proffer invitation and escort.

Now reporter and innkeeper walk along the agency road, past the offices and council house on one side, a trader's store and the Episcopal church on the other. There are enough lights from various windows to make for easy going, and across the wide front of the commissary a number of lanterns hang from the eaves of the porch. They see Indian policemen at the door to the agency doctor's office, a Sioux educated in the East and come home to doctor his people. Behind the church, they can see the dim outline of a Hotchkiss gun and soldiers around it.

"I'd forgotten it's Sunday night," Mrs. Duncan says as the brass bell in the church steeple begins to clang. "But why is the church so dark, and where are the people?"

"There's a curfew now, ma'am," Finley explains. "General Brooke doesn't want a lot of the Indians roaming around the agency after dark. But the preacher rings his bell every Sunday and Wednesday night anyway, just to remind the Christian Indians that they're still Christians, I reckon."

"Then there are some Christians among them?"

"A considerable number," Finley says, and chuckles. "And when the Army came in here, it was amazing how many more wanted to get the white man's religion all of a sudden."

Inside the hotel there is a moment of confusion as Mrs. Duncan removes her large hat and apologizes for being late. Mrs. Finley begins the introductions, moving along beside the larger woman, holding her arm lightly.

"Col. James Forsyth, commanding officer of the famous Seventh Cavalry."

The colonel bends stiffly at the waist, taking Mrs. Duncan's hand. His goatee thrusts forward like a hairy flower bed trowel.

"Your servant, madam."

"Lt. Harriman Martingale, of General Brooke's staff."

"General Brooke sends his regrets, ma'am," the young officer says, bowing and taking Mrs.

Duncan's hand. He lifts her fingers to his lips, and his gallantry surprises everyone but Mrs. Duncan, who quite apparently enjoys it. "General Brooke invites you to be kind enough to visit his headquarters tomorrow at your convenience."

"You may tell your general that I certainly shall."

"The general doesn't care for newspaper correspondents, but I'm sure in your case he'll change his mind," Mrs. Finley says, and giggles. "And this tall gentleman is Capt. George Wallace, who has a troop in Colonel Forsyth's regiment."

"It's a pleasure, ma'am."

"Do I detect a southern drawl?"

"South Carolina, ma'am." He touches her hand for only a moment.

"Even now it does seem strange to have gentlemen from the South serving in the Union Army," Mrs. Duncan says.

"There are a number of us." His voice takes on a sharp note, and Mrs. Finley laughs and touches Captain Wallace's arm.

"Let's have dinner," she says. "Mrs. Duncan, you between the colonel and Captain Wallace."

Mrs. Duncan is large but well proportioned, a fact Captain Wallace can hardly help noticing as he holds her chair. She settles her ample derriere, and as her legs slide under the table, Wallace can hear the rustle of taffeta and silk petticoats. He finds himself wondering how many she is wearing.

"Chicken and dumplings," Finley says as two Indian girls bring in heavy china bowls, steaming and releasing into the room the oily smell of chicken broth and dough. After the girls leave, the talk turns to Indians and everyone looks at Forsyth.

"I suspect Lieutenant Martingale could tell you more than I," he says. "Working in General Brooke's headquarters."

"Everyone believes the end is near," the young officer says, leaning across the table toward Mrs. Duncan. "General Brooke has been having talks with the leaders of those dancers in the Stronghold. Most of them are anxious to come in and have it over with."

"Getting damned hungry, I'd suppose," Finley says.

"Well, they've stolen a few cattle here and there. From the agency herd and from farms of the Indian people on the reservation who've come in here —"

"You say General Brooke has been talking with the leaders of the Ghost Dance?" Mrs. Duncan asks. "From what I'd read, I had supposed it was dangerous to go near the place where they dance."

"General Brooke doesn't go to the Stronghold himself," Martingale says. "He sends people who can get in. Half-blood interpreters or friendly Sioux here at the agency. They act as intermediaries."

"What about that gang of Miniconjou cutthroats in the north? Old Big Foot," Finley says.

"We have information from General Miles that these people are in custody. Under the surveillance of Colonel Sumner's regiment and soon to be taken to one of the forts. I'm not at liberty to say when or to which fort."

"General Miles's plan has from the start been to keep the various Sioux bands in place," Forsyth says. "Keep them from roaming around and coming into contact with one another and creating excitement. Keep them all in place. That's what our troops are doing now, keeping them in place."

"Everyone is confident that General Miles's plan has succeeded admirably," the lieutenant says.

"I'm glad for him," Mrs. Duncan says. "What a burden he carries. You should see the crank mail he's received. Such strange proposals for solving the problems here. And the women who write him. Some want him hanged and others want to marry him."

"General Brooke has received a number of these letters, too," Martingale says. "It's amazing that some of our citizens can be as bloodthirsty as Turks."

"We've got our very own crazy woman right here at the agency," Mrs. Finley says. "You'll likely see her at the boarding school, Mrs. Duncan. What's her name, James?"

"Sickles. Emma Sickles."

"She claims she can speak Lakota, but she

can't. She claims she can settle all this business here, if they'd only let her go and talk with the chiefs in the Badlands," Mrs. Finley says.

"She's the same woman who started the rumor about cannibals. And it's only a fool story. She claimed that during one of the Ghost Dances, an Indian went into a trance and returned to life as a buffalo. He still looked like a man, but he was really a buffalo. And everyone who didn't eat a bite of him would turn into a dog."

"Besides that, the lady dips snuff," Finley says. "There's nothing smells worse than an old lady who dips snuff."

"James, that's a terrible thing to say at the table. But I suppose if that story is true about the man coming back to life as a buffalo, they've likely already roasted him and eaten him." Mrs. Finley bursts into laughter.

"The worst part of that story," says Wallace, "is that it was printed in some eastern newspaper. It was a great disservice to anyone trying to understand and control these people, as well as to the Sioux themselves."

"You continue to surprise me, captain," Mrs. Duncan says. "I would never have supposed an Army officer would have such an attitude. About offending the Indians, I mean."

"It's not a matter of offending them. It's a matter of trying to make our people understand them."

"Do you understand them, captain?"

"No white man can ever understand them.

But even so, even though they can't understand us either, there has to be some effort at both ends to reach a reasonable settlement of differences."

"Actually, they are so primitive," Mrs. Finley says. "I really wouldn't be surprised if there *was* cannibalism among them."

"There has been some of it amongst our own antecedents, I suspect, if one were to go back far enough," Wallace says.

The remark seems to offend Mrs. Finley. For the first time during the meal, she is not smiling.

"That is fascinating," Mrs. Duncan says. "Not what you say, captain, but that you say it." She leans closer to Wallace and gazes into his eyes.

Finley changes the subject, turning to Colonel Forsyth, who has been sitting through the entire exchange contemplating his uniform buttons.

"I understand that your men are taking up a collection to buy presents for the children in the camps."

"Yes," the colonel says. "It's something the officers and men seem to enjoy. Being away from home at Christmastime, they . . . it has become a tradition, I suppose you'd call it."

"You southerners shoot off firecrackers at Christmastime, I understand, captain," Mrs. Duncan says.

"My wife and I have not been in the South for many years, Mrs. Duncan," Wallace says. His referring to his wife instead of addressing the question directly is obvious to them all, and the reason for it is not lost on Mrs. Duncan. She starts to say something but changes her mind and turns to Colonel Forsyth. Lieutenant Martingale once more speaks to the subject of General Miles's genius. The coffee comes and tastes heavily of chicory. At one point Mrs. Duncan mentions wigwams and is corrected somewhat abruptly by Mrs. Finley.

"They are tipis, my dear."

"Heavens, I had no idea there was any difference." Mrs. Duncan laughs. "I certainly have a lot to learn, don't I?"

It is over then, and Wallace and Martingale offer to escort Mrs. Duncan back to the school. The wind is blowing in gusts from the north, and they move quickly with it at their backs, collars up. The agency road is darker now, but there are still a few policemen standing under the eaves, blankets around them. Holding Wallace's arm as they walk, Mrs. Duncan moves close alongside him and he can feel her hips moving. When he speaks, she looks at him with an intensity that is difficult to disregard.

"I suspect they are always there," she says.

"Yes," Wallace replies. "They are always there."

At the boarding school there is a light in the hall, and two of the matrons are waiting for the Widow so that they can lock the door after she comes in. At the entrance is another Indian policeman, watching them. Before going inside, Mrs. Duncan pauses and looks toward the south where there are still some small fires in the Indian encampment.

"That's the camp of the hostiles," Wallace says.

"Hostiles? My heavens, so close?"

"It's only a name for them. They came in late and stopped dancing reluctantly, but they were afraid to stay away. General Brooke has us watching them closely."

"Soon the Badlands dancers will be here, too," Martingale says once more. "Even they are not so hostile after all."

"You sound a little disappointed, lieutenant," Mrs. Duncan laughs. "Well, gentlemen, thank you for bringing me to my door."

And for a moment she stands there beside them, but her hand is on Wallace's arm and he can feel the gentle pressure of her fingers.

"Unfortunately, gentlemen, I can't ask you in for a cup of tea," she says, but Wallace is aware that she is talking only to him. Abruptly, with a smile, she moves back and offers her hand to both of them, like a man. She turns, and Wallace watches her go up the steps and through the open door.

The lieutenant salutes and turns back along the road, but Wallace continues to stand, looking toward the Indian camp. He takes a cigar from his pocket and the Indian policeman moves over with a match, strikes it, and cups it in his hand. Wallace lights the stogie and offers another to the policeman, but the man shakes his head. He wears a wide-brimmed black hat. In the flare of the match, Wallace had seen the broad, flat face and the black eyes.

"Thank you for the match."

"My name is Red Hawk."

"Thank you for the match, Red Hawk," Wallace says.

"I was a boy at the fight on the Greasy Grass."

Wallace puffs on the cigar, and each time the tip of it glows, he can see its reflection in the man's eyes under the dark hat, but he cannot see the expression on the Indian's face.

"At the Little Bighorn?"

"Yes."

"You fought there?"

"Yes. As a boy. I fought on the bluffs above the river."

After a moment Wallace says, "I fought there, too. On the bluffs above the river."

"Yes. I know. I remember you there that day."

For a long time Wallace says nothing. He has a quick little chill at the base of his spine.

"You can remember well. That was a long time ago."

"Yes."

Wallace can think of nothing else to say, and he turns away and walks toward the Seventh Cavalry camp. He can feel the Indian policeman watching him. The cold spot at the base of his spine runs up his back and he shivers, not from the cold wind alone.

10

THE CHICAGO NEWS — An A. C. Hopkins, who went out to Pine Ridge posing as the white Messiah among the Sioux and was arrested and escorted off the reservation by Indian policemen, was for years a traveling salesman of Burley & Tyrell Crockery, Lake Street, Chicago. His old boss said that Hopkins was as good a man as ever went on the road. He came from Iowa originally.

They move about on the hard-packed ground, their shoes kicking up a fine dust, and in the harsh sunlight they squint. Before them is the agency office where the Army has made its headquarters. They are waiting to see the lady correspondent, who at present is inside, closeted with the commanding officer, General Brooke. She has been in the building almost an hour, and they make jokes about what the general is doing in there so long. Quinton Tapp leans against the weathered building and chews an unlighted cigar. Squatting beside him is Chandler Akins of Chadron. These two have a great deal in common. They are the oldest of the correspondents at Pine Ridge, they have both served in the Army, both been blacksmiths, and both have bummed around the high plains at various times in their lives. Akins runs a newspaper in Nebraska, but he has come to Pine Ridge to report the Indian war for the *New York Herald.*

"The war's gone to hell," one reporter says. "When they start sendin' women to write about it."

"Oh, it's gone to hell, all right," another says. "Even Cleaborn can't dig up any blood and thunder to sell to the greenhorns."

"Look at that," Quinton Tapp says softly to Akins. "That greenhorn talkin' about greenhorns. He wouldn't even know how to clean a horse's pecker."

One of the correspondents turns to Tapp with a grin and asks how *do* you clean a horse's pecker?

"With butter. With fresh churned butter."

The crowd continues to tease Cleaborn, but the *Bee* correspondent takes it with a laugh and a shrug. Everyone knows he is the most quoted among them, the man whose copy is printed all over the country. He stutters badly and they all imitate him, spewing out staccato bursts of syllables. He doesn't care. He marches around, his long squirrel coat swinging behind him like a king's robe.

Wilson Krenshaw of the *Lincoln State Journal* walks over to Quinton Tapp, an unlighted cigarette in his mouth.

"You got a match, Tapp?"

"I'm out," Tapp says. He doesn't like this man, and he makes no bones about it. Just another one of the arrogant young sprouts who have been sent here, he thinks. A real bastard.

Akins passes up a kitchen match for the tall young redhead, and Krenshaw grins at Tapp as he gets his smoke going. Tapp scowls and spits, not bothering to take the cigar stub from the corner of his mouth as he does it.

"It's a fact, there's not much to write about," Krenshaw says, moving off.

"Make somethin' up. You and some of these other people around here have been pretty good at that," Akins says. He squints up at Tapp and grins, his cobb pipe clinched between his teeth.

The jibes from Akins have been frequent, but they don't disturb Quinton Tapp very much. Perhaps because there isn't any pretense between them. At least, Tapp thinks, I don't take all that writin' stuff seriously. I know it's mostly bullshit.

"They arrested another dozen soldiers last night. The Indian police. Found 'em snoopin' around the boarding school," Akins says.

"Hell, that's no story," Tapp grunts. "There's nothin' for the soldiers to do, except sit around on these pickets or ride patrols. They need action of some kind, or else they go nosin' around the henhouse, as the sayin' goes."

Krenshaw is still goading Cleaborn.

"That Krenshaw is somethin', isn't he?" Tapp says. "Look at that damned pistol. And he's got a couple of coat pockets full of ammunition.

You'd think he'd get a rupture carryin' all that iron around."

"He's not much worse than some of the others," Akins says. "But your man Cleaborn at least doesn't run around actin' like he was wild Bill Hickok."

"He's hell for silly picture takin', though. Carries that damned Kodak with him everywhere. I saw him yesterday down in Red Cloud's camp. Had some Sioux buck out beside a tipi with a knife raised up, and he was pointin' a six-shooter at the Indian, and somebody else was snappin' pictures of it. Silly damned thing. And he's not my man, either."

All is suddenly still as General Brooke appears in the doorway with Thelma Hanson Duncan. The general is shaped like an oak stave barrel. He glares around at the collected reporters, his short-cropped white hair seeming to bristle.

Mrs. Duncan wears a stylish plaid hat with an enormous feather curling toward the rear and a matching ankle-length coat with the collar buttoned high around her neck. She and the general exchange a few final words, and he disappears inside, the signal for the correspondents to swarm around her. She stands smiling, facing them squarely.

"Some looker, I say," Tapp mutters.

"Wha-wha-what's your first impression of Pine Ridge, Mrs. Duncan?" Cleaborn asks.

"It's a barren, filthy place. I don't see how anyone can live here. I don't see how anyone can expect someone else to live here."

Tapp stands well back from the crowd. But as the questioning continues, she sees him and inclines her head. He touches his hat. Look at that, he thinks. She stands a good head taller than most of the men. She's almost as tall as I am. By God . . .

Cleaborn wants a Kodak picture of her. Others push forward to get into it, and the lanky *Bee* man screams at them and shoves them aside. He finally gets her alone, standing near the wall of the agency office.

"The f-f-first picrure of a la-la-lady war correspondent," Cleaborn stammers. "It'll be a co-co-collector's item."

He clicks the shutter twice.

There is a stampede to see who will escort the Widow to the correspondent's shack.

The shack had once been a storage barn for cornmeal, dried onions, and other agency-grown produce. But now it stands empty of these things, the summer's corn having been eaten off the cob with none left for grinding, and all the garden vegetables consumed almost as soon as they were pulled from the parched ground. The place has been swept clean, and a number of old Army folding tables and chairs have been put there. They establish Mrs. Duncan at a central desk, Cleaborn sweeping the piles of paper off onto the floor with a flourish.

After a short time, one of the Indian hangers-on at the press shack appears with his wife. The man's name is High Dog and he is dressed traditionally, steel ball-bells at his calves, his loosely held blanket exposing a pipe-bone breastplate over a naked chest. He has paint on his face, and his lashes and brows are plucked. Mrs. Duncan is appropriately impressed. The Indian woman wants to sell her a blanket, but she declines. Then an old knife is produced.

"Genuine scalping knife," says Krenshaw.

"My God," Tapp mutters. "They set this whole thing up, like a sideshow."

"They're like soldiers. When they haven't got much to do, they get into mischief," Akins says.

"It's hardly ha-ha-had the blo-bl-blood cleaned off it," Cleaborn stammers.

"It's nothin' but a worn-out trader's skinnin' knife," Tapp says to Akins, who nods and smiles.

Mrs. Duncan pays twenty-five cents for it, and says she needs some fresh air. With the Indians have come the strong scent of wood smoke and grease. The whites move outside. Alone, the Indian man takes the quarter from the woman and slips it into some pocket under his blanket. The two of them look about the room, searching under the scattered papers on the desks and dumping out wastebaskets. The man finds an empty pint whisky bottle and sniffs it. He licks the bottleneck before tossing it aside. They find nothing and finally walk out, past the group of reporters gathered once more around the Widow.

"Mrs. Duncan, do you have any sort of firearm?" Krenshaw asks.

131

"From whom do I need protection?" she asks, and everyone laughs. "But as a matter of fact, my editor did provide."

Holding it by the barrel with thumb and finger, she produces from her handbag a new swing-out Colt revolver.

"That's a model 1889," Tapp says. "Good pistol."

"It's a peashooter," Krenshaw says. "What is that, Mrs. Duncan? A .22 or maybe a .32? A peashooter anyway."

"That's about it," Tapp grunts and shoves his way roughly through the crowd until he is beside the Widow. "It's a fine weapon, Mrs. Duncan. Your editor knows his guns."

"Who pulled your chain —" Krenshaw starts. Tapp wheels on him suddenly, smiling, but his face is cold as the thick lips part over the uneven teeth. Krenshaw moves back a step, almost a reflex as he sees the heavy man's face. He starts to speak, but Akins is between them then, tipping his hat and smiling at Mrs. Duncan.

"Good day, ma'am. I'm Akins, of the *New York Herald.*"

"Of course, I've seen a great deal of your writing. You seem to be one of the few who look at this whole business calmly."

"There are a number of us actually," he says, standing bareheaded in the bright sun. "But the noise of these others . . ." and he waves his hat toward Cleaborn, who nods and grins, ". . . seems to drown us out."

Mrs. Duncan turns to Tapp. "And are you still sending all those rumors in to the *Bee*? It is the *Bee*, isn't it?"

"It's the *Bee*. I send my editor what he wants."

"I see she's read some of your stuff," Akins says.

"If somebody else is likely to write it, I'll write it first."

The other reporters are still now but edging in, waiting their moment. Quinton Tapp is suddenly reminded of a bitch in heat and all the town dogs yammering around, tails up and whipping with excitement. For the moment they are subdued — even Cleaborn — taken aback with Tapp's flash of anger, the tail-between-the-legs hounds, staying back when the mastiff appears.

"I see that the two of you are not armed like Barbary pirates," Mrs. Duncan is saying.

"I suspect Quinton here has one of the largest concealed cannons on the agency."

Tapp pats the bulge in his coat under the left arm. "That's right, but it's not for showin' off."

"Let us hope, Mrs. Duncan, that the intrepid Mr. Tapp does not have to unsheath his deadly metal." She laughs and Tapp does as well, and everyone there knows that had any other of the correspondents said such a thing, there would be trouble. But from Akins, Tapp seems to take it almost as a compliment.

"I suspect there will be no need for Quinton to slaughter any of these poor creatures," Akins continues, "because it appears the situation is well in hand. And speaking of the military . . ."

Lieutenant Martingale has come up leading two horses, one with a sidesaddle. He moves through the other reporters to stand before Mrs. Duncan, where he salutes and clicks his heels.

"Ma'am, General Brooke's compliments. General Brooke thought you might like to tour the agency, and I would be honored to escort you."

"Delighted. And I see the general has been kind enough to provide a sidesaddle."

Why the hell wouldn't he? Tapp thinks. The only women who ride astride are squaws. The young officer turns to the reporters stiffly, pulling on his gauntlets.

"And gentlemen of the press, I have a message for you from the general. General Miles has informed us from his headquarters in Rapid City that the band of Big Foot on Cheyenne River is even now being marched to Fort Meade, where they will be closely watched. Colonel Sumner, who has had Big Foot under arrest for the past few days, is effecting this movement. It therefore appears that all that is left to be done before the reservations can return to normal is completion of negotiations with the Stronghold people, and General Brooke has instructed me that I can tell you the process shouldn't take long."

Now Wallace is there, too, and without a word to the young staff officer, takes the reins from him and touches his hat to the Widow as she turns to him with a smile.

"Why, Captain Wallace," she says. "How nice

to see you again. Will you show me some of your troops?"

"Mrs. Duncan, I am prepared —" Lieutenant Martingale starts but Wallace interrupts.

"It would be my pleasure," he says, and takes her arm as she mounts, going up to the side-saddle with a supple grace that is all the more remarkable because of her size. Martingale is left standing, flushed and tight-lipped, and some of the reporters grin at him and wink.

Quinton Tapp glares after the couple as they ride off toward the Army picket lines near the police barracks.

Akins fills his pipe and lights it. After a few minutes of silence, he stretches.

"I'd better get a few words written about the war's end," he says. "Afternoon courier leaving soon."

They can use the Army wire if they wait their turn and there is no official traffic, but that means each of them can send fifty words only and some Army officer will read those. So they each pay their share to a civilian courier who carries their messages into Rushville each afternoon and leaves them with the Western Union there.

"I'm going over to the game after a while," Tapp says. There is a twenty-four-hour poker session in the rear of the trader's store. "I'm not going to write anything until I feel more like it."

"You'll lose everything you make if you don't stay away from there," Akins says. "One of those fellows is a professional gambler from Deadwood or some such place. They ought to run him off. But even if he wasn't, you're the worst card player I ever saw."

Tapp shrugs and Akins moves off. The other reporters have wandered away. Tapp stands in the warm sun alone. The weather has moderated since dawn, the wind dying and the sky clearing to allow the sun to bake off last night's frost. It is well above freezing now. Somewhere on the west side of the agency, in one of the Army's encampments, a bugler plays "Recall." Along the agency road a few dogs wander listlessly. There are soldiers in front of the office, where Brooke makes his headquarters, and some Indian policemen around the front of their barracks. Everything seems already settled into a slow routine. Most of the agency Indians are in their own camps, moving about as little as possible. Everything has come to a stop, Tapp thinks. A dead stop. Complete boredom.

And now all the soldiers are saying there's little prospect of anything at all happening. Anything Old Man Goodall wants to hear about anyway. And the horse won't bring eighty dollars when he tries to sell it back.

But there is the woman. She, at least, has made him feel better about being on the reservation. He'd met her each of the past four nights, on the road south of the agency. She had come again, as he suspected she would after their first time together. He'd have gone on to her shack or whatever it was she lived in, but she didn't want

136

that. She's got a drunken buck husband or something like that tucked away, that's it, he'd thought. But after the second night, it got too cold for lying around on the ground beside the Pine Ridge–Rushville road, so they'd found the old woodshed behind the boarding school. Well, she'd found it. And so far the police had neglected to check inside it when they walked every night within a few feet of it. He had to be careful, too, because now the woman not only moved well, but she also made considerable noise while she was doing it, and he had to watch that carefully. He didn't want to end up in the goddamned Indian police jail.

Each night when it was over she'd slip away and go back down the Rushville road to her shack or whatever it was, to that drunken buck husband or whoever it was, and he'd feel like one more day had been worth staying at the reservation.

He turns his face up into the sun, and it feels good as he squats there, eyes closed.

That Indian woman is no great looker, like the Widow. But she's a little something special just the same. She'd been to Carlisle Indian School and learned to speak English. All her troubles had started with Carlisle. The troubles she wanted him to help her get rid of, somehow. He wasn't sure how.

He'd suspected something from the first night. That yellow dress, and her drunk as a lord out there on the road. Where did the dress come from? Who was pouring the liquor down her? He had no idea, and he knew she wouldn't tell him. But she'd started right off whining about how she needed to get to Valentine, and he'd have to help her. Since then she'd been wheedling him about it. She wanted to get out so bad, she was really trying to make him enjoy every time so he'd never want to stop. So he'd help her get out.

What the hell, he thinks. How does she think I can help her? She never would say who she wanted to find in Valentine.

Somebody important to her. He had started stringing her along, making little promises that meant nothing. Now, after four nights, it's beginning to feel like he's married to her, and he half dreads slipping into that woodshed, but he knows he can't live out the night without going there. He knows the part he'll enjoy. And he knows the part he dreads — when she starts whining about being set upon by her own people, despised because she'd gone and got herself a white man's education and can talk his language and even write it some. None of her own people want her around, she said, and some would just as soon kill her as not.

"What the hell are you talkin' about?" he'd said. "Nobody's goin' to kill you just because you went to learn how to read and write."

Well, to hell with it, he thinks. He doesn't really care about the woman's problems. There are times each night when something good happens for just a few moments. He always feels it.

But it is gone quickly. He isn't proud of the fact that he uses her and she lets him because she expects help from him. But he doesn't allow it to bother him much that he has no expectation of doing so. He simply doesn't think about it. It isn't the first time he's kept buried a thing that he somehow knows will make him ashamed if he dwells on it. If not ashamed, surely at least not proud. He knows that every man has a few such things buried in him.

The sun is lowering fast in this Dakota afternoon in December, and Quinton Tapp feels a chill. Grunting, he moves toward the rear of Asay's store, where he knows the poker game is still in progress and will remain in progress for as long as the Indian war lasts. Indian war, he thinks, shaking his head and grinning. What the hell! In his pocket is the bank draft from the *Bee*, good for fifty dollars. He hasn't told Cleaborn about it yet, and half the money is his. But a man needs the backing of capital in a game. With a little luck, he can retake that seventy-five dollars he's already lost, and Cleaborn and no one else the wiser. Pay the stuttering little bastard tomorrow sometime.

"What the hell's he going to do with money in this hole, anyway?" he mutters to himself as he slips inside. With the Stronghold gang coming in soon and old Big Foot under lock and key, even Cleaborn can't make a war out of this thing for much longer. We'll be home in a week.

But on Cheyenne River old Big Foot is not

under lock and key, and the man who is supposed to have him there knows it. Sumner, waiting for the Miniconjou chief to come in and talk and bring the Sitting Bull runaways with him, has waited long enough. It is not impatience alone but concern for his future in the Army. If it is discovered that Big Foot is not under close arrest — as indeed he is not and never has been — the wrath of Gen. Nelson Miles will descend with predictable malevolence. So Sumner prepares his troops to march to the camp of Big Foot, to escort him and his people to whatever fort Miles may direct. Sumner is not nervous about the Sioux, for he and Big Foot had talked together and understood one another. He had made the old man realize his own sympathy for the condition of the band. But Sumner is nervous about Miles. So he will march. And because of that, as Quinton Tapp supposes, everyone will go home. At least, some will go home. But not in a week.

PART THREE
THE MEETING

11

NEW YORK HERALD — The news of the surrender of Big Foot and his band of 150 warriors to Colonel Sumner reached here today. The intelligence is most gratifying.

And so Big Foot does not go in. Because of the coughing sickness. He does not go in to speak with the soldier chief Sumner as he had promised he would do. And the time promised for going in passes, and Big Foot lies on his pallet still, dipping the peeled willow stick into a cup of Army honey and sucking it for sweetness. But the taste has grown sour. It has been seven sleeps since any coyote called to him during the night or any hunting hawk in the day to encourage him. There has been only the angry cawing of those *kangi* from the bur oak trees across the river.

"I do not like those birds, the black crows who argue constantly," Big Foot says to Talks, who squats beside his blanket.

Worst of all, he knows the coughing sickness is only an excuse for not going in. He knows the real reason is because he is embarrassed to talk with the soldier chief Sumner now that everything is slipping out of his control. A chief without control is only an old man talking to himself.

"What could I say to the soldier chief Sumner about those Sitting Bull people?" he asks. "He told me to bring them in with me so he could send them back to their own reservation, back to Standing Rock where they belong. Then they all slipped away. So now I cannot bring them."

"You could tell him you have no control of people who once belonged to Sitting Bull."

The old man rises up on one elbow and starts to laugh, but it turns into a coughing fit. One of the women in the room comes over and looks down at him, waiting until the coughing stops. The old man spits into a dirty rag. His eyes are bright and filled with water.

"I cannot control the Sitting Bull people! Of course not. I cannot control my own young men."

Talks looks across the room at Black Coyote who stands in a corner, one foot against the wall. In the crook of his arm is the rifle, his fingers moving on the shining walnut stock. He stares back at Talks, his expression never changing, as though he does not understand that they are speaking of him. His eyes are black as the wings of the crows. Hanging from his mouth is a cigarette, trade store tobacco rolled in newspaper, and he does not squint against the smoke when it comes up across his face like a spider's veil.

"It makes no difference now," Big Foot says. "Sumner will be angry. The white man often neglects to do what he says he will do, but he becomes angry if we do not do what we say we will."

"You can tell him it was the sickness."

"No. He will know I am not that sick."

"You can send me to tell him. I will talk to him."

"No. He will abuse you. I am afraid he will abuse you."

"I know much about the thinking of white men," Talks says.

"But you are too kind." The old man smiles. "And besides, you would probably tell him everything, and when one deals with the white man, he must hold a little back and lie a little. To keep things calm. I know how this works. But you do not."

"Sumner is an understanding man. You said so, and I think you were right. They are strange, I know, but many of the whites are good and truthful men."

For a long time Big Foot looks up at the younger man, a small twisting to his lips. He winks one eye closed, and his old teeth show for a moment in a smile.

"Daughter," he calls softly, and the young woman who has until now been in a corner of the room, staying back to show respect for their talking of un-woman things, moves close. Talks can see her legs and hips flowing under the blanket cloth dress, and the sight moves him.

"Yes, father," she says, her soft eyes moving

from the younger to the older man.

"Tell the story of the owl and the crow," Big Foot says.

For a moment she hesitates, then her voice begins, low but confident, and as she speaks, she looks at Talks.

"There was a crow once, who saw an owl in the sunlight, and he said, 'That old owl is good and just. Why do we abuse him?' And he said, 'I will visit that old owl tonight when my brothers are asleep and apologize for their bad behavior, all that pecking and scolding.' And so that night the crow went to visit the owl, who was kind and just, and the owl ate him."

Talks laughs. "It's a good story, _até._"

"Yes. And like the owl who has his gods that make him act as he does, so does Sumner. Those white chiefs are very strict. When they tell someone to do a thing, it must be done. They are often tyrants. Because each of the white chiefs has a chief himself, telling him what to do."

"I know their ways, father," Talks says, a little out of patience. "I have lived among them. But one thing I know. We should learn from them."

"It would not be our way," the old man sighs. "Just as it would not be the way of that owl to roost with the crow. You cannot change it any more than you can change the way a wood thrush flutes his voice by offering him a bribe of corn."

"But Sumner knows _you_ are good and just. Else he would never have let us stay here all this time in our own village, in our own cabins."

"Yes. But he knows I can be dangerous, too, if I want to be. Just as I know he can be dangerous. And always remember those other chiefs telling him what to do. They have never sat and smoked with me. And they are more afraid of me than is Sumner."

"All right. But our people should do as you tell them. Without all the arguments."

"That too is not our way."

"With such ways I am surprised the People did not perish long ago under the hatchets of the Arikara or the Crow."

The old man's eyes dance. He makes a motion before his face with both hands, as though he eats corn from a cob. It is the sign language for the Arikara.

"Those corn eaters! We frightened them away just by painting our faces. Now the Crow. There was a fighting people. But they had the same weaknesses we had. They liked to argue, too. With their chiefs."

Big Foot laughs again, and again it turns to bad coughing. His daughter bends to pull the blanket around his chin. Talks can feel the warmth of her body near him. It is hard to think of white chiefs and soldiers and the old wars with Crows when such a woman is close to him. When the coughing is finished and Big Foot spits again, she turns and walks away, knowing Talks is watching.

"A man leads and is followed because he has shown his leadership is strong," the old man says, lying flat, staring at the ceiling. "Perhaps my leading is behind me because my strength is behind me."

It is a long talk for the old man. And he is disturbed that Talks belittles the ways of the People, now when Big Foot needs all the support he can get. But looking sideways at the young man, he knows loyalty is still there. He will not turn his back on the People or on Big Foot. The old man closes his eyes and mumbles to himself as all old men do. This is the way, he thinks. It was the way his father thought and his grandfather, too. Sometimes those around him can understand his words, and sometimes it is as though he speaks a foreign tongue.

There is a great commotion outside, and someone shouts that Red Beard comes. The old man rouses himself.

"Who comes?"

"Red Beard. The one called Dunn by the whites," Talks says. "He comes with one of his half-blood friends."

"The man who sells chickens and eggs?"

"Yes. The man with the ranch across the river."

"He has been a friend for a long time," Big Foot says.

"Father, he also signed a paper, with other white men along the Cheyenne River, asking the great white chief in the East to send more soldiers."

"Yes. I have heard about that."

"He is not such a friend as he pretends, perhaps."

"Maybe he had to sign the paper," Big Foot says. "Maybe the other white men expected him to sign it, and he did so that they would not be angry."

Red Beard is not in the camp of Big Foot to sell butter and pullets. Yellow Bird comes into the cabin of the chief to explain why the white man has come. He wears his medicine bird headdress, a stuffed crow, the wings extending down over each of the old man's ears and the tail feathers hanging behind like a scalp lock. Over his forehead is the bird's beak, partly open in the eyeless head. As Yellow Bird moves, the bird's head moves as well, as though it talks.

"That Red Hair Mouth is here," Yellow Bird says, "with a message from the soldier chief Sumner."

Big Foot sits up on his pallet with a loud grunt, pulling the blanket over his shoulders. The old man is excited, and he waves one hand at Yellow Bird.

"All right, send him to me, quickly. I want to talk with him."

"He's got one of those half-bloods with him," Yellow Bird says. "More white than Sioux. I don't like those half-bloods any better than I like the Hair Mouths."

"All right, let the half-blood talk with the people outside. But send Red Beard in to me."

Yellow Bird is reluctant, almost stubborn. For

a moment he stands glaring. He is excited, too, in a way that makes his eyes shine, and Talks does not like what he sees in the old man's face. Suddenly Yellow Bird pulls up his Ghost Shirt and reveals a Remington pistol.

"This is for the Red Hair Mouth and his half-blood friend," he says, then turns to the door.

Big Foot is suddenly angry and shouts at the medicine man.

"I want to see that white man." Talks is surprised at the strength in the old chief's voice.

Soon the red-bearded white man appears. He is short, and his hair hanging beneath his wide hat is red like his beard and equally unkempt. He is unarmed, except that under the greatcoat he wears there may be a small pistol. But the People are not afraid of this man. He has been among them many times, selling his eggs and chickens.

Red Beard and Big Foot greet one another, but there is no social talk.

"We have been friends for a long time," Big Foot says. "Now you come with a message from the soldier chief Sumner. Tell me what it is."

"I went to the soldier camp. To sell eggs," Red Beard says. "Colonel Sumner said you had promised to come in and talk with him but had not."

"No. I was too sick, as you can see. And the Hunkpapas who were here have gone, and we needed time to find them again. It is an embarrassment to me that they were my guests and are now gone."

"Sumner was angry."

"I thought he would be."

"He said his chief had told him to take you and your people to one of the Blue Coat forts and keep you there until everyone stops dancing," Dunn says. Now Yellow Bird and Black Coyote are back inside the cabin.

"And what will Sumner do?"

"He had his soldiers ready to come, but then he asked me to come instead and tell you this."

"When will he come?"

"His soldiers are near now," Red Beard says. "He will come and ride with you and the People to one of the forts."

"It is what he wanted to do at first, before we stopped here at our camp," Talks says.

"Yes," Big Foot says. "It is what he wanted before."

Yellow Bird has begun a soft chant in one corner of the cabin, and he has a gourd rattle that he shakes, making a whisper like snakes running through corn husks.

"It will be all right," Talks says. "They will be friendly with us, even though Sumner is angry. He has said he is your friend. They will take us to Camp Cheyenne and give us tents to keep off the cold and food for the children."

"Are you sure?" Yellow Bird cries, and he has begun to shuffle about the room, keeping time with the rattling of his gourd. "Are you sure the Hair Mouths will be friends? Are you sure?"

Big Foot waves his hand impatiently and Yellow Bird shuffles back to his corner, but he continues to dance silently.

"Is it true, Red Beard," Big Foot says, looking at the white man with his eyes hard and unblinking, "will Sumner be friends with the People?"

The white man looks around, furtive as a caught fox. Talks watches his eyes dart like the spider bugs on summer water, here and there, never still. The white man opens his mouth to speak. Lakota words come so fast it is hard to understand them, and as he speaks, Talks cannot help but distrust this white man, distrust him more than he has ever in his life distrusted a white man before.

"The soldiers will come at night. They will make you go with them," Red Beard is saying. Yellow Bird moves closer once more, bending forward to listen, his gourd rattle silent. "They will be ready to shoot if anyone causes the least trouble. Some are anxious to shoot. I listened to their talk. They said they would send more soldiers than the gravels in the Cheyenne River. While you sleep. And when they have you with chains on your arms and legs, they will send you and all your men away to a great iron house on an island in the sea."

"You heard Sumner say that?" Talks asks, and his voice is hard and loud in the small cabin. Red Beard looks at the young man for only a moment and then turns back to the chief.

"You must go, my friend," Dunn says.

"Wait. You heard Sumner say these things?

About the shooting and the iron house in the sea?" Big Foot asks.

"I heard his soldiers say them. And then Sumner said to me, 'Come and tell Big Foot we come to take him to a fort until the dancing stops.' "

"Sumner is our friend," Talks says, his voice large again. But the chief raises his hand and Talks is silent.

"You must leave," Red Beard says. "You must go to the south, to Pine Ridge. You must leave now because there is no time to lose."

"But this is my home. We harm no one! A few of my headstrong young men may wave their rifles or steal a cow now and then, but —"

"You must leave quickly," Red Beard says, breaking in. "They will come . . ."

Talks is quickly across the cabin floor, and the white man gasps as the young Indian takes hold of him, hands pulling at the collar of the greatcoat.

"What are you telling this chief?" Talks hisses. "Why are you so anxious, white man, that the People leave Cheyenne River?"

"It's true. I overheard them talking," Red Beard says, trying to pull away from the young man because he does not like what he sees in the young man's eyes. "They were making secret plans. I heard them."

Red Beard's eyes dart back and forth again. Talks releases him, pushing him away with disgust.

"I told you," Yellow Bird shouts. "I told you."

He turns and runs out of the cabin, and they can hear much shouting. Black Coyote pulls Dunn through the door, and everyone shouts at the white man as he runs to his companion.

"It's true, they will come, and they will shoot," he shouts. He turns to his half-blood friend. "Tell them I have spoken the truth."

"It is true," the half-blood shouts. The two of them turn their horses and gallop out of the camp. The people run back and forth, cackling, like chickens under a soaring hawk. A number of the older men — the elders — run to Big Foot's cabin and crowd inside. And the young men outside the cabin begin to gather up horses. They wave their rifles and shout.

"*Upelo! Upelo!* They are coming. The Hair Mouths are coming."

Like flames in dry grass, the alarm goes through the camp. They hitch wagons and run from the cabins with blankets and pots.

Inside the cabin of Big Foot, Yellow Bird is shouting at his chief.

"Now you see? Now you see? We must go quickly to the south. We must go to the Stronghold. There we can join our brothers in the dance, and we can make our songs to the coming Messiah and be safe."

"You're a fool," Talks shouts. "The dance has brought these soldiers down on us, and you still insist on doing it."

Yellow Bird is almost ready to leap on the younger man, but Big Foot speaks, and the voice of the old man stops everyone in his yammering.

"We will decide," he says loudly. "We will decide now. But we will not fight among ourselves."

"Red Beard lies," Talks says. "He wants the Miniconjous away from his ranch, away from his cattle. He thinks we will steal his cattle and eat them . . ."

"And we will," Yellow Bird says.

"He wants us all off the Cheyenne River, and he would lie to make it so," Talks says.

"We must go to the Stronghold," several shout.

"What Red Beard says is a lie."

"How do I know?" Big Foot asks.

"If you think it is a lie, stay here, Man-With-A-Loud-Mouth," Yellow Bird says to Talks. "But must we leave our women and children with you to be slaughtered?"

"He lies," Talks says, his voice hard but not shaking as Yellow Bird's voice shakes.

There is then a deep silence and they can hear the crows again, for the commotion outside has gone silent, too. And they can hear the fire in the stove and the wind beating harder now against the walls of the cabin. Black Coyote slips into the room and goes to the chief and bends down.

"Father, we have only a little time," he says. "I will take a few of the young men with rifles, and we will ride to meet the soldiers."

"No, you can't do that, I refuse to allow it."

"We will make time for you to get away, father," Black Coyote says, still gently. "We will kill only a few of them."

"No, you must stay." And Talks sees the light of cunning come to the old man's eyes. "What would I do without my young men around me? I want all those with rifles to be close around me, and do not forget to have your ammunition with you."

He looks at Talks and shakes his head slowly.

"We cannot take the chance that Red Beard is lying," he says. "We must go."

There is a shout of gladness from the others and they go out.

"I will stay and talk with Sumner when he comes," Talks says. The old man looks up at him. One of the women is braiding his hair, a small gray plait down either cheek and a meager scalp lock behind. Across the room, another of the women is rolling blankets, and a third is throwing kitchen utensils and some loose rifle ammunition into a wooden box.

"I ask you to come with me," the old man says. "Perhaps on the road I can make them understand that we must go to Pine Ridge agency and not to the Stronghold. We will go to the agency and surrender and be with our brothers the Oglalas. But you must help me. I need you to help me turn them away from the Badlands."

For a long time Talks waits for the old man to say more, but Big Foot is silent, and so the young man turns away to prepare himself. He is a young man strange to his own people. His mother and father are dead long ago, and he has no sister or brother. Nor wife either, for which the Miniconjous think him crazy. They know he is not crazy like the ones who sit all day allowing the spit to run from their mouths and speak only foolishness. Nor is he one of those strange men who try to get other men into the bushes with them. But he is unlike any of the other young men.

Even his new desire for Big Foot's daughter has been well hidden, and only the old man and his wives know of it. And of course, the young woman herself. But to all others he appears to make a life of doing nothing but helping old Big Foot. Some say this is devotion and others call it ambition. But no matter what it is, he goes now to prepare his trip away from Cheyenne River because Big Foot has asked him. But he knows somehow that it is not right.

"Wait," Big Foot calls. Talks turns again to the old chief as Big Foot motions one of his women to bring the rifle from the corner where it always stands. Big Foot takes it in both hands and offers it to Talks.

"I don't want it, father," Talks says. "To have it is to use it. And we stand no chance if we use our rifles against the white man."

"Please take it," the chief says. "I trust you not to use it except to protect the People. I would feel better knowing you had it hidden under your blanket."

Talks takes the rifle. Along the stock are a number of brass tacks, making a yellow design against the grain of the wood. He works the action, snapping down the lever, and watches a bright golden shell with a blunt gray slug slip into the chamber as he closes the breech. It makes a solid sound like a heavy door closing and locking. He can smell the oil from the rifle and feel its smooth surface under his fingers. Along the barrel he can read the stamped inscription "32 Winchester Center Fire." He lowers the hammer with his thumb, and saying nothing more, turns and goes out of Big Foot's cabin.

People are running back and forth, many shouting, many deathly silent with fear. One of the few dogs who has escaped the stew pot dashes among the horses and the people, yapping with excitement. Horses are being saddled or hitched to the wagons. There are a few travois. The wind blows the horses' manes and tails. Yellow Bird goes from family to family, telling them to hurry, warning again and again that the Hair Mouth Blue Coats come. He has a rifle now, and he waves it as he shouts. Black Coyote is mounted already, his face with fresh daubs of black paint across the high, hard cheekbones. He encourages everyone to hurry, too, making his little barking sound. With him are many of the young men. Talks sees their weapons, and there are more rifles than he had ever thought were in the band.

Talks watches a smile grow on Black Coyote's face as the young bodyguard sees the rifle in

Talks's hand, and somehow it makes him very angry.

Since they have stopped living in tipis, the Miniconjous cannot move as quickly as they once did. But even so, in a short time everything is loaded. The wagons and travois pull into line. The bodyguards have their horses close to the cabin of Big Foot, waiting for the chief, and the older men are busy seeing to the organization of the march. Finally, when Big Foot appears at the door of his cabin, weak but walking on his own, everyone is waiting. Talks and another young man help the old chief into the back of his wagon, and they are ready.

"It is cold," Big Foot says, and Talks helps him pull the blanket over the bony shoulders. His old eyes search Talks's clothing. "The rifle?"

"Yes, father. Under the wagon seat. When I leave the wagon, I will take it under my blanket."

"Good. That is a fine rifle. You keep it near."

Beside the wagon now is Big Foot's daughter, and Talks turns to her. She holds the reins of her spotted pony.

"Tie him to the wagon and ride with your father," he says, making his voice brusque as though he were giving orders to the bodyguards.

"I will see that he stays warm," she says, and her teeth show in a smile.

How do these things between men and women go on, Talks thinks, even in bad times, even when the old world is being blown away like dust before the winds? But they do, maybe even more so in bad times. He climbs up into the wagon seat and speaks to the team, and they start.

The wind has grown ugly, and already there is cold spit in it. Darkness is coming fast from the east, like a great silent cat, black and menacing, filled with unknown things. Once more Talks speaks to the mules and flicks them with the ends of the lines. They move to the head of the column and start south.

"We will watch from the hills," Big Foot says. "If the soldiers come, we can decide what to do. If they don't come, we can go back to the cabins."

"They will come," Talks says. "They will come, but we will not be there to meet them."

Big Foot pretends he has not heard. But, Talks thinks, I don't believe we will ever go back again.

The darkness grows quickly. Soon a number of the men go to the front of the march with lanterns. They move through the night, lighting the way. It is growing much colder. And many times Big Foot coughs. We should be back there in that cabin, Talks thinks, with a warm fire for the father, and ready to take some more good beef from Sumner. But we are here . . .

He looks into the night ahead and at the small glow of the lanterns bobbing along in front of the mules. The cold and the darkness have closed around them, and looking back he cannot see any of those who follow. We are started, he thinks. And there will be no stopping now until we are in the Stronghold or at the Pine Ridge agency. And both are more than one hundred miles away. It has begun to snow.

Once, the young woman rises behind him and says her father is sleeping, and her hand lies on Talks's back. He can feel the warmth and the strength of her fingers. He thinks again, Yes, this woman and man thing goes on, even in the worst of seasons.

12

DULUTH TRIBUNE — A dispatch has been received from Colonel Sumner stating that the Big Foot and Sitting Bull Indians who surrendered to him a few days ago have escaped and are making for the stronghold in the Bad Lands.

Just to the west of the Indian police barracks is a large hospital tent, headquarters of the Seventh Cavalry at Pine Ridge. For this winter Wednesday evening, everything has been moved out except the coal-oil stoves and two tables, one at either end. On one board are laid out boxes of candied dates and English walnut meats frosted with sugar, sliced pineapple and pears, canned spice cake and raisin cookies, cinnamon apples and peanut brittle. On the other table is a fifty-gallon Army washtub filled with an amber liquid and chunks of ice from the agency icehouse.

The officers of the Garry Owen regiment are holding open house in celebration of Christmas Eve. The fruits and nuts have come by rail from the East. The punch was made on the scene, a family recipe of Captain Wallace's. He explains the formula to the regiment's most popular guest, Mrs. Thelma Hanson Duncan of the *Chicago Herald*.

"For those who enjoy punch, it is tasty and potent," he says. "There are three parts light rum, one part dark Jamaica, one part peach brandy, one part burgundy, the juice of a dozen lemons for each gallon of liquor, four parts water, a fistful of brown sugar for each tub of mixture, and a dash of ground nutmeg."

"I've never heard that particular recipe," she says, sipping the brew from a white china Army coffee cup which she holds in both hands.

"Everyone does it his own way," he says.

"Tell me, captain, how did you manage the liquor on this Indian reserve?"

"By special permission of the agent, Mr. Royer. Who, I suspect, had some goading from the general."

"How nice to be able to break one's own rules in the name of Christmas."

"Actually, the lemons were more a problem than the rum and wine. But we managed to deprive the Rushville civilians of a few dozen."

People arrive and depart, invitations having been designed to move guests literally in one end of the tent and out the other. Except for a few special people — General Brooke, of course, and the Widow Duncan — no one is encouraged to overstay his welcome. This is not because of niggardly impulse on the part of the Seventh Cavalry officers but because of the size of the tent. There simply is not room enough for everyone at once.

The agent and his wife stay for a short time, he avoiding the members of the press as best he can. General Brooke stays only a little longer, nibbling peanut brittle and talking with members of his staff and line field-grade officers, who effectively shield him from the correspondents. They, on the other hand, seem perfectly happy to do their drinking without the usual barrage of queries. Except for the Widow Duncan.

"Captain Wallace, what does it mean, this Big Foot being loose?"

"It means we must catch him before he can join the Sioux in the Badlands. If he gets to the Stronghold, it will strengthen the resolve of the fanatics already there who want to ignore the agent's order to come in and stop dancing. Right now that would be a great misfortune because it appears the Stronghold people are about ready to pitch it all in and stop this Messiah nonsense."

"How does the Army propose catching him?"

Before Wallace can answer, Wilmot Cleaborn moves up, cake crumbs in his drooping moustache.

"I don't drink, captain, but the cakes are d-d-delicious," he says.

"What about those escaped Indians, captain?" the Widow asks.

"Yes, I'd be interested to know a-a-about them, too."

"Well," Wallace hesitates, looking at Cleaborn.

"You understand that plans can only be revealed in confidence. So many of these people can read now . . ."

"Of course, we know that," Mrs. Duncan says. "But surely, for our own information . . ."

"Yes, f-f-for our own information?"

"Well. Units are screening the countryside between the Stronghold and Big Foot's last known location at Deep Creek on the Cheyenne River. To intercept him before he can reach the Badlands. Here at Pine Ridge we don't expect to get involved. Our job will continue to be keeping the Stronghold people under observation. One of the units north of White River will catch him."

"I'm afraid I don't know where these rivers are, captain."

"The old Big Foot camp was on Cheyenne River, about one hundred miles northeast of where we stand," Wallace says. "That stream flows from west to east, eventually into the Missouri near Fort Sully. And flowing parallel to it and about fifty miles south of it is the White. Now the White is north of us about . . . oh, about twenty-five miles, and then it curves down closer to us in the west. But never mind that. The thing to remember is that the Cheyenne and the White run almost parallel as railroad tracks up where Big Foot is loose. We think he'll come straight south from Deep Creek to the White; then, staying on the north bank, turn west and march directly toward the Badlands. The Stronghold is just north of the White. Do you see?"

"No. But that's enough geography for now. May I have another cup of this terribly good punch?"

In the tent there is little concern for what might be happening north of the White. The officers of the Seventh and Ninth Cavalry regiments express sympathy for their comrades in other horse units, like those in Sumner's command north of the Cheyenne River who must this very night be out in the cold trying to catch the Miniconjous. But they laugh and go back to the washtub. The wind outside has begun to gust, making the canvas walls of the tent snap and flutter. It blows out of the east and drives the temperature down. At Fort Sully the Signal Service Weather Station instruments are registering eighteen degrees now at nine P.M., and the barometer is rising, which means it will be colder before the sun comes again.

Only a few women appear at the open house because there are only a few at the agency. They are treated lavishly and with great pomp by the officers of the regiment. Even the Episcopalian minister's wife, who is flustered by the attention because she has received none such as this since the administration of President Buchanan. The washtub must be refilled once, and this time the formula is not so strictly observed, and the taste suffers. But no one seems to notice. Many of the correspondents have come back in for the second time. An officer from the Ninth and one from the Seventh have an argument over who has the best troops, the Ninth man saying his Brunettes will outfight any white outfit.

Once more, Wallace escorts Mrs. Duncan across the agency to the boarding school, but this time they are alone. They walk close together, she holding tightly to his arm. She seems content to be silent, and he is aware that from time to time as they walk, she looks at him and smiles.

"You must come to Fort Riley when all of this is over," he says. "Our accommodations are better, you will find, than they are on an Indian agency."

"I might accept that invitation. If you promise me a long interview on your days with Custer."

"That isn't exactly what I had in mind," he says. "I had supposed you might like to see how the Army really lives in garrison."

"Or perhaps just a nice visit, without having to worry with my editor's assignments."

"Yes. You could meet my wife. I know you would enjoy knowing Carrie."

"Your wife? Of course." But then she says nothing more and he is embarrassed and a little angry with her, but he isn't sure why.

"Christmas must be a terribly lonely time for a soldier away from home," she says. "I suppose at these times you think of home, don't you?"

"Yes," he says, a little surprised that she has caught his feelings. "I think of little Otis and of my wife, of course."

"Do you ever get homesick for South Carolina?"

"I think a great deal about it lately," he says. "But there were unhappy times there after the war. When I joined the regiment, we were assigned to occupation duty and my own unit was in South Carolina."

"That must have been dreadful for you," and she increases the pressure of her fingers on his arm.

"A fine old lady once said to me on the streets of Columbia that her people hated the Yankee fighting army but the hatred for the Yankee occupying army would last through seven generations."

At the front of the boarding school, they pause and her eyes are on his face as she leans close to him.

"Since the last time, you'd never imagine what I have managed to have brought in from Rushville."

"No. I'd never imagine."

"Tea. I have a nice tin of spice tea, just right after all that delightful punch you made."

"Well, unfortunately, I have to inspect our picket lines," he says, and his words come haltingly. She continues to smile, with the same warmth, as though he had accepted the invitation.

"Perhaps another time, Captain Wallace," she says, and turns away from him and goes into the school.

The party ends well before midnight, and the sentry on the Seventh Cavalry horse picket line watches the last to leave. They are laughing too loud, talking too loud. He rubs his cold fingers along the barrel of his Springfield carbine. He has that very afternoon lost his gloves in a dice game at the Ninth Cavalry mess. He grumbles to himself in a heavy German accent.

Wilmot Cleaborn goes to the back of Asay's store where the poker game continues and finds that his colleague Quinton Tapp has not been there all evening.

"He lost all his poke," someone says and laughs. "And yours, too, Wilmot."

Cleaborn shrugs and sits at a corner table under a smoking oil lamp. He takes paper and pencils from his squirrel-skin coat and begins to write an account of the plan for catching Big Foot. "The cutthroat gang of Big Foot," he calls it. But he has been riding patrol all day with the black troopers of the Ninth, and his nervous energy finally deserts him. He slumps onto the table and sleeps.

Wilson Krenshaw is sleeping too, in one of the rooms at the Hotel de Finley, his own account of the new terror and danger stalking the reservation already completed. In the next room — the combination lobby-parlor-dining room — Chandler Akins reads the newspapers the evening courier has brought from Rushville. In the *New York Herald*, his own stories are generally run after Cleaborn's, which go to the *Herald* through the Associated Press. He smokes his corncob pipe and shakes his head as he reads.

169

Along the Seventh Cavalry horse picket line, the last patrol comes in and the men begin to unsaddle. They grumble as they feed and rub down the horses, damning the Sioux and all other heathen. The sergeant in charge watches them closely, moving back and forth, feeling their horses with his hands.

"Get that sweat off, boys," he says. "You'll have a horse with distemper, and you'll have to walk back to Fort Riley."

Fitzpatrick joins the line of soldiers.

"You can't see a goddamned thing among them hills up north," the detail sergeant says to him. "A whole regiment of red savages could ride through and who'd know the difference?"

"Well now, lad, we can always hope if such a bunch was to come out, you'd hear 'em or run smack into 'em," Fitzpatrick says.

"What's this business I hear about some of these sons of bitches roamin' loose somewheres, about to cause trouble?"

"Big Foot's band, supposed to have been under lock. But give the boys up north the slip. He's a cruel bastard, they tell me."

"What's it mean to us?"

"Not a damned thing, likely," Fitzpatrick says. He raises his voice. "All right, lads, get on to the mess tent. White beans and corn dodgers, and coffee straight from the pits of hell."

After they've gone, Fitzpatrick moves along the line of horses, patting them, running his hands across the withers to see if they've cooled. He comes onto Captain Wallace suddenly in the darkness.

"By God, cap'n, you give me a start," he says. He can smell the rum on Wallace's breath. "A good party, sir?"

"So-so. Where's the horse picket guard?"

"Likely down at the far end of the line."

"He's one of our boys, isn't he?"

"Yes, sir. One of them German recruits we got in just before we left Riley."

Wallace holds out a box.

"Take one of these. See how you like 'em."

Fitzpatrick takes something soft from the box, and his fingers feel the gritty sugar. He pops it into his mouth.

"By God, good, cap'n."

"They're dates. Sugared dates. Here, take the box. Give some to the German boy."

"You bet, sir," Fitzpatrick says. Wallace has moved off into the darkness and Fitzpatrick calls after him.

"Just like one of them desert heathen sheiks, ain't it, cap'n, eatin' these little palm fruits."

Wallace makes no reply, moving on to the tent he shares with a number of other officers. He pauses outside for a moment, and he can hear them talking, wondering where they'll be riding on Christmas Day. Carrie will have lit the candles on the tree by now and have put them out, too, he thinks. And will by now be in bed, warm but lonely, looking through the window that opens onto the elms along the rear of Officers' Row, and beyond, barely visible on a moonlit night, to the rising rimrock. He doesn't know what the weather is there, but he imagines moonlight, because they have so often been there in bed, looking out and whispering together. But tonight . . .

He is disappointed that he has missed Christmas Eve with his wife and son. This he had looked forward to for over a year. It would be the first time the boy would realize something special was happening, the first time he would see the lighted candles and the presents and the holly and know it was different from other days. Last year, on his first Christmas, he was too young to comprehend.

Wallace and Carrie in these first months of the child's life had found pleasure in watching day to day as the brain developed, as the eyes grew large with each new understanding. It was the delight of growing up all over again, relived for them both, as they watched their child. The dim and obscure memories of their own childhoods growing again before their eyes. And each time he looked at the boy, he would think that someday he too would share the same feelings with his own children. Grandchildren? It is almost too much for Wallace to grasp, the thought of grandchildren someday. So far off . . .

He looks at the sky. In the east the clouds have begun to break up and a few stars show through, brittle and blue white in the cold blackness. He thinks again of Fort Riley and the moonlight through the bedroom window, the rimrock hanging in the distance above the flat plain of the river. And he can hear the whippoorwills and smell the heavy honey scent of the black locust blossoms, as though it were spring. But the wind does not feel like spring, and he goes into the tent.

13

BOSTON TRANSCRIPT — There seems to be little basis in fact for the story currently appearing in much of the press that the Pope has been asked to act as mediator between the United States government and the Sioux Indians.

—————⊰●⊱—————

The cold wakes Quinton Tapp and he lies for a long time in the darkness, not knowing where he is, hearing the sounds of voices and laughter from somewhere nearby. Then he makes out the gray outline of the partly opened woodshed door and he knows. His fingers reach out to explore the rumpled blanket on the dirt floor. The Indian woman is not there. But he finds the bottle and knows even before he lifts it to his lips that it is empty. She had finished it before she left. As though it was worth stealing.

The man from Rushville who brings liquor onto the reservation had come in with a large special order that afternoon, hidden as usual in the water barrel hung from the side of his wagon. But when Tapp finally got the man away from the Seventh Cavalry camp, there was little left.

"I had rum and lots of wine before, but that

was for them Army officers," he had said. "All I got is a few quarts of this here peach brandy. Take it or leave it."

Quinton Tapp had taken it, although it cost a dollar a bottle. Now his mouth is sticky and his teeth coated with the thick syrup, grainy and sweet. His head throbs. It had been a bad evening. Ruby Red Hawk was unwilling to do anything but argue — in a soft whisper even though they had seen none of the Sioux officers near the boarding school this night. She had squatted there in the darkness on the blanket, squatted like the heathen savage she was, and told him he had to get her out of there, out of Pine Ridge agency and the reservation. She had to get to Valentine or even to Omaha. Like a wife, he had thought with a start, she's talking like a wife.

"You take me out," she had said, "or I go myself."

"You haven't got a horse," he said. "And Valentine's over a hundred miles off. You got fare for a ticket on the railroad? Hell no!"

He offered her the bottle, but she pushed it away.

"I don't want. I want to know when you'll take me to Valentine or Omaha."

"Oh, for God's sake." He'd ought to paste her a good one in the mouth. Some women even enjoyed it when somebody gave them a good lick. But somehow, he knew he'd never hit her.

The argument had upset him and it disturbs him now to think that perhaps there is more to

Ruby Red Hawk than simple physical release. Until now she had needed him. She wanted to get to Valentine, but there was more than that, too. She needed his hands and his kisses. It was better with her than with any whore he'd known. Better even than with that brakeman's wife in Omaha. It is unsettling to think that this well-shaped Indian woman may mean more to him than the pleasure of having her naked breasts under his hands, of pushing himself into her in all his final fury and hearing her gasp with surprise, each time a little different from the last, each time a little better.

He thinks of the night she finally told him about herself. Her name, she'd said, was Ruby Red Hawk. When she went off to white man's school in the East, they asked her what her full name was, and she just happened to think of Ruby and she added the Red Hawk because that was her brother's name and she liked it. The school people had fussed awhile because she was supposed to be named Willow-on-the-Prairie or some such thing, but she told them she'd had a change made in honor of coming east, and they'd swallowed it. So they took off the yellow tag that had been on her coat to inform any interested train conductor along the way that she was headed for Carlisle Indian School, and they enrolled her and taught her how to read and write English. And she'd been Ruby Red Hawk ever since.

Her father and mother died of measles in one of the epidemics that swept across the reservations from time to time. They never get accustomed to civilized diseases, Quinton Tapp thinks, but die off like flies from the damnedest things. And the only family she'd had left was that brother, and he was busy with his own family and trying to turn himself into a white man by being a reservation policeman.

And the damnedest thing was that the brother didn't like her having gone to Carlisle.

"What the hell do you mean?" Tapp had said. Whispered, actually, as they lay in the shed. "If he's a policeman, he thinks like a white man. Else he wouldn't wear that damned badge and push his own people around."

"No. He says school for Indian men, not women."

"Aw hell, Ruby, if he's a policeman . . ."

"No. He said that. He said white man's school for men, not women."

And that was all she'd tell him. Only that nobody at the agency, nobody in the entire reservation or Sioux nation, wanted her, and she needed to get to Valentine because someone was there who could help her.

"Well, to hell with her," he mutters, determined to refute what he feels by verbally abusing her. "Heathen savage."

He peeks through the door before he slips out. There are no policemen in sight, and he thinks maybe they've had a Christmas party of their own. He starts along the agency road, shaking his head, his mind groggy with the peach brandy.

He is cold and sore and despondent. An old image comes to his mind, he doesn't know why. Of the bony lady, his aunt, who had reared him. She had reared him hard, scrubbing his ears each morning until they hurt, sending him off to school or the fields with sometimes ragged but always immaculate pants and shirt and a tin pail full of baked sweet potatoes for his lunch. Only she always called it dinner. And he had never tasted candy until he was old enough to steal it for himself. The first time she'd caught him with only half of the striped candy cane eaten. He'd spent that night in the attic, locked in after a session with the man's razor strap.

"You're dirt and no good," she would yell at him. "You're bad as your mother. Just dirt and comin' to no good end."

And then he thinks of the Widow, and her uppity ways and her sniffing around Captain Wallace. For an instant he finds it intolerable, this high-toned bitch coming out here to prance and parade around like some kind of royalty. He mutters to himself, some of the words coming aloud, as though he were actually talking to Thelma Hanson Duncan.

You'll go back to those sweet-smellin' sheets, Widow, and write all this Poor Heathen swill in your newspaper that never prints a lie. And you'll say how the poor savage red man is gettin' stomped and clubbed by people like me and shot by people like the Army officers you're always swoonin' around.

No sir, your kind don't have the stomach for it. You come out and take a quick peek and then hurry home. All you've got the stomach for is sendin' somebody else out here to do it all. So you can sit back there and talk about how bad it is and say you never had a damned thing to do with it. What you don't know, and much less write about in those pretty newspapers where they never print any lies, is that we don't club or shoot many of these bastards. We just stand back and let 'em die from your white man's diseases and your eastern-made whisky and your Congress starvin' 'em to death. And you send out somebody else to kill their game and fish out their streams and cut their timber so you can have nice lap robes and pine-sided houses and dried trout in glass jars on the saloon bars where your fancy gentlemen can munch on them while they're sippin' peach brandy or some other shit. You run up and down the railroads you had scum like me build, and you don't even look out the windows to see that we don't have to shoot or club these miserable bastards because all the red niggers just naturally drop off like flies from a sickness called civilization.

Go ahead and scream your fool heads off about how mean we are to these greasy savages. But you know who'll be right here as soon as the dirty part is cleaned up. You will, and your kind. Pushin' right in as soon as you don't have to worry about one of 'em gettin' a belly full of tiger sweat and shootin' somebody's head off or makin' a bonfire out of your house and barn to cure a few scalps. Just come on out after the job's done, and you don't have to worry about 'em except to name a street for some tribe or put up a statue in the park with this scrawny little bastard on a horse with a hand up over his eyes like he's lookin' out at the approach of one of your whisky drummers.

You and your kind have taken away all the good times that once were. For me and the heathens, he thinks. I wish you'd just left it to all us heathen, white and red. We'd knock hell out of one another and have a good time at it. And maybe I'd feel better about it all.

Here you've got me sympathizin' with the damned Sioux, dirty, back-shootin' Sioux. And, for eighteen dollars a week, they've even got me writin' the kind of stuff that excites them and makes them feel better about changin' this whole country out here.

Quinton Tapp has reached the side of James Asay's store, and he leans against the wall, panting in the darkness as though he'd run a long way. Then he is sick, and the peach brandy coming up is worse than going down. He gags and spits and blows his nose with his fingers.

From the Hotel de Finley come the sounds of laughter and loud voices. Some of that group of which he is supposed to be a part. Correspondents. But he detests them and, thinking about them, spits again.

14

THE ROCKY MOUNTAIN NEWS —

TREACHEROUS CHIEF FOOLED SOLDIERS

IS PLAYING HAVOC

BIG FOOT & HIS BLOOD DRINKERS CAPTURE TWO WHITE WOMEN

Ranch Looted by Cutthroats

Squaw Runs Around Naked

HORSES & CATTLE KILLED

Before ice comes on the rivers is an undecided season. Cold walks forward a few steps and then backs away, so on one day there is wind and snow and on the next warm sunshine, until finally cold makes up his mind to come and stay. Then the rivers freeze and the snow grows in crusted fans around the stubble of dead prairie grass and the chokecherry stands naked. Even the sumac gives up the last of its red leaves and they are driven across the land like bloody lance points thrown away. And the low running clouds make the whole world look like the bottom of a slate-colored pool.

But before the cold comes is the undecided season and it is such a time now, south of White River where Big Foot's people have stopped to rest at a place called Cedar Springs. They have stopped because the winds have grown sharp and the cold painful, with particles of ice and snow blown against the faces of horses and men, too. They watch their old chief grow sicker, and many who shouted against him before, making their usual arguments, are silent now. The old man has what is called pneumonia, and his people watch him because they know he is very sick.

They have come quickly to this place, away from the Cheyenne River, pushing each day until darkness and then sometimes on into the night, the men walking ahead with lanterns. They had come to the Badlands Wall, a great steep place that slopes sharply like a buffalo's face. They had brought their animals and wagons down the Wall, working carefully as great chunks of hard-packed soil slipped from beneath the hooves and wheels, rolling and rattling ahead of them to the bottom. Everyone came down, and they were in the valley of the White River. They had crossed it, leaving behind somewhere the soldiers they knew were trying to find them and take their sick chief and the young men to a white man's iron house on an island in the sea.

And because they had captured one of the soldiers' half-blood scouts and then after talking with him allowed him to return to the Blue Coats, they had learned much. They had learned the soldiers thought they were riding directly to the Stronghold. It had been told to them that the soldier chief General Miles thought this, and it was a good argument not to go there.

And so because of this and because of the sickness of their chief, and perhaps a little because of the fierce look of Talks now that he carries the rifle, they had agreed with Big Foot and said they should go to Pine Ridge agency. Not to the Stronghold in the Badlands where the dance might go on, but to the Red Cloud people. Yellow Bird still grumbles that surrender to the white man is foolish, but he has been overruled. Black Coyote complains, too, saying the Sioux now act like timid white women hiding their chickens from the wolf with an apron. And he continues to wear his black face paint and stroke his rifle.

They have made a shelter for the old man and try to keep him warm with a fire of cedar branches. These flare up with a loud popping, like shod horses walking through rabbit ice on a cold morning. The shelter is suddenly filled with the smell of resin and a quick bright heat, but only for a moment, and then it is gone and the wind feels its way in once more. His women feed him as best they can. But it is hard to make good soup from parched corn. They have no fat, nor bone marrow, and the Army honey is gone, too. Talks thinks, If we had stayed on Cheyenne River and gone with Sumner, we would be eating beef now. But they had not stayed on Cheyenne River. And old Big Foot grows weaker.

"Are they all here? Are the People all here?" he asks. Talks tells him they are, camped along the gully where the shelter has been made, resting and hiding from the wind until the chief is well enough to move again.

"I will stay here for only a little while, and then we must go on," Big Foot says. "The *osní* may come to stay. The cold may come to stay."

"We will go soon," Talks says. "But first, you sleep. We are close now and soon will be with Red Cloud's people."

"Yes. Red Cloud."

The old man pulls the blanket over his face, and his breathing is hard and loud in the small canvas shelter. The younger man waits until he is sure the chief is sleeping.

Almost since the start of their running, Talks has been the go-between for the chief and the other leaders. When the old man does not feel like arguing, he sends Talks to do it for him. Some of the other men may not like Talks because they are jealous or because they do not appreciate a younger man taking such a strong place in council. Yet even these know he is honest and will not deceive them. More unhappy with this new power than any of the others is Talks himself. He says little about it, nor does he tell the others of his worry over the old man. He is glad they are going to Pine Ridge agency, but he knows now even more surely than before that they should have stayed in the Deep Creek cabins on Cheyenne River.

"What do our scouts say about the soldiers in the north?" he asks Black Coyote.

"The soldiers have not come south of the Wall," the young bodyguard says. "They think we are still north of the White River."

"Good. Now, the father wants to send two men to Pine Ridge to tell the Red Cloud people we are on the way. That we will join them soon, in peace."

"Do we tell the white men, too?"

"No, we tell our brothers, the Oglalas," Talks says with some harshness. "We will wait to tell the white man anything. We will wait to see how he acts when he finds we are here and going to the Pine Ridge agency."

"Those white soldiers will never know we are here until we come marching into the agency," Black Coyote says. But Talks shakes his head.

"They will find us," he says. "They will find us soon. And another thing. The father says that when they do, our young men must remain calm. No *kicízapi*. No fighting!"

Talks turns away from the young man who still wears black on his face and strokes his rifle. Talks goes along the steep gully where they have taken shelter from the hard blowing wind. He can still hear in his thinking the hard breathing of Big

Foot, like clabbered milk being poured from a pail into a crock bowl. It saddens him that now the old man may be dying, here in this cold gully and a long way yet to go.

Then Big Foot's daughter is beside him, coming out of the darkness without speaking, but standing close. As the wind sharpens, he lifts his blanket and she moves against him. They stand together, under one blanket, and his arm is around her shoulders. His hand is on her breast and he thinks, how firm yet soft it is. It will be the fountain of life for my children, he thinks, and the blood pounds through his whole manhood. He does not speak, but he can feel her heartbeat and his own, and the smell of her is sweet.

She moves back then, her fingers touching his face once, gently, before she walks back into the darkness toward her father's tent. And even in the night, Talks has seen her smile and now watches in his mind as her body moves.

For a time he stands in the darkness, the tiny wisps of snow swirling down into the gully and around him like gnats around the face of a sweating man in summer. Only now it is cold. He remembers that for the white man and the Christian Indians this is Christmas Eve. He thinks of the celebrations at Carlisle, evergreen trees hung with brightly colored paper and burning candles, singing, and fat oranges a man could eat with the juice running down his chin. They'd had roast turkey once, for Christmas Day. The first he had ever eaten. He has not tasted turkey since, and tomorrow he knows his Christmas dinner will be a mouthful of parched corn and a wad of beef jerky.

He has had plenty of time to think about Ghost Dancing and soldiers and the People. Driving the old man's wagon all this way, the slender bundle in back under the blankets making a terrible breathing. He knows that Big Foot's heart is good and that the old man's only deception with the white man will be for diplomacy. But he does not know the hearts of all the others, or what they might do. Especially the hotbloods.

He knows that the hearts of many white soldier chiefs are good, too. But not all of them. And there are hotbloods among the Blue Coats as well. One has to worry less about the leaders than the others, he thinks. Who can tell what they will do? How can a dangerous mistake be avoided? What will the gods arrange to cause mischief?

Talks knows what the Messiah dancing is about. The People grasping for a last hope when little hope is left. He knows that shattered hopes can bring disaster. Mistakes a man makes in not-hungry times are unimportant. But now the same mistakes can turn into dangerous things. He is beginning to know the weight of leadership.

Is it better to be dead than hungry? He doesn't know. But the idea of death does not frighten him. Like the rest of the People, he believes dying is only a part of living and no man is ever complete without it.

Yellow Bird has come up and stands near him, and Talks brings his mind away from thoughts of danger and of death. The old medicine man stands looking into the darkness, and finally he speaks.

"And so we go to *wazi blo* agency. To Pine Ridge."

"Yes. The father would have it so. He is sick."

"You have seen white man's diseases and know of them. Do you think Big Foot may die?"

Talks looks at Yellow Bird for a moment, and there is suspicion in his mind that the medicine man may be speaking with some desire or expectation. But he brushes such unkind thoughts aside.

"It is not a white man's disease, like the spotted sickness," he says. "It is a disease of winter and of the very old, like distemper in horses. And he may die of it, yes."

There is a long silence before Yellow Bird speaks again.

"And we go to Pine Ridge."

"Yes."

"And we will stop at the trader's store on the way."

"Tomorrow or the next day, depending on the weather and how fast we can move, we will stop and rest and buy supplies at the trading store at Wounded Knee."

"Yes. At Wounded Knee."

15

ST. PAUL PIONEER-PRESS — At Pine Ridge, recent lights seen in the north have been explained by General Brooke's scouts to be hay stacks burning. Indians in the camps of the friendlies when pressed said it meant their brothers would be on the warpath soon.

The weather had blown in like midwinter for two days but has moderated now, and even hours after sundown the temperature is well above freezing. Scattered clouds are blown before a gentle wind through the pale night sky, their dark masses edged with lacy white in the glare of a moon coming full. They make shadow patches that move ponderously on the land, gliding across ridges, slipping down the hills, dipping into gullies and out again, like silent ships sailing through an ocean of moonlight. Watching, Capt. George Wallace almost expects to see a broad iridescent wake glittering behind them as they pass.

He stands on the porch of the post office at Wounded Knee, a tiny building, dark now, and silent since the trouble began and almost every-

189

one moved into the agency. For a while there had been dancing among the Indians who regularly lived here along Wounded Knee, in sight of this front porch, and Louis Mousseau, postmaster-trade store operator, had left for what he considered a safer temporary habitat. But Louis is back, having come with the four troops of the Seventh Cavalry, and he is even now behind his counter in the store across the road, dispensing the items from his shelves and barrels to soldiers who have come to spend their money before the bugler plays "Tattoo."

Louis had stocked his store completely from the wagon of supplies brought from Pine Ridge agency. And a good thing he'd brought that wagon of stuff, because the store had been thoroughly looted by passing Sioux after his departure, leaving all the shelves bone-bare for the unfortunate scavenging prairie mice. Now he has some tinned meat, plug tobacco, chewing gum, dried apples, and other things almost completely useless to soldiers.

The tiny settlement is spread before Wallace in the moonlight. A long, low valley bisected exactly by the agency road to the south that runs from the post office to the bright night horizon. At less than five hundred yards are the tents of the soldiers, set in neat rows with guidons marking each troop area, west of the road. At about twice that distance is a sharp gully that winds away to the west toward two ridges of high ground. On those ridges Wallace can make out the shape of two Hotchkiss guns. At least, because he knows they are there, his mind sees them whether or not his eyes do.

On the east side of the road, almost even with the post office, is the combination store and house of Louis Mousseau. The postmaster-trader has turned his living quarters over to the officers of the Seventh, so that those who desire may sleep there rather than in the tents provided by the regiment. Farther along the road is a scattering of Indian cabins, some sod, some scrap lumber. They are all dark. The order has been passed among the soldiers to stay clear of them, although Wallace can hardly see what anyone would want from these dilapidated, deserted shacks. Behind the Indian cabins, to the east and almost hidden until one walks right to its steep banks, is the creek called Wounded Knee. Its clear and cold water flows north toward its mouth at White River.

The agency is about fifteen miles to the southwest, White River somewhat farther than that to the north. We are close enough to intercept Big Foot if he opts for the Stronghold, Wallace thinks, yet well centered on his most likely avenue of approach to Pine Ridge if he decides to go there.

His mind turns to Fort Riley and Carrie, and then he is angry with himself as the mental image of the Widow Duncan intrudes. But it lasts only a moment, and he pushes all of it from his thoughts and watches the activity across the flat valley. There are still cook fires going at the far end of the troop encampment where the kitchens are and where the cooks and their helpers are just now scrubbing out the last of the supper pots and pans. At the trade store soldiers pass in and out of the door, and when the door opens, the bright orange lamplight spills out into the road. On the porch there Wallace can make out dark shapes and now and then the pinpoint of a cigar or cigarette. These are NCOs, he knows, collected to gab before the last rites of the day — "Tattoo" and the checking of tents in the encampment to ensure that each young soldier is in his place and not gone stooling, as they always say. Wallace can think of no reasonable cause for any soldier to go absent without leave from here, a long way from any friendly settlement and in a country that might grow suddenly hostile.

After all these years it still fascinates him, this movement of an Army, albeit a small one, across the land, completely independent of everything around it, creating its own world as it goes. What had been a barren little crossroads settlement with hardly more than two dozen shabby structures — including henhouses — now a busy military operations center, with all the wagons, limbers, horses, equipment, ammunition, kitchens, tentage, weapons, and men that that entails.

Half the regiment had been moved here as soon as it was evident that Big Foot was loose and south of the Badlands Wall and White River. Wallace and everyone else at Pine Ridge agency had hoped the troops along Cheyenne River would corral the old devil and get him into Fort Bennett or somewhere for safekeeping. But they hadn't. And Wallace smiles as he thinks about how General Miles must be reacting. Wringing out a lot of tail and blistering some hide, too. The men of Sumner and others had likely ridden hard, but all in the wrong places, and Big Foot had slipped south and across the White before any of them had supposed he could. All they could do, those northern units, was report the tracks they'd finally found going over the edge of the Wall and down to the river.

So everything had changed at Pine Ridge. What had been a mess for those units along the Cheyenne suddenly became everyone's mess. And where was the old bastard heading? At first everyone had supposed it was the Stronghold, where he could join with the dancers. But with the Miniconjous south of the White, it appeared more likely he was headed for the Pine Ridge agency. But to do what?

Whatever it was, the Seventh had been alerted to cover the eastern approaches to the agency, and four troops had moved to Wounded Knee under command of Maj. Sam Whitside, a fuzzy-faced veteran, tougher than a bull hide and well liked by all the officers and men. Colonel Forsyth and the remainder of the regiment were still at the agency, waiting for Big Foot to show himself. Waiting.

"Find the old rascal and determine his intentions," General Brooke had said. "But by all means, find him!"

Determine his intentions! There's the rub, Wallace thinks, and smiles to himself as the phrase occurs to him.

From the cluster of dark shapes at the trader's store, one detaches itself and moves across the road. Wallace recognizes at once the short, powerful body of his first sergeant, even though it is largely hidden now under one of the new-issue winter coats that come almost to the ground. Fitzpatrick has a cigar clamped between his teeth, and he removes it to salute.

"Evenin', cap'n," he says.

"Good evening," Wallace says. "Some of our people at the store?"

"Not now. There was. A few, sir. For tobacco, most of 'em."

Wallace says nothing. He continues to look out across the bright valley.

"Not much in the store for a sojur," Fitzpatrick says. "Unless he's cookin' his own grub. What's a sojur goin' to do with such as flour and cornmeal?"

Wallace looks at him and shakes his head.

"Are you cold?"

Fitzpatrick grins and looks down at his coat.

"No, sir, but I ain't had a chance to wear one of these nice infantry coats."

"No one could trail you," Wallace says. "You're brushing out your own tracks."

He steps off the porch, and they walk together

along the road toward the tent encampment.

"Any horses lamed today, sergeant?"

"Two, sir. Nothin' serious. Shoes on one and a good pack on the forelegs of the other will have 'em back to service in a couple days."

"How many men on sick call tonight?"

"None turned into hospital, sir. We left three back in Pine Ridge. There ain't many turn sick at night. Only in the mornings, before duty call. But once there ain't nothin' ahead but sleep or card playin', they don't turn sick unless they're dyin'."

At the far end of the tent city, a number of large Sibleys have been set up. One is a hospital; the others, kitchens and officers' quarters. For those not sleeping in Louis Mousseau's house.

"Be sure lights go out when the horn blows," Wallace says. "All this gambling is bad enough in daylight hours; I won't have it after 'Tattoo.' "

"No, sir. You know, the gamblin' now isn't too bad; it's been so long since pay call. But some of these lads will gamble for anything. Or on credit until the old moneybags comes again. They're usin' horseshoe nails for chits in some games. Some are playin' for chewin' gum. Cap'n, if you was to take soldiers out and leave 'em naked, they'd play for the horseshit, I reckon."

"Good night, sergeant," Wallace says. The stocky man salutes again and wheels off the road and toward the tent area. But Wallace remains for a while in the road, looking at the moon and the clouds and the land.

He can make out a sentry on the high ground to the west. As he watches, the man moves back away from the brow of the hill, and Wallace can now make out clearly the Hotchkiss guns. The moon makes a delicate tracing of silver along their barrels and around the muzzles that face toward the valley.

16

Walking back to the agency under the bright moon, Quinton Tapp has been stopped three times. Twice by troop sentries and once by an Indian policeman. The fact that one of the troopers was a black man from the Ninth Cavalry and the policeman was Ruby Red Hawk's brother has done nothing to improve his disposition. By the time he reaches the boarding school, his patience has almost run out and he is swearing under his breath.

"Damned niggers," he mutters. "Damned redskinned heathens. And that damned woman . . ."

He'd gone to the woodshed at dark, before the moon rose to its full brilliance, but she had not come. After a while, he slipped out past the Army sentries and through the Indian camp south of the agency, cutting back finally to the Rushville road. The camp dogs had barked at him, and a few of the men had come out and stood silently, watching him pass, their broad-brimmed hats pulled low over their faces.

Once on the road he'd walked until he passed the place he first had seen Ruby Red Hawk sprawled drunk beside the road. Perhaps a mile farther along he had come to a shack like so many Indian homes on the reservation, well back from the road.

He had stopped, standing in the growing moonlight, wondering if this might be Ruby's place. A scrawny dog ran out at him, yammering hysterically, and he had no decision to make because there she was, coming from the shack where no light showed. She was moving toward him, and he could see a shotgun in her hands.

"It's you, ain't it?" she had called.

"Yeah. Are you aimin' to shoot me?"

"I knew you'd come down that road."

"Well, are you aimin' to shoot me?"

"Not unless you try to come in here. You turn around and go back now."

She waved the shotgun, and although there was bright moonlight by then, he couldn't be sure if the hammers were cocked. The thing looked like an old-fashioned Ithaca ten-gauge, and such a cannon loaded with mustard seed would be painful. She likely had it stuffed with tenpenny nails.

"Go on back. I'm finished with you, man. You ain't gonna take me nowhere. You're just after me. You're just like a randy old bull, after me all the time, but you ain't gonna take me off this damn' reservation at all."

"Now Ruby, you know you had some good times, too. Here we've got a fine warm night. What would it hurt if we . . ."

She waved the gun again, and he knew then it was cocked because he heard the hard metallic sounds of the hammers rolling back.

"Go on back. I'm leaving for Valentine myself. You get on away from me, you old randy bull."

"All right, Ruby. But why don't you come on with me for a while?"

"I ain't goin' with you no more. I'm goin' to Valentine."

"Listen, Ruby. I sure am thirsty. Can I come in and get a drink of water and —"

"Damn you, man, get on back." She raised the shotgun to her shoulder. He started along the road toward the agency, looking over his shoulder.

"You shoot a white man, you'll catch seven kinds of hell, you bitch," he shouted.

"You go on, man, don't you come back here, ever."

The dog had run after him, yelping wildly until he'd taken a handful of rocks from the road and sent the mutt back toward the shack with a few accurate throws. As he walked along, his arm hurt almost as much as his pride, and he rubbed it with his left hand as he muttered curses about heathen women and large-gauge shotguns. Then the first sentry stopped him because he had made no effort to slip back into camp, but came storming along the road, still talking to himself.

"You gonna get yo head blowed plumb off, white man, out here wannerin' aroun' on the road after dark," the black soldier had snickered.

"Kiss my mule," Tapp replied, heading for the poker game.

By moonset Quinton Tapp is back in his bed behind the parsonage, and he's thinking, My God, twenty dollars. I won more than twenty dollars. It's got to be a good omen. A damned good omen. I may even pay Cleaborn back a little tomorrow.

So something good had happened that day — after the woman with that shotgun, and not coming back to the shed with him, probably not ever, and those fool reporters who he heard were offering a reward to whoever found Big Foot first. He has to laugh, thinking about Cleaborn and Krenshaw and a few others among the correspondent corps. They'd ridden out with the troops of the Seventh Cavalry to some place called Wounded Knee twelve or fifteen miles away, and they'd stayed one night and the next day were back at the agency. They don't like sleepin' on the ground, he thinks, and chuckles in the dark. Went out there yesterday thinkin' there'd be a big fight. But there was nothing but the same old business, so they turned tail and came back to their beds at the Hotel de Finley.

If anything really happens around here, I'll feel it in my bones. I'll know. At Wounded Knee or anywhere else, I'll feel it beforehand. I'd bet on it. I'd bet the whole twenty dollars.

Well, he thinks, Christmas come and gone. Doesn't make one helluva lot of difference. If I'd been in Omaha, I'd have been drunk all day and maybe at the brakeman's house — dependin' on where the brakeman was, of course — and he chuckles again.

But I ought to turn over a new leaf for the comin' year. Try to find me a nice decent woman who's not married to some other peckerwood, and stop drinkin' so much sour mash whisky. With the thought of sour mash, he licks his lips.

I wonder if that crazy red nigger woman is really goin' to try and get to Valentine on her own.

17

BLACK HILLS DAILY TIMES — Weather for December 28, 1890: According to the U.S. Signal Station at Spearfish, there is more unseasonably warm weather ahead for Deadwood and the rest of the state. Today, the maximum temperature is expected to be in the low 50's and the minimum will go only to the mid-thirties late tonight. The warm spell is expected to last for about two or three days and then freezing temperatures will return. Skies are expected to remain clear for at least two days and winds will be from the south generally with a velocity of only 2-to-3 miles-per-hour. Thus far during December, there have been two meteors sighted from the Spearfish station, both early in the evening.

<hr>

The warm sun and the soft winds come once more to the land of the Lakota, but Big Foot grows worse with the sickness of cold weather and old men. They have arranged bows on his wagon and stretched canvas across it to make a tent, and inside, with the sun bright, it is warm, almost like a sweat lodge. But the old man stays under his blankets and shivers. Blood has begun to run from his nose. He lies on his side so it will not stain his coat, but some of it gets on the blankets and makes evil-looking wet places in the wool, like the wounds in a deer's side where small bullets have gone in.

After two sleeps, the last cold spell has passed, and now the People are anxious to move quickly and be with their brothers in Red Cloud's camp. And be near a trader's store where they can buy flour and coffee and maybe some dried meat. At Pine Ridge, where so many of the Lakota are gathered and so many soldiers, too, the agent might issue some fresh beef. If not the agent, maybe the Army.

Scouts had returned from Pine Ridge with much news. The people of Red Cloud, they said, wait anxiously for the arrival of their friend Big Foot. But what is more important, the scouts said the dancers in the Stronghold had agreed to come into the agency and turn in their guns. Maybe, some of the elders said, if Big Foot were to arrive at the same time he could be even better at soothing hot tempers and making brothers recently angry at one another happy once more to be together.

"We must all be brothers, now that the white man presses in against our land and our people," someone had said.

"Hair Mouths," Yellow Bird had said and spat. "Even the dancers in the Stronghold are acting like old women."

Now, when things might be going better, the People mostly ignore the medicine man and his ravings.

"No one can bind up old wounds among brothers like Big Foot," they had said. "*Koképe sni yo!* Don't be afraid."

But with this hope of something good, there was also the dread of another thing. The scouts had said there are now troops at Wounded Knee, directly across the road that the People will take to Pine Ridge agency. So there had been a conference with a great deal of shouting and arguing.

"Go to the south," many said. "Around the Blue Coats. Come into Pine Ridge agency alone and proud."

"If it is not these Blue Coats, it will be others," Talks had said. "Let us go in now and have it over. Our people need rest and food, and our chief is sick."

But the arguing had gone on. Finally, Talks had said harsh words and the older men had been offended, but at last Big Foot told them what the People would do.

"This young man is right," he had said. "We must go straight in. Besides, *omápisni yélo*. I do not feel good. I am too sick to go around them any longer."

"They will take our weapons," Yellow Bird had cried.

"We will give them a few of our weapons," the chief had said. Then he smiled, blood running from his nose. "But we will keep a few, too. A people must never be completely unarmed."

So they had started directly toward Wounded Knee. Because the soldiers were near, Talks had left Big Foot's wagon to one of the other young men and caught up his pony to ride ahead with the scouts. He had felt the daughter of Big Foot watching him from her place in the wagon under the canvas. When he was mounted, he reined close to the wagon and bent down, his face close to hers.

"He sleeps now," she had said.

"Good. It will be all right. We will buy meat for him at the Wounded Knee trader's store."

He placed his hand over hers.

"Soon, we will stand together again under my blanket."

"Yes. I would like that," she said.

Then he had pulled away, feeling the heat rising inside him again.

Talks had left the rifle of Big Foot under the wagon seat, but Black Coyote and the other scouts had rifles in their hands.

"When the Blue Coats see those weapons," Talks had said, "they are going to be unhappy."

Nobody said anything. They sat around him on their ponies and stared at him with dark, unblinking eyes. They held their rifles with the butts on their knees, the muzzles up like the points of lances.

"Do you want the Blue Coats to start shooting as soon as they see you?"

"What we want is not what the Blue Coats will do," Black Coyote had said. "They will do what *they* want. And if they decide to shoot, we will have something to shoot back."

Some of the other young men had grunted and shaken their weapons. Talks had known it was useless to argue. And besides, Black Coyote was probably right. So they started, riding along American Horse Road toward Porcupine Creek, where the band would stop and rest when the sun came straight overhead.

And now the sun is there, straight overhead. The band is not far behind as the scouts come to the last ridge before going down into the valley of Porcupine Creek. Talks stops them and sends Black Coyote ahead. The young warrior with black on his face makes a low barking sound as he rides forward. He does not go all the way to the ridge but stops just short and then rides along so that he can look into the valley, but anyone there can see only his head against the sky. Talks thinks, Yes, this is a good young man, as Big Foot has said, but it is too bad he was born in the wrong time and not in the days when the Sioux were chasing the Crow from the Black Hills.

Black Coyote stops riding and stands for a long time. He raises his rifle above his head.

"What does that mean?" Talks asks, for these young men have had no practice in stalking together or in war and its signals.

"Maybe he sees something," one of the other

young men says. Talks rides up carefully and looks into the valley of the Porcupine. The young bodyguard is smiling, his teeth white in his black-painted face. At the stream below, Talks can see four men. They are watering their horses, standing with reins held loosely in their hands as the animals drink. Two are in civilian clothes and two are wearing the uniform of Sioux scouts. Seeing them, Talks feels the hair on the back of his neck go stiff, and his skin seems to move.

"Two half-blood scouts of the Hair Mouths," Black Coyote says.

"Yes, and two Oglala scouts."

"Let me shoot the two Oglalas," Black Coyote says. "As a punishment for scouting against their brothers."

"No. You will shoot no one."

They watch the four men and the horses drinking.

"What do you think they are doing here?" Black Coyote asks.

"Looking for us."

The white man's scouts are talking together. They are unconcerned. And Talks is puzzled that such men as these, two half-bloods and two Oglalas, are not aware they are being watched. They should feel our eyes on them, he thinks.

Finally, the white man's scouts begin to tighten saddle cinches and look to bridles and bits. From their saddlebags they take corn and feed the horses, holding the grain in cupped hands. The horses are white man's horses, big-boned and heavily muscled, and they need grain or else they would soon be head down and unable to run. The men still talk and laugh, and some of the sounds reach the ridge, but Talks and Black Coyote cannot understand any of the words. Talks leads his small party down a gully toward them, the unshod ponies moving quietly. As Black Coyote is suddenly on them, his rifle menacing, they look up startled and afraid, shocked to see the black on the young Miniconjou's face.

But Talks is there quickly and speaks to the men in the tongue of the white man as they stand with corn cupped in their hands.

"We are of the band of Big Foot," Talks says. "We will not harm you. But keep your weapons where they are, on the saddles. Who are you? *Nitúwe hwo?*"

One of the half-bloods drops the corn in his hand and moves to stand near Talks's pony, looking up as he speaks, shading his eyes with one hand.

"I am called Little Bat," he says in Lakota. "I am a scout and interpreter for Major Whitside, who is at Wounded Knee."

"Is this the soldier chief at Wounded Knee?"

"Yes. He has been looking for you, to ride with you back to Pine Ridge agency."

"And you will take our weapons," Black Coyote says. The man called Little Bat glances at the young black-painted warrior but then looks again to Talks, because it is obvious Talks leads here.

"Big Foot will be here soon," Talks says. "We

will wait for him. You and these others move over there to the shade of that bush and sit down."

As the four men move, Talks feels good. It is the feeling of power that men will do what he says to do. It is also good that suddenly there seems no reason to be afraid that trouble will start between them, with shooting and blood. But most of all, it is the power. He had never lusted for it, yet now that he tastes it, the flavor is good and it makes him a little drunk at first. He begins to understand that maybe it is like this with all men who suddenly have power. It is a hard thing to find, yet once a man has it, harder still to give up.

"Maybe we ought to shoot at least one," Black Coyote says, his teeth showing. Talks knows the young man is trying to frighten the four white man's scouts, but it is an opportunity for him to make his authority felt again.

"No. We will do them no harm."

"Maybe we ought to cut off their hair," Black Coyote says. "That would not harm them. One does not feel his hair being cut, unless the knife comes too close to an ear."

"We will do nothing to them. See to their horses. I don't want them running away."

"You lead like an old woman," Black Coyote says, but there is no anger in his voice. He looks at the two Oglala scouts. "Maybe you have Oglala leaders that are like old women, too. Maybe that's why you are wearing the

HairMouth's uniform and scouting against your brothers."

Black Coyote rides up the ridge toward Wounded Knee to watch for soldiers. Talks is glad he is there, not only because it takes the young hotblood away from the others where he complains about the way things are done, but also because Talks trusts him in these games that are like war must have been in the old days. He sends four other young Miniconjous in other directions to watch as well. To be surprised now would be bad, especially after taking the four white man's scouts prisoner.

Squatting on the bank of the creek, Talks makes designs in the soft earth with his fingertips. His thoughts are heavy in his head, and he knows this comes with power, too. I need to know what to do, he thinks, so I hope the old man is not long coming. And those young men I sent out, they will not be sentries long. Not even Black Coyote. They will tire of that and go off looking for something else to do. When the old man comes, he will decide. Until then, I hope nothing else happens, and especially nothing else that might cause shooting. Now for the first time he feels uneasy about not having that old rifle with him.

He walks over to the four prisoners who squat in the shade of some low brush along the creek's high-water bank. They are smoking, and the young Miniconjou who watches them with his rifle in the crook of his arm smokes, too. They watch Talks but say nothing as he comes to them. Then the man called Little Bat hands Talks his tobacco sack, and Talks takes it and rolls a cigarette in the fine white paper of the white man's cigarettes, not the bad-tasting newspaper they must usually use.

"Is the trader's store at Wounded Knee still there?" Talks asks.

"Yes. It is there," the man called Little Bat says. "It was not there for a while, because the white man went in to Pine Ridge agency. But he came back with the soldiers. So now the trader's store is open again."

"Do they have this white man's tobacco and paper?"

"Yes. I was there before I rode out on this scout. I bought that tobacco there. There is flour and sugar, too, and other things your people can buy."

"We need things like that. Is there candy?"

"Yes. There is candy."

Talks smokes for a while, looking at the white man's scouts, and their eyes look back squarely and do not shift. He thinks it is a good sign.

"This Major Whitside, is he a good man to the People?"

"Yes. He is a fair man. Soon now, when they hear you are coming in, Colonel Forsyth will come to Wounded Knee as well. He is the chief of Major Whitside."

"And what sort of man is this Colonel Forsyth?"

"He is a good man, too." The man called Little Bat hesitates. Then he goes on, looking squarely into Talks's eyes. "He does not know the People so well as Major Whitside does. But they are both good men and fair."

Talks looks at the man called Little Bat, and then grunts and turns away and goes back to his drawings in the soft earth.

The sun has hardly moved when the People come over the eastern ridge and start down into the valley of the Porcupine. Talks does not wait but rides out to meet them, telling the chief what has happened as the wagons and horses and travois come on and cross the creek before stopping to rest at midday. Soon the old man, lying under his blankets but raised up on one elbow, is listening to Little Bat tell of the Blue Coats.

"They have been looking for you," Little Bat says.

"Good. I am going straight in," Big Foot says, and he coughs and spits blood. "Go and tell the soldier chief at Wounded Knee that I come. Go and tell him."

The old man lies back down, and one of his women pulls the blanket up over his face. Walking away, they can hear him coughing.

"That old man is sick," Little Bat says.

But Talks speaks of something else. He says to Little Bat, "Send two of your men. One Oglala and the other half-blood. Send them to say we come in. I want you to stay here. You and the other Oglala."

Little Bat looks at him and smiles.

"I want you here because you speak our tongue," Talks says.

"So do these others."

A great many of the band have come near, looking at the white man's scout. Some of them look angry, but most are only curious.

"I don't want to talk with Oglalas who wear blue coats," Talks says. "I want to talk with you. Now send these two others to Whitside, as I have said."

So two of the white man's scouts ride back over the west ridge. The man called Little Bat and the one Oglala remaining squat in the shade of the high-water brush. Talks goes back to the old man's wagon, but he makes no conversation there, only leans against a wheel and looks at the two white man's scouts. The Oglala smokes again, and his eyes are down. But the man called Little Bat still has his head up, his eyes on Talks.

Near the two prisoners Yellow Bird stands, and Talks watches him, too. The old medicine man has a rifle in his hand. He sways back and forth, his lips moving but making no sound. His face is freshly painted. I do not like that old man, Talks thinks. Behind him, in the wagon, he can hear Big Foot coughing.

18

NEW YORK HERALD — The half-starved, half-clothed Sioux threaten an uprising. The ration appropriation got half-way through Congress and got stuck. And now the red man has the audacity to complain. So shoot him, of course! He is nothing but an Indian and has no vote and therefore no friends.

———————⟆●⟅———————

The squadron of the Seventh Cavalry at Wounded Knee does not wait for Big Foot to come in but goes out to take him along the line of march. Four troops of the regiment form and ride past the squalid Indian houses and the post office, Louis Mousseau on the porch of his store waving as they pass.

"The newspaper folks are going to be mad as wet bees," Louis thinks. "All of them gone back to Pine Ridge agency, and here we are about to catch old Big Foot and his boys."

The column moves east along the road with K Troop on the right, B Troop on the left, a section of Hotchkiss guns between them along with the squadron commander Maj. Samuel Whitside. These are followed by the remaining two troops and the assistant regimental surgeon riding the box of an ambulance, its canvas hood looking like starched linen in the sunlight. Along each side are the black stenciled letters *U.S. Army.*

Off to either flank along the ridges are the outriders, always two horsemen together with carbines ready. Sometimes they are as far as half a mile from the line of march. These flank watchers are veterans, picked carefully for their experience. If anything happens, they will be the first struck. But at least, far from the road, they are free of the ranks of the close column, free of the sergeants' watchful eyes.

The troops say little as they ride. When they do speak, it is with laughter coming too quickly and somehow strained. Their knuckles show white as they grip bridle reins. Capt. George Wallace can sense the electric excitement. And although he has ridden out like this before, it has its effect on him as well.

First Sergeant Sean Fitzpatrick rides up, his face red and wet with sweat under the short visor of his forage cap. He has the black leather strap fixed tightly beneath his heavy chin, and the whole appearance is one of a small French kepi holding the man up by the neck. Wallace acknowledges the salute with a short wave.

"Cap'n, some of these men is nervous as pregnant mice," Fitzpatrick says.

"Maybe someone ought to sing to them," Wallace says. Fitzpatrick grunts and stares across the rolling expanse of plain. There are few trees near the road. Along some of the ridges are pines, mostly stunted. Only in the draws can timber of any size be seen. For the most part, the land rolls away in treeless billows.

"Them red heathen could hide a regiment within pistol shot of a white man, and he'd never know they was there," Fitzpatrick says. "And some of these young sojurs are beginnin' to sweat about that."

The young soldiers, Wallace thinks. Going into a possible fight for the first time. Learn quick or die, maybe. You teach a man only so much about how to act under fire, then instinct and luck keep him alive. His own instincts had been good apparently, and his luck as well. Now the excitement is still there and the fear, too. But he has grown accustomed to fear. No, he thinks, you never really grow accustomed to it. But Wallace has come to satisfactory terms with it, and handles it to the extent that his troopers are never aware that he has the taste of it in his mouth before any shooting starts.

"A body might expect that at least once in this here Army they'd give us experienced sojurs all around," Fitzpatrick complains.

"You have to watch them closely, Fitz," Wallace says. "You know it just never works in such a perfect way. You just have to watch the young ones. But one thing. If there's to be shooting this trip, then the other people have to start it."

"And they damn well may start it, too," Fitzpatrick says. "I heard them scouts talking. Old Big Foot said he was comin' in. So now why are we all randied and goin' out after him? It might make him mad as hell."

"It might have been safer to wait for him, that's true. But I don't think the major wanted to chance playing it safe."

"How's that, cap'n?"

"Look what happened to Sumner up north of White River. He waited for the old devil to come in, and the next thing anybody knew, the whole kit had slipped off."

"I'd still like to meet these Miniconjurs on my ground instead of out here."

"Unfortunately, they decided not to come to Fort Riley, didn't they?" Wallace says. He glances back along the column. "Fitz, police the rear files. Keep it closed up."

Fitzpatrick wheels out alongside and trots back toward the rear. The young recruits watch him pass, expectantly, eyes bright and faces wet with sweat, their cheeks smudged with the dust already collecting there.

"Have patience now, lads," one of the sergeants is saying. "Have a little patience, and you may get the chance to decorate your tent with some Sioux hair before nightfall."

"This ain't no shootin' yet," Fitzpatrick calls as he passes. "And see none of you make it one. You hear that? You just keep them heads up and them peckers down until you're told what to do."

And then the Sioux are before them, fanned out along a low hogback in what looks like a skirmish line. In their hands are rifles, and the tails of many ponies are done up in a bun. Some of their horses are painted, too, with designs across the shoulders and forelegs. The squadron outriders come fogging in, their gallop setting up plumes of dust pointing into the main body from either flank. Over the brow of the hill the rest of the Miniconjous appear slowly, coming on behind their young warriors. Leading them is a wagon with a lopsided canvas stretched over willow bows. Riding beside this wagon are a number of men, some of them young and painted, and most of them carrying weapons. One of these, his face striped white and black, waves a new Winchester above his head and makes sharp barking noises.

"Listen to that cur dog bark," one of the noncoms says.

"If them red beasties start to scald us, he's the first son of a bitch I'll kill," says another.

Whitside has begun to give his troop commanders their instructions.

"Skirmish to the left and right, leading troops, on foot. Horses' holders to the rear. Unlimber your guns, sir."

As the little artillery pieces swing around and are dropped, their trails kicked into the dirt of the road, the cavalry begins to form its own line. K Troop peels off to the right, forming a long double row of men. As the troop turns back to the front, the order to dismount runs along the line, and the men go down, carbines now in their hands. Every fourth soldier remains mounted, takes the reins of the riderless horses, and moves back about fifty yards. These are veterans who can handle four horses under fire. It runs the percentage of recruits along the line even higher, a fact every officer and noncom has at the front of his mind. Wallace trots his horse along the rear of his formation, and some of the men look back at him, their eyes white in dust-grimed faces. Across the road, B Troop has deployed, too. Between the two troops are the cannons.

"We'll give 'em a taste of shell," one of the artillery men shouts.

"Injuns damn well don't like wagon guns."

"That may be so, boys, but old Fort Riley never looked so good."

"Keep quiet in there and listen to your sergeants!"

The line of Indian men comes on, close enough now that features and the designs of paint on faces can easily be made out. The artillery officer gives a quiet command, and the Hotchkiss breeches come open with an oily rattle, ready to receive the shells. But Whitside raises one hand slightly and the gun crews stand waiting, one man holding a shell ready for the open breech.

Wallace prepares his command.

"Load," he orders.

The big hammers of the Springfields roll back and the awkward breeches are pulled up, and into the chambers go the brutal lead-nosed 45–55 rounds. The breeches are pressed closed with a gentle click, the noise of it running down the line like fingers softly snapping at an officers' mess quadrille. They stand half-turned from the advancing line of Sioux, holding muzzles up, but the weapons cocked and ready to be brought to shoulder.

"Easy," Wallace says softly. "Keep those muzzles up."

Fitzpatrick moves along the line, too, dismounted, his Colt six-shooter in his hand.

"Don't stick your fingers in them trigger guards yet," he says. "Keep your finger out of them trigger guards; now boys, just do what I tell you, and we'll all get back to Kansas in a piece."

The advancing line of warriors finally stands, holding in their nervous ponies while the leading wagon with the crooked canvas top comes on slowly toward the troops, passing through the young painted men who still hold their rifles ready. One of Whitside's interpreters rides out to meet the wagon, and soon the wagon halts, too, not fifty yards from the soldiers. There is an exchange between the half-blood interpreter and the wagon driver, and then a signal, and Whitside turns to Wallace.

"Come along," Whitside says. "You men hold it steady."

The two officers ride out to the wagon, where the canvas is being partly held aside by two women. As they pull up alongside, they can see an old man lying on the wagon bed, holding himself up on one elbow. His head is bent to one side, and blood running from his nose stains the blankets pulled over his shoulders. One of the women bends to him and wipes at his nose with a rag, doing little except smearing the blood across the old man's face. His cheeks are very wrinkled and his ears seem to Wallace monstrously big. Behind each of them is a small gray plait of hair that hangs down almost to the old man's shoulders.

Little Bat has come over now, and Whitside acknowledges him with a curt nod, and as they begin to talk with the old man in the wagon, a young Indian in white man's clothing rides near. He holds a rifle, but at his side, and his face is not painted.

"My name is Talks With Horses," the young man says in English. "I have been to Carlisle and can talk the white man's tongue."

"Good," Whitside says. "You have already met the man called Little Bat, and here is another of my interpreters."

He bends into the wagon from the saddle and holds out his right hand. The old man takes it in his and they shake for a few seconds, each looking into the other's face.

"I am happy to see you, Big Foot," Whitside says.

"I am happy to see you," the old man replies. "I am very sick."

Little Bat translates, and the man called Talks With Horses listens intently, frowning slightly. As the talk continues, more people crowd close around the wagon. But to Wallace, it seems the

221

tension has suddenly dissipated. Even so, nearby he sees the young man who barks like a dog, and the eyes in the painted face glare at him. Behind him are a number of the tribal elders, and there Wallace sees a man who looks nearly as old as Big Foot, and he wears what Wallace knows is a Ghost Shirt. On his head is an outrageous feathered hat, a stuffed crow it appears to be, and Wallace turns away to hide his smile.

"The father has been very sick," Talks With Horses is saying in the abrupt and sometimes unintelligible Carlisle English. "He very sick now."

"Yes, I am sorry to see that," Whitside says. "We will have one of our white doctors look at him."

After Little Bat has interpreted that speech, Talks With Horses says again, "He very sick. Since we left Cheyenne River. But more sick now as then."

"Young man, I am glad you're here," Whitside says to the Indian called Talks. "You can listen to what I say and tell your chief if what my interpreter says is right."

"Yes, I will do that."

Whitside turns back to the old man, who seems to struggle to keep himself propped up off the wagon bed.

"I have come to escort you in to Pine Ridge agency," Whitside says. As Little Bat speaks, Big Foot has a coughing fit and the blood runs down across his upper lip. The woman daubs at it with the stained cloth.

"Yes. I am ready to come in. I was coming in anyway."

"Good. We will camp tonight and feed your people at Wounded Knee." Whitside pauses a moment, looking around at the crowd gathered near the wagon. "I need a council with my people," he says.

"Yes, you can do that if you want to," Big Foot says.

Whitside and Wallace and the two interpreters move away from the wagon, holding their horses close together as they talk. Once more Whitside looks around at the crowd of Indians and along the line of warriors who still stand not far away and facing the troops.

"I've got to take all these weapons, and their horses, too."

"Wait a minute, major," Little Bat says. "You try taking these weapons now, and there's going to be hell to pay."

"They look mighty mean to me," the other interpreter says. "I'd hate to try taking those rifles, major, or the horses either."

"I don't see much choice," Whitside says. "Those are orders right down from Miles."

Little Bat shakes his head, and he and the other man look at Wallace, and he knows they are imploring him for support.

"Major, I think maybe they're right," he says. "Right now they look calmed down, but if we start taking their guns and horses, it could get

223

ugly quick, sir. Why not ride them into Wounded Knee, feed 'em a good bait, and in the morning disarm them?"

"A good feed would take a lot of sting out of 'em," Little Bat says. "From what I've seen, they ain't had much grub in the past few days."

"Old Miles would skin my ass," Whitside says. "But I think you're probably right."

He scratches his bristling beard, looking once more at the line of young warriors. He shakes his head.

"All right. I'll send a heliograph message back to Pine Ridge agency and ask the colonel to bring out the rest of the regiment. By morning we'll simply overawe the bastards, I hope. How many fighting men you think they've got here, Bat?"

"Maybe a hundred and fifty. But their women would fight, too. It's a tough bunch, major."

"How many guns?"

"Maybe one hundred repeaters."

"Damn! That's a lot of rifles," Whitside says.

"You've seen a lot already and under those blankets are more, I'd bet."

"What the hell do they do with them? They don't hunt anymore."

"Major, a rifle is important to these people. Just to have it. When a Lakota man gets his hands on one, it's pure hell takin' it away from him."

"Yes. I knew that without asking, but . . ." Whitside looks at the group of young men around Big Foot's wagon. "Let's hope the whole regiment lined up tomorrow will convince them they'd best cooperate."

"I ain't too sure," Little Bat says.

"Major, the old man may be suspicious about this little talk we're having without his man Talks With Horses here to listen in," Wallace says.

"I've been thinking about that, too. We'll tell him we've been discussing his health. That old man is sick, no doubt about that. Let's bring up the ambulance and carry him in to Wounded Knee in that; let the sawbones start wipin' his nose. That old wagon he's in hasn't got a sign of any springs."

They all nod.

"Good. That's what this conference has been about. Now let's ease these folks into Wounded Knee before somebody decides to dispute us."

Back at the wagon, Little Bat explains that Big Foot will be more comfortable riding in an Army ambulance, and Talks With Horses relays his own sentiments to the same effect. The spring vehicle is brought up, and four soldiers lift Big Foot from the wagon and into the ambulance, sliding him in on a stretcher. They roll up the canvas and tie it on either side so the old chief can look out as he rides.

"This is a fine wagon you've got," Big Foot says. An old woman is with him in the ambulance and a younger one as well. The troopers nearby look at her and wink and grin. A fine-looking piece, some of them say.

Then they are lined out for the camp at

Wounded Knee, the two troops that trailed coming out leading going back. Following them are the Sioux, and then the cannons and B and K troops. Wallace feels intense relief. But it pains him to acknowledge that he is a little disappointed, too. The troopers and the young warriors with rifles continue to look at one another, but with more curiosity than malevolence.

Before moving back to the head of the column to be with Whitside, Wallace calls Fitzpatrick and instructs him.

"Get those hammers down, Fitz."

"You want 'em unloaded, cap'n?"

"No. Keep rounds chambered, just in case. But hammers down."

"Goddamn, I sure hate havin' these green recruits lettin' hammers down on live chambered rounds, sir. It's a good way to get a horse's foot shot off."

"Can't be helped. Do it. I don't want some chance shot to start a war."

The dust is worse now than coming out because the column is moving along the road where the earlier passage of the squadron has churned the hard-packed earth into powder. They ride facing the lowering sun, too, and eyes are squinted against it. The whole column seems immersed in a red luminous fog. The dust creates a light of its own, from deep inside where the late sun's rays have been bent and reflected and refracted until finally the shining appears to be coming out instead of going in. People walking beside the wagons and travois cannot be seen except for their heads, which float above the glowing haze. But it is only a short distance to the valley of Wounded Knee, and nobody complains except a few of the file closers at the extreme rear of the column.

Wallace is at the head again when Whitside issues his instructions.

"George, send a detail on in, and set up five Sibleys, just south of our own troop tent area. Three can be used for any of these people who don't have shelter. One for our interpreters. I want them close to the Sioux. And one for Big Foot. Put an oil burner in that one and some extra blankets. Get word to the surgeon that I want him to do everything he can for the old man. Have the commissary detail break out a ration of bacon and bread for these people."

"Where will we camp the rest of them, major?"

"On south of our camp. I want 'em at least a hundred yards from those Sibleys I mentioned. In the open space between we'll disarm them in the morning. Post some guides for these hoot owls to get 'em into their camp. I don't want any of them wandering off."

The column moves along the road between the post office and the trader's store. At that point the Indians break from the line of march, many of them, and crowd inside the store to buy sugar and coffee. The following soldiers are ready to intervene, to move them on, but the officers pass word among them that the Indians should be allowed to buy whatever they can afford.

"It's better to pamper 'em a mite than to shoot their guts out," one noncom says.

"That's your own goddamned opinion," another replies.

The pause gives the quartering party time to get set, so when the Sioux move once more, soldiers are ready to show them where they will bed down. Big Foot's ambulance pulls out of the column and waits until the Sibley tents are erected. Talks With Horses remains beside him, and the young woman is still in the ambulance. All the others move on. As Wallace rides past, the surgeon calls him.

"It's a bad case of pneumonia. Not much can be done. We can try to make him comfortable."

"The major wants you to do what you can," Wallace says. Back in the road he watches the camp forming farther along. The Indians mill about for a time before starting to pitch their tentage, like old dogs, Wallace thinks, turning around before lying down. Then he is suddenly aware that not a single rifle is in sight.

"Where the hell are the rifles?" he mutters.

Fitzpatrick joins him and they watch the camp taking shape. The Miniconjous fan out on the west side of the road just short of the deep gulley that runs toward the high ground, where Wallace sees the cannon going back into position. When all the band gets in, their tents will run from the road all the way to the base of the ridge. A pony herd is forming just west of the Indian tents.

"By God," Fitzpatrick says. "I don't see any rifles now."

"Yes, and I'm not too happy about that."

An Army wagon is driven through the Indian camp, and the people crowd around it, taking the bacon and hardtack soldiers hand down.

"Maybe I'm just spooky," Wallace says. "We've been lucky so far."

"They seem terrible calm to me," Fitzpatrick says. "It ain't too natural."

"I just hope they don't break somehow."

"Well, I'll tell you one thing, sir. I'm sure as hell glad they ain't five hundred of them bucks."

"Fitz, I'm glad there's not two hundred."

"The rest of the regiment gets here, we'll count about four hundred ten or more men, I guess. Not countin' them Oglala Sioux scouts."

It is growing darker, the long shadows running out from the ridges and the deep purples and blues creeping up from the low ground. The waning moon casts little light and only later will make the landscape silver for an hour or more before setting. The evening star is a single speck of light in the western sky.

The two men start back up the road toward their own camp when Fitzpatrick reaches out and touches Wallace's arm. They see the young warrior with the paint-blackened face near the road at the edge of the Indian camp.

"It's that Cur Dog," Fitzpatrick says.

"Is that his name?"

"It's what the lads are callin' him. Didn't you

hear him barkin' like a dog back there when we found 'em?"

"I can't recall."

"He's a mean-lookin' bastard, ain't he, cap'n? And he's got a new Winchester. I seen it."

As the two white men ride on toward their camp, the young Miniconjou watches them, his eyes moving in his motionless head. His hands caress the smooth stock of the rifle, hidden now beneath the folds of a blanket that drapes his shoulders. His lips are parted, and in the last light his teeth gleam like the whites of his eyes above the dark stripes across his nose and cheekbones.

On the ridges to the west, the Hotchkiss gun crews dig in their trails, carefully aiming the little cannons directly at the Miniconjou encampment.

PART FOUR
THE HOPE KILLERS

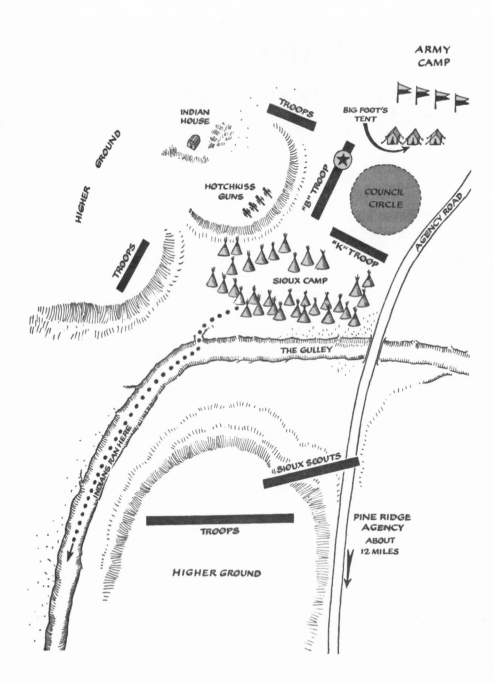

ARMY CAMP

TROOPS

INDIAN HOUSE

BIG FOOT'S TENT

HIGHER GROUND

HOTCHKISS GUNS

"B" TROOP

COUNCIL CIRCLE

TROOPS

"K" TROOP

AGENCY ROAD

SIOUX CAMP

THE GULLEY

INDIANS RAN HERE

SIOUX SCOUTS

PINE RIDGE AGENCY ABOUT 12 MILES

TROOPS

HIGHER GROUND

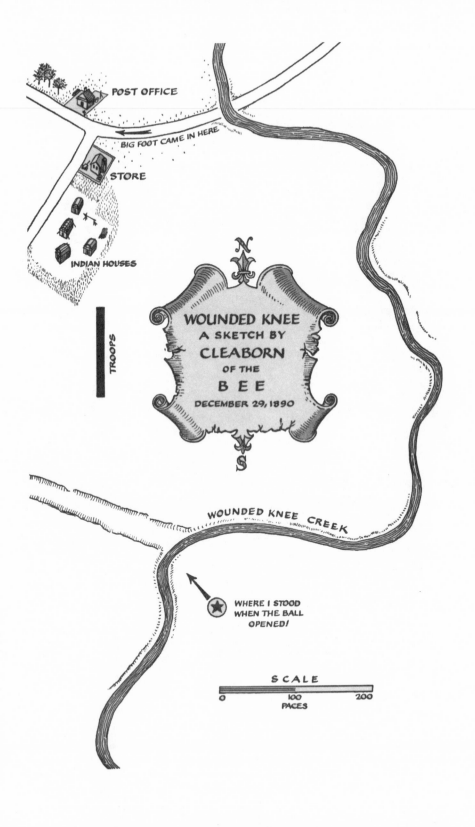

POST OFFICE

BIG FOOT CAME IN HERE

STORE

INDIAN HOUSES

TROOPS

WOUNDED KNEE
A SKETCH BY
CLEABORN
OF THE
BEE
DECEMBER 29, 1890

N

S

WOUNDED KNEE CREEK

WHERE I STOOD
WHEN THE BALL
OPENED!

SCALE

0   100   200
        PACES

19

OMAHA BEE — Old Big Foot is in tow. As the military approached, the hostiles formed a line of battle with guns and knives. An Indian who was later identified as Big Foot walked out toward the soldiers and said he wanted to speak to Major W. Dismounting, the latter walked out to the chief.

"I am sick. My people want peace," Big Foot said.

Major W. said, "No parley! Surrender or fight!"

The response came: "Surrender."

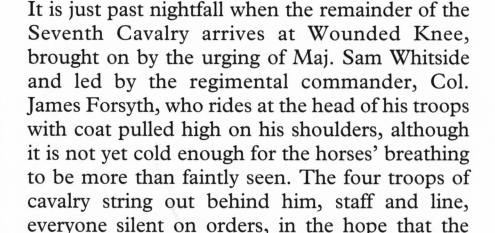

It is just past nightfall when the remainder of the Seventh Cavalry arrives at Wounded Knee, brought on by the urging of Maj. Sam Whitside and led by the regimental commander, Col. James Forsyth, who rides at the head of his troops with coat pulled high on his shoulders, although it is not yet cold enough for the horses' breathing to be more than faintly seen. The four troops of cavalry string out behind him, staff and line, everyone silent on orders, in the hope that the command can slip into camp without the Indians knowing it — hence avoiding the possibility of unnecessarily frightening them. It is a faint hope, because a part of the column is a troop of Oglala Sioux scouts, many of whom have relatives in the Big Foot band.

Midway in the squadron are the newspaper reporters. Wilmot Cleaborn has rented an open buggy, because he is unaccustomed to horses, and with him rides one of the Pine Ridge store-keepers with a small keg of whisky. To celebrate with the officers of the Seventh, he has said, for this quick and bloodless end to the fake war. Beside the buggy ride Chandler Akins and Wilson Krenshaw on horses obtained in one fashion or another at the agency. All the other correspondents have stayed at Pine Ridge to await the arrival of the dancers from the Stronghold.

Before they left the agency, Quinton Tapp had seen the keg of whisky.

"What are you aimin' to do with that?" he'd asked.

"Share it with the regiment's officers," the storekeeper had said.

"Hell, it's not enough to wet a man's whistle, as the sayin' goes. It's barely enough to give 'em all a decent breath."

A little later, as the troops were forming up to make the march to Wounded Knee, they had seen Tapp riding out on the Rushville road, going south in the late afternoon sun.

"Where's your pardner headed, Wilmot?" Krenshaw had asked.

"Rushville. To f-f-file a story for me. A-a-about

the end of the war," Cleaborn said. "And I suspect he'll s-s-stop by that Indian squaw's house
on the way back. He's been s-s-sniffing around
there."

"The old boar and the sow," Krenshaw had
said, and laughed.

"At least he won't be around," Akins said. "So
you can talk about him all you want and feel safe,
can't you?"

Krenshaw scowled, but he said no more about
Quinton Tapp while Akins was in hearing.

Moving across the darkening ridges, there had
at first been much banter and laughter. Tensions
were eased now that the dancers were coming in
from the Badlands and old Big Foot's bunch was
safely under cannon muzzles once more. This
scare would soon be over, the soldiers back at
Fort Riley and the pleasures of Junction City, the
newspapermen returned to their various towns
and cities. Many would be forsaking the dust and
bad food for linen tablecloths and flush toilets,
electric streetcars, and wall-mounted telephones.
It is a prospect even the fire eaters enjoy because
they, too, are bored with trying to make a war
where there is none.

"Now I wonder why the Widow didn't come
along?" Krenshaw had said.

"Having tea with the g-g-general," Cleaborn
said.

Some of the soldiers, hearing the remark, had
laughed.

"I understand General Brooke has offered her

a horse and an officer to escort her anywhere she wants to go," Akins said.

"I th-th-think they're all missing out," Cleaborn had said. "Since Sitting Bull was k-k-killed, this Big Foot's the m-m-meanest and most d-d-dangerous old savage on the plains."

"Wilmot, you've been reading too much of your own copy," Akins said, and nobody laughed except Cleaborn.

After darkness came on and the cavalcade neared Wounded Knee, the order had passed down the line to stop talking and smoking. Soon Whitside's scouts had come out to meet them and guide the command into the north end of the valley, away from the Indian encampment.

Now, as the horses move past the post office and peel off to the west where the new arrivals will make a tentless camp, the smell of bacon cooking is heavy and sweet in the valley. They can see fires around the Miniconjou tipis to the south because it has been a long time since the Sioux made their fires in holes to hide them from observation across the flat plain.

Once the camp guard is established and the horses tended to, the officers gather in Capt. George Wallace's tent. Colonel Forsyth is among them. They crack open the keg from the Pine Ridge agency store and pass tin cups around. The talking is subdued, and to the sentry walking nearby, his carbine slung, it doesn't seem much of a party. After only a short time the officers begin leaving Wallace's hospitable quarters and going toward their own bedrolls. The three correspondents have been invited to take part in the small celebration, too. When Whitside leaves the tent, Akins walks with him through the darkness toward Louis Mousseau's store, where the major is quartered.

"From what's been said, it appears your capture of Big Foot went rather smoothly."

"It was a little scary at first. But he was of the same mind as ourselves. He wanted to come in here peacefully. His young men, I guess, finally accepted it."

"I had understood you made threats at the time."

"No. We skirmished two troops and ran out the Hotchkiss guns, but when I rode out to talk with the old man, I made no threats. Their young men were acting like prairie chickens about to mate, feathers ruffled and strutting around stiff-legged. But hell, Chandler, even those young bucks didn't come to fight."

"And Big Foot is really sick?"

"About near death, I'd say."

"And tomorrow?"

"Well," the old soldier says. He hesitates a moment and then shrugs. "We disarm them and ship them off to . . . well, Chandler, I'm not really at liberty to say."

"All right, major. I thank you for what you've given me."

But there is something disquieting about the coming day. Walking along the road toward the post office, where he plans to sleep along with the other two reporters, Akins finds 1st Sgt. Sean Fitzpatrick inspecting his guards. The two men stop and talk quietly.

"Oh yes, they've given us the plan already," Fitzpatrick says. "And I ain't likin' it worth a damn."

"How's that, sergeant?"

"All them Sioux men we'll get in a bunch. Right in that cleared space in front of the Sibleys . . ."

"Where old Big Foot is sleeping tonight?"

"Yeah, right in front of them Sibleys. Their women and kids we'll keep in the Indian camp. Then we'll form B and K troops in line, facin' the men and between them and the Indian camp."

"Between the men and their families?"

"Yeah. But that's not what bothers me. Although a man could get knifed from the back while he was watchin' the men. But what bothers me, sir, is being so close to them red bastards. When we start takin' their guns away, we ought to be standin' off a ways, where they can't get at us so easy if they feel inclined."

"I think I understand. Those two troops will actually be right cheek by jowl with them."

"That's it, sir. The two troops will be in an *L* shape so's to box in the men on two sides — south and west. Then off to the east a good distance will be G Troop. The rest of the command will be back even farther yet, surroundin' the whole kit. Them Oglala scouts, too. They'll be mounted and across the valley south of here."

"Whose plan was this, sergeant?"

"Hell, sir, I don't know," Fitzpatrick says, and laughs. "Us poor old helpless sojurs don't never know who tells us what to do, we just do it. Say, why didn't Tapp come out with you fellows?"

"I'm told he's squirrel hunting," Akins says, moving off. He can hear the sergeant laughing behind him. What he has just heard worries him. When experienced noncoms like Fitzpatrick smell trouble, it is usually not long in coming.

He pauses in the road to look at the star-flecked night, and as he does, a bright meteor drops like a wounded firefly down the sky from almost directly overhead. Its brilliant scratch across the black dome lasts for fully fifteen seconds, etching a silver path between the last two stars of the Big Dipper handle, then plunging toward the horizon before burning out in the atmosphere. Akins doesn't believe in signs, as some of the Miniconjous just down the road might. So he dismisses it from his mind and goes to his bedroll.

Eighteen miles away, sitting on the mare in the middle of the Rushville–to–Pine Ridge road directly before the house of Ruby Red Hawk, Quinton Tapp sees the meteor, too, and watches it burn through the blackness. Then once more, as he has already done a number of times, he calls her name into the stillness of the night. The

241

mare fidgets under him as he shouts again, then again. There is no answering sound but the soft wind blowing through the tattered stalks of parched corn in back of the shack, making the whisper of silk rubbed against silk. He nudges the mare's flanks with his heels and she moves in closer, where Tapp calls once more with the same result. Off to the east, there are two coyotes quarreling, now and then breaking into a full-throated duet. He slips down, opening his coat and feeling for the Smith and Wesson in its shoulder holster. But he leaves it there. He steps across the porch and reaches for the door, but it is already open and he moves inside.

Across the dark, single room, Tapp can make out the gray rectangle of a rear door, also open, but he can see nothing else until he strikes a match. There is a table in the room and on that a coal-oil lamp. He moves over and lights it, and after he has replaced the blackened globe, looks around the room. The light cast is a dirty rust color, giving the small room the appearance of an ancient sandstone cave. There is a three-legged stool, a bunk bed with a straw tick, a large woodbox, a kitchen stove with one leg broken off and supported with a chunk of wood that might once have been the tip of a fence post. Tacked to one wall is a faintly colored calendar picture of a pale Jesus holding his hands out over a flock of smudgy white lambs.

Quinton Tapp is aware of a strange, yet some-how familiar, odor. It is the smell of smoke and

242

fat and of something else he has never been able to define.

It's like crawlin' into an old goat shed, he thinks, where the goat hasn't been for years but is somehow still there. Except this isn't goat. It's Indian. Pure heathen, red-nigger Indian. There is something about it thick and musty and somehow exciting too, and warm, like the inside of a cowhide glove left wet in the sun until it's steaming.

For an instant he wonders if when they come into a white man's house they smell something strange and say to themselves, That's a Hair Mouth white man smell.

On the stove is a battered pan. There is a hardened ring of grease around the inside and there, too, a number of bones, small bones. He inspects them closely and thinks, By God, no wonder that feisty dog hadn't come out to bark. She's ate it.

"Well," he mutters softly, "wherever she's gone, she went with a full belly, I reckon." The bones had been picked clean, almost as though polished.

Something in one corner catches his eye, and he moves over holding the lamp and sees a corn-husk doll. A muscle in his belly tightens, and the hair along the back of his neck moves. He takes the doll up and peers at it closely in the lamplight and sees that a small, pinched face has been drawn on it, probably with a bit of charcoal. He suddenly knows the woodbox is not a woodbox at all — wadded in it is worn cotton bedding.

"I'll be good goddamned," he says aloud. "A crib. It's a damned crib for a baby. At least for a small whelp."

The breeze swings the rear door on noisy hinges and Quinton Tapp jumps, drops the husk doll, and reaches for the pistol before he realizes it is only the wind. He shudders again, looking down at the crib and the doll beside it on the dirt floor.

"I'll be goddamned," he whispers. He sits on the bunk bed, the lamp on the floor between his feet, and takes a pint bottle from inside his coat. The heat of the lamp is on his legs, and he can smell its oily vapor. He drinks in long, hard swallows and coughs, wiping his mouth with the back of his hand.

That was it then, he thinks. A little red booger, right here in this shack. That's why she never wanted me in here. She didn't want me to know about that kid, that little red-nigger whelp. Because she figured that if I knew she had this kid, then I never would take on the job of getting her out of this place.

But where did the kid come from? She never mentioned a husband. Not that a husband is required, he thinks, taking another long pull at the sour mash.

Valentine. She'd wanted to get there in a hard way, any way she could. Then maybe whoever it was knocked her up was there, in Valentine. A white man. Could be that's why she was afraid of her own people. Not just the Carlisle thing, but the Carlisle thing plus a half-white, half–Hair Mouth whelp, bastard legally and racially as well.

"It's a girl, I'll bet," he says to himself.

A baby girl. Sure as hell a little half-white baby girl. Every night that she'd come to the agency, looking for a man to set her free from this place — he looks around the dilapidated shack — getting drunk, laying up with men, doing whatever she thought might help, that little baby was left right here, in this shack, in that crib. Lying there awake and looking up into the blackness and hearing the coyotes and maybe prairie mice in the cupboard.

Across one wall is a wooden shelf, and there a broken can of what was once baking powder, turned on its side. And nothing more.

The coyotes are silent now, and there is only the faint sound of the wind and the creak of the rear door on its hinges. Tapp blows out the lamp and outside finds a well in back with a low curbing. He draws up a bucket of water for the mare, then beds down on the porch. He doesn't want to go back inside the shack somehow, and he leans against the wall, his legs stretched before him on the hard-packed ground, sipping from the bottle until it is gone. Then he rolls on his side and pulls his coat collar around his ears. There ain't a thing I can do about it anymore, he thinks, even if I wanted to. Come mornin', I'll ride up toward Wounded Knee and pick up the Seventh when it's bringin' in the Big Foot bunch and forget all about this damned woman and her little girl whelp.

How would it be, havin' a little whelp around all the time? How would it feel to have put somethin' on this earth by a thing you've done, and then have to raise it and take care of it and protect and feed it? In fact, how would it be to have a wife, and a place to come back to each time you've been gone, where the fire is made and the table set with meat, and the bed warm and ready? A place where a man didn't have to jump up and grab a pistol each time he heard a limb brushin' against the house in the night. How would it be to own things, things other than a horse and a shotgun, but chairs to sit in, a glass closet to hold a woman's nice things, a gold watch fob for Sunday?

Well, he thinks, the time for all of that may be past for me. I made the choice years ago. It's a waste of time, thinkin' about some little whelp runnin' through the house makin' a mess of everything and requirin' attention so it can grow up decent.

A screech owl makes its trembling call very close by, probably in the rafters of the shack. In his mind Quinton Tapp can see the little brown bird with the horned head. He pulls his coat tighter. Then he thinks, I wonder how old that little girl might be? Lyin' down here in the dark, waitin' alone for her mother. Then he is asleep.

20

CINCINNATI POST — On this sunny Sabbath, Major Whitside of the Seventh Cavalry is said to have captured old Big Foot and his followers, surprising the renegades at Porcupine Creek. The rest of the regiment left Pine Ridge late in the day to assist. Tomorrow, December 29, the entire band will be escorted in. The Indian troubles can safely be said to be past.

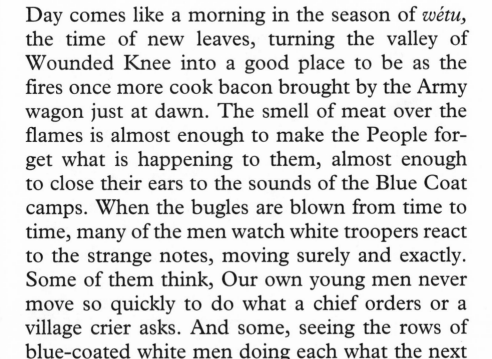

Day comes like a morning in the season of *wétu*, the time of new leaves, turning the valley of Wounded Knee into a good place to be as the fires once more cook bacon brought by the Army wagon just at dawn. The smell of meat over the flames is almost enough to make the People forget what is happening to them, almost enough to close their ears to the sounds of the Blue Coat camps. When the bugles are blown from time to time, many of the men watch white troopers react to the strange notes, moving surely and exactly. Some of them think, Our own young men never move so quickly to do what a chief orders or a village crier asks. And some, seeing the rows of blue-coated white men doing each what the next man is doing, and he the next, and so on down the line, become uneasy with the sight, as they are uneasy with white man's machines, because they do not understand it. Their eyes go to one another, then quickly turn away so that the apprehension will not show.

Once they have finished their own breakfast of meat and hardtack, the Blue Coat soldiers move away from their tents and begin to form long lines. The new sun makes a bright shining along the barrels of the short guns they carry. Seeing these, many of the young Sioux smile because they know the soldier guns are the same kind of single-shot carbines carried into the fight at the Greasy Grass when Custer was killed and Crazy Horse was alive and when the People and their brothers were as many as the grains of sand along the rivers in muddy season time.

A few of them even talk about those times. They tell once again the stories of that afternoon when the soldiers under these same flags rode down to Miniconjou Ford on that Montana stream the whites call Little Bighorn and were turned back to the hill where they all died. Of course, the swallowtail flags then had been red-and-white-striped with a circle of white stars, and now they have two large red and white stripes with the white man's letter symbols on them. It is a good day to remember, that afternoon on the Greasy Grass more than fifteen summers ago. But that was then and this is now, they think, and today it is the soldiers who are as many as the grains of sand, and there are those wagon guns on the hill besides, ready to sting like wasps. So the men do not smile long, nor do they tell many of the good stories from the old days.

To the south, they can see their brothers the Oglalas dressed in soldiers' blue uniforms and wearing fur hats and riding horses, grain fed, with *U.S.* branded on their flanks. And some of them think it is too bad these Oglalas, who now scout for the Hair Mouths, have not been branded on the flank, too. The Oglalas are forming a line across the valley just beyond the deep gulley and short of high ground where there are more soldiers, these on horses and holding their carbines muzzle up in the new sun.

"They are going to kill us," Yellow Bird says, his old teeth grinding at a fat chunk of bacon.

No matter what Yellow Bird says, most of the Miniconjous are calm with the warmth of the morning sun on their heads. Many are still hungry and think only of the bacon cooked on sticks held over the open flames of campfires. A few are troubled with bad digestion, partly because they are unaccustomed to fat pork and partly because the soldiers all around make them nervous. They nibble at the meat and try to look calm so the women and children will not be disturbed. From the edge of their eyesight they watch all the lines of soldiers forming, and they look at the little cannons on the hill to the west where they can also see an abandoned house. An Oglala lived there once, they think, and he bought his coffee and salt from that trader's store up the road and visited with the other Oglalas who had once lived in the shacks clustered near the post office. But whoever he was, he had gone, his wife and children with him. Near his house stand the cannons, the nasty little wagon guns, and the soldiers who work the guns sit on the porch of the abandoned house and smoke cigarettes rolled in fine white paper.

Outside the tent where Big Foot lies, Talks stands in the morning sun, a blanket across his shoulders and draped to his knees. The rifle of the old man is hidden under Talks's blanket. He chews a piece of bacon brought by the daughter of Big Foot. The oily texture reminds him of the days at Carlisle when there had been pork almost every day. These white men sure like to eat pigs, he'd thought. Now he tries not to think of Carlisle at all, or anything taught there about the white man and his ways. Now he tries only to think as a Miniconjou thinks, so he can anticipate what the young men might do. He finds it hard to think only as an Indian, and he blames that on Carlisle, and for the first time he is unhappy that he has gone there.

A few people move back and forth across the open space between the Indian village and the Army tent where Talks stands and where Big Foot lies inside, breathing with heavy gasps. An elder of the tribe goes into the tent from time to time, but mostly the elders stand and talk, near the tent of their chief. Children run back and forth, too, playing in the warm sun, rolling willow hoops, and laughing. Sometimes the Blue Coat medicine soldier comes and listens to Big Foot's breathing with a black tube that hangs from his ears. Inside the tent the oil stove still burns and it grows very hot, yet each time Talks goes in to see the old man he lies shivering under his blankets. It is better just to stay out of the tent, Talks thinks, better to stand here in the sun and watch the People and wonder what they might do.

Big Foot's daughter brings Talks another chunk of *kukúse,* the white man's bacon, and some hard bread. He stands chewing it, liking the feel of it between his teeth. The young woman stands for a moment near him and they speak only with their eyes in a language Talks does not completely understand. But he likes it. Then she turns and walks away. He eats, thinking of her slender brown fingers as she held the meat and bread up to him. But other things push aside his thoughts of the woman.

He cannot stop thinking that it would all be better if they were back in their cabins on Deep Creek along the Cheyenne. As the old men come to Big Foot's tent, he avoids their eyes because he knows he cannot reassure them as they would like him to do, knowing the white man's way as he does. They have fed us here, he thinks, and promised to do us no harm. But before long they are going to tell us something that is bad. It has all been too good so far, and soon the bad must come. The way of the People is not to worry, and sometimes that makes them panic when a bad thing comes because they have not thought about it in advance.

Yesterday most of the young men were painted and waved guns in their hands, plain for the soldiers to see. I hope the soldiers have forgotten about those guns, Talks thinks.

"Look at that Talks," Black Coyote says to the other young men. "Now he's a tribal chief and acting like an old man makes him look like one. But he still hides the father's rifle under that blanket. Maybe he's a good chief."

Talks is not concerned with what Black Coyote says. He is watching the Blue Coat chiefs gathering for a talk. They point and make gestures he cannot interpret, looking toward the lines of soldiers around the ridges and across the valley.

The interpreters come to Big Foot's tent, and Talks follows them inside, holding the rifle close to his side under the blanket. The half-bloods who speak for the white men say that the Blue Coat chief wants to speak with all the Miniconjou men. They want a small council, and would all the men please come to the open space between the tent where Big Foot lies and the Indian encampment. The words are kind and friendly, and the white soldier chiefs seem to be asking, not telling.

"All right," the old man says from his blankets. "We will ask them to come."

A village crier goes over to the Indian camp and walks between the tents, telling the men to assemble, to listen while the white chief talks. After a while, they begin to come, smoking and joking among themselves to show their independence. First come the old ones, and behind them the young warriors, who do not joke and laugh, but only smoke and look angry. They hold blankets around their bodies. Behind them, the women remain in the camp, making things ready for the trip to Pine Ridge agency and the people of Red Cloud. There, too, the children still play, some with the wet of bacon grease still on their mouths.

The men come and form a wide semicircle, like a strung bow, sitting on the ground cross-legged, their blankets around their shoulders and covering their knees, except for the young men who stand behind in little groups. The old men smoke, watching the Blue Coats and the front of Big Foot's tent, still joking and talking. Black Coyote stands back from the elders and away from any of the other young men, smoking a cigarette rolled with white man's newspaper. Talks is happy to see that his face is scrubbed clean for the first time in many sleeps, and the other young warriors as well, coming now before the white soldier chiefs without the defiance of paint across their cheeks. But their eyes are still defiant. Talks knows what is hidden under their blankets, and once more he thinks, I hope the white soldiers have forgotten those rifles.

While his own men gather, Talks can hear behind him and behind the tent of Big Foot the soldier little chiefs with stripes on their sleeves calling out orders he does not understand. He can hear other things, too. The crows have begun to call from the ridges, and in the Indian camp a dog barks, running with some of the children. The sky is blue with only a wisp of cloud toward the west, lacy like the smoke from Black Coyote's cigarette. Heavy in the air is a smell of cooked meat and coffee and horses.

The Blue Coat chiefs walk to the front of Big Foot's tent, and with them there are others Talks has not seen before. There are all the half-bloods who interpret and a man with a long dress — *siná súpa,* a black gown — who is called priest in one of the white man's religions, one taken up by the Oglala chief Red Cloud and some of the other Lakotas. Except that Talks knows of no Miniconjou who has become a Catholic. And there are others. One is tall and with a drooping moustache, wearing a squirrel-skin coat. Beside him, another young white man with red hair, and from his coat Talks can see the butt of a pistol thrust out like a stag's hoof. Then an older man, smoking a pipe made of a corncob. None of them, even with the pistol protruding from be- neath the coat of the red-haired man, look dan- gerous. They are talking and joking, too, like the Miniconjous.

A white chief with eyes the color of summer sky comes near, and he speaks to Talks, smiling with large white teeth under a moustache like corn silks. He says his name is Wallace, but Talks does not reply. He is thinking of his people's name for these white men — *hínsma wicá*, Hair Mouth. He saw this man the day before, when Big Foot placed his hand in the hand of the chief with a bristly face, the one called Whitside. Now Whitside is there as well, walking with a soldier chief with a beard like the tail of a shrike.

This is the man who starts the talking, and his half-blood interpreters change his words into Lakota so the Miniconjou men will understand.

"My name is Colonel Forsyth," the soldier chief says. "I have come here to greet you and to bring greetings from the big chief General Miles, who wants you to know we mean you no harm. These soldiers around you are my soldiers. They will escort you to a place of safety until the danger is past and you can return to your home at Cheyenne River."

It would be good, Talks thinks, if we could go there now. But he waits and says nothing. Most of the older men nod and puff their pipes and cigarettes as the words are told to them, but the young men make no sign, standing in the rear and watching.

Two lines of soldiers have started from the Blue Coat camp. One group marches under a red-and-white swallowtail flag with a *B*. These move along the west side of the little group of Miniconjou men and stop, the soldiers about five paces apart, making a fence between the men and the Indian camp near the ridge where the wagon guns stand. The other group, with a *K* on their flag, move along the road to the west of the council then turn back sharply to join the end of the first line. These K Blue Coats stand between the men and the Indian camp too, on the south side. Talks looks around and sees that the council is now almost surrounded with Blue Coats. The B men to the west, the K people to the south; across the road to the east and some way off are the ones on horseback, too far for him to see their swallowtail flag plainly. And finally, on the north, are the tents and the one where Big Foot still lies and beyond that the Blue Coat camp. The soldiers who have just come up to stand between the Sioux men and their families hold their carbines casually at their sides, butts on the ground. Talks looks beyond these soldiers who stand close to the Miniconjou men and sees another mounted troop on the hill just south of the wagon guns, overlooking the pony herd. Then due south, even beyond the Indian village and the gulley, are the Oglala scouts and another mounted white troop, maybe two.

"I have brought these soldiers here," Forsyth says, and he speaks of the B and K men, "so that we can talk without the interruption of the women and children walking back and forth from your camp."

That is your first deception, Hair Mouth, Talks thinks. He looks at the two lines of soldiers, and they are very close to the Indian men, only a few paces away. The two troops make the shape of

256

a cupped hand, and our men are in the palm of it, he thinks.

But maybe they are so close they would be foolish to start shooting, he thinks. Maybe they would not come so close if they were planning to do any shooting. It would be very confusing and dangerous to their own men, too, if they started anything so close to us. And those wagon guns could not fire on us without hitting their own men. Of course, they could fire on the camp. He glances quickly at the camp where the children are still playing between the tents, then looks away. They are too close to us anyway, he thinks. I can smell them. To start a fight so close would be foolish. Maybe we will be all right.

Talks suddenly stiffens. Something the Blue Coat chief has said makes him stop thinking about what might happen, and he listens closely as one of the half-bloods speaks the words in Lakota, and as the words come and with the troops standing so near with their carbines, the men of the band begin to move nervously and look around with fear and anger.

"Now before we travel to the white man's place where you will be safe and sheltered and fed, I must ask for all your weapons!"

There it is! Talks thinks. They did not forget seeing those guns yesterday. There it is, the bad thing he had been afraid would come. He looks at Black Coyote, still puffing the newspaper cigarette, and the young man's eyes glitter in a face turned harsh. From the squatting men comes a low grumbling, like the sound of a mule with a belly full of alkali water. It is a bad thing to ask any Sioux man for his weapon.

"We will talk with our chief," Talks says in the white man's tongue, and Forsyth says it is all right. Talks and Yellow Bird and another tribal elder go inside where Big Foot lies still coughing and bleeding at the nose. His old eyes watch them closely and Talks believes he has heard the talk outside and knows why they come.

"Yes, I knew they would want the guns," he says. One of the white man interpreters comes in, the one called Little Bat, and he stands back so the others can speak together.

"What should we do, father?"

"Give them a few old guns. Keep the good ones," Big Foot says.

"Yes, keep them," Yellow Bird whispers. "If we give them our weapons, they will kill us all."

"If they'd wanted to do that, they could have done it long ago, standing far off with their wagon guns," the old chief says. "But a people should never be completely disarmed."

The man called Little Bat speaks. "They will not harm you. Their big chief Miles would be very angry if any of his soldiers harmed you. I think he would punish anyone who harmed you without just cause."

Looking at the half-blood, Talks believes he speaks what seems the truth. But the big chief is far away, and those soldiers out there under the swallowtail flags with *B* and *K* are very close.

"General Miles only wants you safe," Little Bat says.

"He wants us in his iron house, or dead," Yellow Bird says.

Big Foot lifts one hand from beneath the blankets and Yellow Bird is still.

"Listen. Give them a few old guns. Keep the good ones. A people must never be completely unarmed."

"This is a bad mistake," Little Bat says, but old Big Foot lies back and pulls the blanket around his face and closes his eyes.

So the runners are sent to the village and they return with a few old broken guns. Mostly they are guns the children have been playing with that will not shoot. These are placed on the ground before the white soldier chiefs and Talks knows what they will do. The one with the bristling face who shook the hand of Big Foot yesterday becomes more angry than all the others. Talks understands much of what he says.

"Hell's fire, sir, we saw a batch of good repeaters yesterday. These aren't what we saw. Let's get the old man out here."

Forsyth nods and a number of soldiers and officers go into Big Foot's tent and carry him out. As they prop him up on a blanket roll in front of the soldier chiefs, the Miniconjou men move silently but make a quivering among them, like a pony herd when wolves come close, and Talks can almost feel the heat of their anger rising in them. In the rear, the young men are becoming excited, moving aimlessly and glaring about like dogs before a hailstorm.

"We have asked your people for their weapons. But all they bring is these."

"These are all we have," Big Foot says, and Talks begins to understand how one deception leads to another and that to another. "All the rest we burned on Cheyenne River when the Blue Coats there asked us to do it."

The second chief, Whitside, speaks angrily. "We saw repeating rifles. And a lot of them, yesterday, in the hands of these young men."

Old Big Foot coughs and then smiles and waves one hand weakly as he speaks, and the tribal elders murmur and nod with his words.

"Young men are very hard to control. For an old man like me, it is even harder. They are tough and headstrong and hard to control. But they would not deceive you."

Even though Big Foot tries to make a joke of it, which is a fine trick of diplomacy, the men behind him are tense and growing angry. The white soldier chiefs are angry, too, but it has not touched their young men yet. The soldiers called B and K still stand unconcerned, holding their carbines down at their sides. Only slowly, as the talk continues, do the soldiers begin to sense it and their eyes go bright.

The soldier chiefs are talking together again, low so that none of the Miniconjous can hear. They point toward the Indian encampment, behind the line of soldiers under the swallowtail flag with the *K*. Soon, some of the white chiefs walk around to the Indian camp, a number of their soldiers with them. One of these groups is led by the man called Wallace, and as he comes to the village Talks can see him laughing and talking to the women and patting the children on the heads.

"I do not like Hair Mouths who touch our children," Yellow Bird says, and he rises from his place near Big Foot and begins to move restlessly among the young men, whispering with them. And along the lines of soldiers, Talks can see many young faces gone white now and fearful because the young Indian men are staring at them with hatred. But there are others along that line who are not young at all, but with hard and lined faces, and sky-colored eyes that glare back at the young Miniconjous, even though they still hold their carbines loosely at their sides as though they were fly switches.

"Big Foot," Forsyth says, "I am sending my men into your camp to find the weapons Major Whitside saw yesterday. Only officers will go into the tents and your women will be treated with respect."

Big Foot does not speak but seems almost asleep except that even in the warm sun, even with blankets around him, he shivers and clutches his coat tight around his throat. From the tent where he has slept, the young woman comes and wipes the blood from his nose with a cloth, then turns and walks back, eyes downcast.

Little Bat tells the white soldier chiefs this woman is Big Foot's daughter. Some of the soldiers standing near laugh when they hear this and speak words Talks can understand.

"Daughter, like hell."

"Young tipi squaw for cold winter nights."

"You men keep at ease," the one called Whitside says sharply. But the anger rises in Talks to hear these white soldiers speak so of an old chief probably dying and his daughter who wants only to look after his comfort.

Many of the men are now looking toward the Indian camp. The search parties move from tent to tent, the man named Wallace still smiling and talking with the women and children. As he and other Blue Coats come from the tents, they bring nothing in their hands. Watching it, Talks feels a little triumph growing in him, and pride, but it is suddenly finished as Wallace and the other white soldiers begin to lift women up from the blankets where they are sitting. And some rifles are found under the women. The young warriors mutter, and Yellow Bird has begun to prance around among them, chanting so softly no one can understand his words.

"What's that old bastard doing?" one of the little white chiefs with stripes on his sleeve asks.

"He's about to cause trouble," the man called Little Bat says. All along the line of men under the B and K flags, Talks can see faces white, the skin drawn tight over cheekbones. Like faces with no blood, he thinks. It is beginning to look very

262

dangerous to him, and he moves back away from where the soldier chiefs stand, closer to the young men of the band, but he says nothing to them.

In the Indian camp, the women are being treated with kindness by the man called Wallace, who still smiles and shows his teeth beneath the corn silk hair of his moustache. But some of the soldiers are dumping wagons and travois packed for the trip to Pine Ridge, scattering pans and clothing and other things across the ground. A few find knives, which they take, and some find other metal tools like hoes and needles and awls, and they take these, too.

Now Yellow Bird's chant has become loud enough for the young men to hear, and Talks hears it as well.

> The prairies are great, the prairies are great.
> They will swallow the bullets of your
>   enemies
> You cannot be harmed by the weapons of
>   the white Hair Mouths,
> For their bullets will fly into the great
>   prairie.
> The prairie is great!

When the soldiers return from the village, they carry only a few rifles and many other things no one has ever used as a weapon. All of it is dumped on the ground before the white chiefs, and they look at it and Talks can see their anger grow. They talk together, the white chiefs, and it has become a time for wet hands and tight chests because now Talks knows they will ask to search the men.

Some of the old men go forward at once and drop their blankets to show they have no weapons. But none of the young men go forward. They begin to move away from one another, no longer standing in groups but singly, all over the cleared council area, and most of them face their village now, looking past the soldiers, angry at the sight of wagons and travois dumped and the things scattered among the tents. Talks is with them, and he hears Big Foot speak to the young men through his choking throat.

"Don't let your anger carry you away. Don't do a quick thing. Stay back, away from the white soldiers, and do what they say."

Talks wonders at these words. Is the father telling them now to give up their weapons and not keep back any at all? He sees that it no longer matters what the old chief says. The young men are not listening. They are facing the K soldiers, eyes hard and mouths drawn down. In this small council space, Talks knows there are about 120 Miniconjou men. He can see there are about the same number of K and B soldiers, but all the Blue Coats have arms, and even Talks does not know how many of the Sioux men are armed.

Yellow Bird has begun to throw dust in the air, chanting. Some of the dust falls on Big Foot and he tries to scold Yellow Bird, but his voice does not work and he coughs, shivering in his blankets. But Yellow Bird stops chanting and throwing the dust and squats down. Talks can hear a sigh along the line of Blue Coats, and in his mouth is a bitter taste as though he has been sucking a brass cartridge case.

But there is no time for thinking of such things for suddenly there is a shout, and everyone jumps like a buck deer surprised as he drinks.

Black Coyote has thrown back his blanket and stands now near the line of K soldiers, his bare chest painted, and holding the new rifle in one hand above his head.

"This is mine and I paid for it," he shouts in Lakota, and none of the soldiers understand. "To have it, you must pay for it. You must pay if you want to take it."

Old Yellow Bird is up at once, chanting again, throwing dirt into the air.

"That fool," Talks says to himself, and starts toward Black Coyote, who continues to walk in front of the soldiers waving his rifle and shouting in their faces that they must pay him for it if they want it.

The Blue Coats step back, recoiling from the young warrior, still unaware of what he is saying. Their eyes have gone glassy and their carbines are up now, not pointed but not held casually on the ground either. Yellow Bird begins to blow an eagle bone whistle.

Talks hears a half-blood interpreter say, "We've got to stop them raising all this hell, colonel. It's right on the edge."

265

Before he can reach Black Coyote, Talks sees a soldier move out from the K line, a heavy man like a whisky barrel with little chief stripes along his sleeve. He runs to Black Coyote and tries to pull the rifle from the young Miniconjou. They stand there, pushing and shoving against each other, their hands on the gun, swearing into each other's faces, and Talks tries to reach them. Along the lines of soldiers there is some shouting now.

"Look out, boys, they're going to break."

"There's another goddamned rifle, there's another one."

"Hold steady there, you men, hold steady."

Talks is almost there when the rifle fires, muzzle still up as the two men pull against one another. The explosion cuts across all other sounds and they are stilled, cut off suddenly like breathing after a kick in the belly. The crows on the far ridges stop cawing, water in Wounded Knee Creek runs for a heartbeat without any sound, and even old Big Foot's full throat closes for a moment and is silent. Then as he sees but does not want to see, blankets are dropping to the ground from the shoulders of young men around Talks, and there are the guns, coming up, and the guns along the line of soldiers, coming up, all on the same string, and the sounds of the hammers cocking back as loud as hail striking sheet-iron roofs.

"Wimáca yelo!" a warrior shouts. "I am a man!"

"My God, boys, they've broke."

266

"They're gonna shoot, boys," he hears the K soldiers call.

"Fire. Fire at the bastards, fire!"

The council space is crushed and smashed in a round, red ball of deafening noise, and the black powder cloud instantly obscures almost everything, and Talks can only dimly see the Indian village where the women and children scramble for shelter as the bullets from their own young men cut through the line of K Blue Coats and on into the Miniconjou tents.

Through the smoke, too, the dim line of soldiers, weapons up and making orange tongues of flame licking toward the young men and the old as well. The only thing Talks can see clearly are the rows of brass buttons standing like tiny suns, gleaming through the dense cloud. But then there is the white chief named Wallace, moving behind the K soldiers, his mouth open under the corn silk hair of his moustache.

Talks drops his blanket, and the rifle of the old man comes up in his hands, tight against his shoulder. Along the barrel he sights into the eyes of the white chief, and as he does, Wallace looks at him with the pale, summer sky eyes, almost smiling as if he was still playing with the Sioux children, and Talks can see, too, the white teeth under the corn silk hair. He does not know he has pressed the trigger until the rifle slams against his shoulder. He sees the man called Wallace jerk like a struck dog, and his soldier hat flies off along with a large part of his head, and then he is down in the smoke. Talks takes a step, the old man's rifle down now, and then he falls, too, his legs gone like wet rags as the soldier bullets strike him. When he falls, his face plows into the hard ground, and he feels his teeth cutting his lips, then only the thundering above his head, but for a long time he still hears the eagle bone whistle.

21

CHICAGO TRIBUNE — When the demand for a surrender of arms was made the Indians replied by opening fire. The soldiers returned the fire and a terrible slaughter took place. They shot them down wherever found, no quarter being given by anyone. The Indians' first volley was almost as one man, so they must have fired 100 shots before the soldiers fired one. But oh! How they were slaughtered after their first volley!

───────◆───────

For 1st Sgt. Sean Fitzpatrick it had never happened like this before, this holding, clutching, pressing close together with an enemy in the moment before the deadly surge, feeling the breath, looking into bloodshot eye, smelling him, and knowing the wild, animal sense of terror and defiance and courage. Then breaking free as the rifle explodes, pulling back, each torn from the other in a last spasm, everything else forgotten except the will to live. Each, too, knowing their mortal danger. The heavy Colt coming up from the holster and leaping with the smoke and flash, the quick, expressionless eyes, black and suddenly hooded, but glaring still. The slugs going home with flat thuds like the slap of a hand against wet putty, the young Indian collapsing, looking somehow ridiculous with his face and arms burned red by the sun but his now naked and punctured chest, hidden so long beneath a white man's coat, pale and fish-belly colored, streaming out the life in a torrent where the bullets go in. The tall form misshapen and slipping down, but still a target. No longer a threat, no longer dangerous, but a target still as the revolver leaps again and again, Fitzpatrick unable to control it and shooting it empty in a frenzy of almost convulsive passion released after the long tension. A frenzy of killing, but of despair, too, and a growing sickness in his guts.

Then for only a few seconds having become predator, he is man once more and staggers back into the line of his own troops, reloading mechanically, running along the line shouting orders and encouragement, the stomach cramps gone as suddenly as they came. By God, he thinks, I knew we were too close to the bastards.

He fires again, into the smoke and dust and yelling, still close but at least not near enough to them now to hear the metal strike flesh. All around the crash of gunfire breaking like unexpected rip thunder tearing across the senses, but above all that he can still hear the sudden rush of breath from the man they'd called Cur Dog, the gasping out of life's air when the first shot went home. For the rest of his own living nights he will hear that sound in sleep, waking to it, sweating, and clutching his hands to his chest, over and over again.

At the center of the flaming circle, a young Miniconjou with the new Winchester of Black Coyote now in his hands crouches, singing a death song as they did in the old days, leering, the rifle waist high, pointed like a lance. He sings and works the lever smoothly. The leaden slugs go toward K soldiers and some on beyond them and into the Indian village where everyone is running. To the young Miniconjou, the soldiers are only dim shapes through the swirling smoke. Like the old-time warriors in certain bands who staked themselves to the ground with an arrow through the sash, pinned to that spot, defiantly holding their place against any enemy until death came, and only then no longer fighting, he moves in a small circle, prancing, chanting, his slender hands quick and sure on the hot Winchester, fingering in the fresh rounds, the plump, deadly cylinders of brass and lead. Deadly, ferocious, and beautiful in his graceful movements, singing, teeth bared like a snarling wolf. Staked to that single spot by will alone, waiting for the relief that only death can bring. And soon it comes.

One of the half-blood interpreters standing with B Troop is staggered with the surprise of the first blast and tries to bring up the long Marlin rifle he holds, but a dark figure bolts through the dust and is on him, a bread knife raised. The blade comes down and slices off the end of the half-blood's nose, leaving it dangling by gristle like an overripe cherry stubbornly clinging to the limb. The knife goes up again and the half-blood swings the muzzle of the rifle, and with the blow the Sioux stumbles back, and before he can recover, the rifle is up and the shot fired. The Indian goes boneless and flops down.

The half-blood sways like a drunken man, pulling at the end of his nose, blood running down his arm and splattering his coat and the Marlin, but the end of the nose will not come off, and he finally leaves it dangling and starts to fire. The blood gushes into the breech of the gun, and as it grows hot, the half-blood smells the odor that meat makes, thrown into the embers of a fire until it is blackened.

Within the thick smoke now boiling across the council circle, rising from the dense cloud like an old bird with tattered feathers, Big Foot is on his feet, throwing off the blankets and lifting his arm and crying out in a voice unheard in the din.

"Stop, stop, you are killing us."

And then the wasping bullets find him and he goes back to the ground, like a dirty rag, the arm still reaching up, fingers of the wrinkled hand splayed out and reaching, reaching. He settles back almost gently, the blood from his nose still wet on his lips, and after a tremendous quiver like a great doll, lies broken and thrown aside.

The woman, seeing her father struck, runs from the tents where flying metal is already shredding the canvas. She goes toward him across the blazing circle and falls, too, hit quickly and unable to reach the old chief, unable to revive him with her cries. And they are choked off soon, like the gaspings of a tiny bird caught in the hand, fingers tightening on the throat. She tries to crawl, but the life runs out quickly, and she is a long way from her father when she is finally still.

Along the K Troop line, beginning to melt away, scatter, and disappear, one of the old soldiers stands, a three-time sergeant but reduced in each instance for insubordination or drunkenness, sober now and waiting calmly for his shots. He expects the bullets to find him, standing still and erect, but they pass, and finding a dark form in the growing pall of smoke and dust, he lifts the carbine, sights, and fires. Levering up the breech of the Springfield and sliding in another of the fat shells, others held between his fingers and dangling like golden sausages at the carbine's hand guard, he lifts the weapon again, waits for a target, then fires. Veteran of the Bighorn, a boy with Reno in that dreadful valley, veteran of other fights since, with the Nez Percé and Cheyenne. And all the while, in Montana in seventy-six and in between, hating the memory of the Yellow Hair Custer who led them to disaster. But now, in this savage moment, he speaks to the young soldiers near him, loud enough to be heard but somehow softly, too.

"Slow, lads, slow, and take good aim, and kill the red bastards. Shoot slow, lads, and get one for old Custer, ever' shot!"

273

Coolly he stands and shoots and waits for the returning hornets, but although some come close enough for him to hear, none touch him. He shoots and continues to speak until soon he is alone and no one is close enough to hear, but his voice drones on.

Whitside, running back from the council circle now ablaze with gunfire and obscured with dense smoke and dust, screams for his horse and mounts, driving in the blunt spurs that make the horse grunt and leap forward along the rear of B Troop's line.

"Get mounted, get mounted, they're going to break. Hurry, hurry, don't let 'em get away."

The B Troop commander, responding to the major's shouts, begins to bring his troopers back to the horse picket line. A few horses have broken free and dash across the open spaces between the clouds of smoke, and one has been hit hard and is down at the hindquarters, trying to drag himself about by forelegs only, screaming. The B Troop commander runs over, still on foot, and lifts the Colt, and when the slug strikes, the horse flops down sideways.

Krenshaw, eyes popping from his face, unhurt in the first scalding fire, now advances boldly into the circle, shooting his new pistol, exultation on his features as his hat is swept off and his red hair streams across his wet forehead. After a few steps his gun is empty, and he backs away and finds another, dropped by a soldier, and empties it, too, laughing.

Behind him, Cleaborn flees, his squirrel-skin coat standing out behind as he runs back among the tents of the Army encampment. Well away from the shooting, he dives behind a tent, then after a moment on his face, sits up and heaves a sigh and tries to catch his breath. Later, he will write, "With Colonel Forsyth and Major Whitside, I stood when the firing started within touching distance of the treacherous devils. The only thing that saved all of us from death was that the Indians had their backs to us when they began firing at K Troop."

Old Yellow Bird, the eagle bone whistle still in his teeth, holds a rifle and scrambles crablike toward the Sibley tents where Big Foot had lain. He can hear the white Hair Mouths shouting, feel the weight of their bullets over his head. He can hear a pony from across the valley, from the herd of the People, hit and screaming, and there in the smoke and dirt and flying metal, he thinks of the Greasy Grass and how the horses of the Yellow Hair had been hit and started to die. But, he thinks, Lakota ponies screaming are much worse to hear than the big stupid horses of the Hair Mouths.

A bullet cuts his Ghost Shirt across the shoulders, and he soon feels sticky liquid running down his arms as he crawls, running down between his fingers. By then he is close to the tents and is thinking, Oh please, let me kill one of their chiefs, just one, let me kill just one. And he is inside one of the big tents, panting, lying for a moment, still thinking, Let me kill just one.

Along the B Troop line, near the Sibley tents, a young soldier only two months out of Germany buckles and falls, like a blue lump on the ground with dust powdering his back. Holding his belly, he gasps softly, "Muttie, Muttie."

"Look, sergeant, the tent," another trooper shouts. A number of them turn now in that direction. "That's a rifle at the flap, look out."

A number of them fire, bullets tugging small black holes in the canvas. Near the line of tents a stack of baled hay has somehow caught fire, and as his soldiers spray the tent with bullets, the sergeant runs across and takes one of the blazing bales, hoists it quickly with his knees, and dashes it against the tent. Inside he can hear the defiant chant, and still shots come from the flap. The canvas flames quickly, sending up a billow of smoke that obscures the brightening sun. And inside, the bullets find a can of kerosene left the night before by the surgeons to fuel Big Foot's stove. When the fire reaches it, the tent is gone in a blossom of violent flame and smoke, an orange ball raging out to singe the eyebrows of the soldiers firing into it, then gone as quickly as it came. The chant and the firing from the tent are finished, and the tent itself in only a few seconds. On the ground, beneath a smoldering scar of blackened canvas, lies the humped-up form. A rifle juts out like a cannon from an emplacement. One hand is visible, still clutching the rifle, the skin peeled back from the flesh, the nails somehow white, like pearls.

The sergeant tries to spit but cannot and backs away, his own Colt hot to the touch in his hand. He is still aware then that there are troopers firing into the smoking ashes of the tent.

"Cease fire, goddamnit, can't you see he's dead?"

And for a terrible moment, one trooper, eyes glazed and face black with powder smoke, turns on the sergeant. His carbine is cocked and almost comes up to fire on the sergeant, when suddenly the soldier shudders and expression returns to his face, and he wheels away. In that heartbeat, the sergeant knew what was about to happen, and his own hand had tightened on the revolver, ready to kill the soldier. But now it is past, and the sergeant tries to spit again but cannot.

At the K Troop line, the young Sioux standing only a few feet off, the fight is furious and violent, a frenzy of movement and smoke and muzzle flashes. Unlike the horses farther down the valley, crazed with fear, screaming and running against a wire fence, these men are crazed with killing, thrown back on old instincts for survival, and they lash out blindly against the threat, merciless and mindless, like cornered silo rats, maddened with the rage of it. After the first crash of gunfire, each side recoils, leaving some of its number on the ground, a few still thrashing across the bloodied ground before they are still.

With the first shots, three buggies along the road, with the Wounded Knee trader and friends who have come out from the agency to watch, lurch away in a headlong dash up the valley toward the post office. There are white faces of the riders, looking back at the fight behind them, and a hat sails off and comes to rest in the road. One of the half-blood interpreters who has run back among the Army tents and crouches there sees the buggies, horses running hard away from the firing, and he begins to laugh. He can hear the strike of lead in the canvas of the tents around him, hear the blasts of gunfire and the screaming horses, all the din of the fight. Yet watching the buggies race away he cannot stop laughing.

In the swirling smoke and dust at the council circle a veteran trooper goes down quickly, all his strings cut. He swears, feeling nothing but knowing he is hard hit.

"Where the hell's it at?" he mumbles.

His hand, with only a little sensation left in it, discovers the gummy hole in his thigh and he swears again. It is a small puncture, but as he feels behind the leg there is the shredded flesh and he groans.

"That's a .45–55, sure as hell," he says aloud. "That's a goddamned B Troop shot. They've ruined my leg, they've ruined my leg."

Having suffered three gunshot wounds during his service, he clenches his teeth to await the pain he knows will come as the nerves regain their sensitivity after the shock of the striking bullet. But before that happens, darkness crosses his eyes and then his mind, and he lies bleeding and motionless as the warriors from the circle begin to leap over him and dash toward the Indian encampment.

Some of the blue-clads are caught in the rush of the Miniconjous. One young K trooper, a mass of straw-colored hair beneath his hat, stands staring, eyes bugged, teeth bared, unaware of the metal tugging at his baggy sleeves. His fingers release the unfired carbine, and it falls to the ground, still cold. A dark figure runs toward him out of the smoke, face half shot away, and the boy stands slack-jawed, watching the figure fall. Somehow, mesmerized, he stands and is not hit, untouched in the storm, like a sheep in the slaughter chute waiting dumbly for the hammer.

On the hill above the pony herd, the gun crews are ready at the little Hotchkiss guns, but at first there is no target in the smoke below them.

"Hold your fire," an artillery officer shouts. "You'll hit your own people!"

"Look! They're running toward the Indian camp."

"Lay on the tipis, lay your guns on the tipis!"

The crews heave the guns into position.

"There they go! Shoot now, men, shoot."

The first cannon bellows and heaves back in a cloud of smoke, and the odor of sulfur carries along the breeze from the guns as a second and then the third and fourth fire. In the Miniconjou village, a shell strikes a wagon at the rear axle, blowing off a wheel and killing instantly an Indian woman who has been trying to get her pots and blankets loaded. The wagon bed tilts crazily, and a baby falls out to scramble on the ground toward its mother, coming up tight against the still-warm body and lying there with black eyes wide and crying.

The others, seeing the warriors come running from the circle and seeing, too, the shards of metal now ripping their tents and their wagon horses, grab up children and start to run south toward the ravine, some of them screaming and keening. And beyond the ditch the Oglala scouts, seeing the Miniconjou brothers rushing toward them, rein back up the slope to the lines of cavalry waiting there. As they pull into the line, the officer there, veteran of the Little Bighorn fight, shouts his instructions.

"Horse holders to the rear! On foot, prepare to volley! Be careful of the tads and women, men. Be careful where you shoot!"

Across the valley, Chandler Akins stumbles up the slope toward the battery, his coat flapping like a Ghost Shirt, his leggings plain below the coat, and he hears slugs going into the ground around him. My God, he thinks, somebody's shooting at me. Somebody thinks I'm an Indian. Those fools . . . He drops his pipe but runs on, then goes back down the slope to retrieve it. By now the artillerymen are shouting and waving, and the troopers on the far side of the council circle below cease firing at the newsman as he goes on up the hill.

Coming out on the crest, he hears the men around the guns, yelling at one another, and the sergeant, too.

"When them breeches open, get that shell in there, damnit, ain't you men had enough drill with these brass toothpicks?"

Akins lies there panting, then turns and looks back into the valley below. The large tent where Big Foot lay during the night is smoldering embers now, and before it the council circle, where the smoke and dust has begun to blow aside, is covered with low figures, lumps on the scarred soil. The line of B Troop is moving to horses, still intact, but at the other edge of the council area the K Troop line has been scattered and is no longer a line, most men still there turned now and firing toward the village and the gulley beyond where the figures can be seen running, except for a few who pause and kneel and crouch, firing back toward the soldiers. The tents and wagons of the village are being shattered with the cannon fire, and in their impersonal search for the fleeing warriors, Akins knows that some of the figures on the ground must be women and children. Many of the Miniconjous are in the gulley, some firing over the lip, and the shellfire creeps into that area.

"What a bloody mess," Akins says. "What a tragic, bloody mess."

Near him, a gunner looks over and grins, holding another shell ready to go into the breech when it opens.

"We'll drive their ass out of that ravine, sir, you can bet."

Akins clamps the cold pipe between his teeth and chews on the stem.

"What a tragic bloody mess."

Still, a few run from the circle, up now after falling prone with the first shots. There is a young Miniconjou, rushing through the K Troop line, and suddenly before him one of the little chiefs of the Hair Mouths, gold stripes on his sleeve. It is too bad, the young Miniconjou thinks, running now against this white man who is a little chief with stripes on his arm and a veteran fighter. But as the big pistol comes up in the Hair Mouth's hand, it snaps dully, the hammer going down on an empty chamber, and the young Miniconjou shouts and clubs the Hair Mouth with his only weapon — a large stick. He shouts again as he sees the dulled eyes of the soldier, and he throws his arms around the man sliding to the ground. He has the pistol and holds the limp body against his own with one hand as he searches through the soldier's clothes for ammunition with the other. He feels the strike of bullets and shouts once more as he realizes fire has struck this Hair Mouth hanging on the crook of his arm.

Dropping the Hair Mouth, he runs on toward the village, but then he is struck as well and going down scatters the bright brass cartridges along the fine sandy soil. He crawls along, scooping them up, fingering them into the loading gate of the .45. Then he rolls into a small depression and from there begins to shoot, shouting a defiant song. The shapes turn before his eyes, flashing blue-and-gold forms that are blurred in the sunlight and dust, like painted ponies dashing across his vision. Then the pistol is empty, and he lies, unable to move, but still singing even after a soldier runs up and bends to him, pulling the gun away from his fingers. The soldier stands over him, watching him with carbine ready, but doing nothing as he listens to the song. The Hair Mouth says a thing the young warrior does not understand, and he continues to sing, but the words are weaker now and come with difficulty from his dried lips.

The People run. The men, carrying guns they've picked up from the ground or the ones they had hidden beneath blankets from the start. The women run, too, alongside the men, some carrying rifles as well. And among them are the children, dogs barking hysterically at their feet and tripping them. They all flee through the village where ponies run about aimlessly, dragging half-destroyed wagons among the tents that have begun to burn. The People, the first of them, rush into the gulley and across it, seeing their brothers the Oglalas in Army uniforms falling back to the ridge where the lines of cavalrymen wait. The exploding shells follow them, snapping at their heels with sharp cracks like close thunder. Some stay in the gulley and hide. Some stay there and fire from the lip, back toward the soldiers at the council circle, at Hair Mouths anywhere they can be seen.

And when one of the blue figures falls, they shout with exultation, but the wagon guns continue to search for them.

From the village, some of the wagons pulled by walleyed ponies clatter out into the road and along it toward the post office and the trader's store, women and children in them bouncing like corks on the flood. Soldiers ride out and take the reins and draw the wagons farther up the road, away from the din and the shelling. Finally there are a number of them drawn up before the store and the post office, the women keening and the children crying, soldiers sitting around them, watching with silent faces.

Back at the circle, where the firing has stopped and the smoke is drifting away, the Catholic priest kneels with a wounded trooper. Down the priest's back is an ugly knife wound which he ignores. Two paces away is a dead Miniconjou youth, the knife still in his hand as he lies face up, eyes open to the sun but unseeing. Down the line a young soldier crouches on hands and knees, hat off, hair falling. He retches with the fear that comes now, after he has stood firing in the line where the warriors ran through. Unwounded but vomiting, his body convulses until the man called Little Bat comes up and bends down to him.

"Are you hit, boy?"

Eyes watering, the boy looks up and stares for

a moment before he speaks.

"Hit? No. Good Lord, why did those devils start this hell?"

The half-blood straightens and looks toward the flaming village and the smoke beyond. His mouth tightens.

"They think you started it, boy."

There at the ravine lies a small Miniconjou boy, his arm still thrust through a willow hoop. A chicken, not seen by anyone before, is running there wildly and abruptly is gone in a black flash and a flurry of white feathers, like a goose down pillow suddenly exploded in the shell burst. Beyond that, some of the People surge up toward the line of Oglalas and troops, but the fire comes quickly, disciplined, and a number of Miniconjous stagger and a few fall. The rest run back into the gulley and start along its course, those with guns firing as they go. An old man, somehow escaped from the council circle, leads them, his arms up and his chants urging them on. The shards from the exploding shells seek them out, and alongside at some distance ride mounted troops. On the ridge an officer rides along his line, shouting.

"Stop firing there, soldier. That's a woman," he yells.

The trooper looks back at him, his teeth bared in a grimy face.

"Well, by God, sir, she's firin' at me," but stops firing, as he sits back on his haunches, swearing softly. "The bitch hit old Ryan, goddamn her red soul."

Across the valley, a trooper rides out of the smoke to G Troop, a small Indian boy hanging from the crook of one arm. He goes to an officer and salutes.

"Got a tad here, cap'n. What should I do with it?"

"Up the road there with those other women and children."

"Ma's blowed all to hell, cap'n."

"Yes, damnit, you don't need to tell me that. Take him on up there where I told you."

To the south, the troopers are mounted again, riding far beyond the people running along the ravine.

"Don't let them get away. Head 'em off, boys, before they get loose on the prairie."

As they spur along, one trooper falls off his horse, and a veteran pulls up and sees that this is a recruit, unhit, but unable to stay in the saddle.

"Goddamned raw troops and raw horses. Get back up in that seat, you lard-headed bastard!"

But no sooner is he back astride than he goes off again, this time with a chest wound from a long shot out of the gulley. The veteran reins back and dismounts and kneels over him. The fallen man reaches up and grabs the veteran's shirt, soaked with sweat by now in the sun.

"That river. That river behind the ranges. What is that river?"

"The Republican, son," the veteran says.

That's one of our good Fort Riley rivers."

"Last summer, I fished a river like that at home . . ."

His hand falls away from the veteran's shirt, and after a moment the old soldier rises, shaking his head. Then he is up and after the rest of the troop.

In the gulley, an old man shouts.

"Kill the Hair Mouths. It will be *anpétu síca,* a bad day, if we do not kill many of them."

But even those not trying to hide, those still fighting, they remember another old man saying their shirts would turn aside bullets. But they have seen the brutal red marks of many bullets on those shirts this day, and when they hear the old quavering voice, they grind their teeth because they know it is a bad day no matter how many Hair Mouths they kill. But in a little while the old man is down, too, and silent.

Now the shooting has grown scattered, in little clusters of sound far up and down the valley. Huddled figures are herded out of the ravine, mostly women and old men, with a few children, and moved toward the road by mounted soldiers, watching with bright eyes, their weapons ready.

Far to the south, beyond the people in the ditch, a cry goes up among the troopers.

"Mounted men! There are more red niggers off to the south on horseback."

"Agency people come out when they heard the shooting. It's agency people."

"Hold your fire, men."

287

They move toward the group, perhaps fifty in all who have drawn to a halt and seem to watch for a moment. Then there is a burst of fire from them, and dust kicks up at the feet of the troopers' mounts.

From the ditch the People watch.

"Look, it is our brothers the Oglalas from Pine Ridge agency come out to help us."

"The Hair Mouths shoot back now."

They watch as the mounted Indians far to the south turn their horses away and ride off beyond the ridges. Slowly, seeing this, the ones who are still left in the ditch throw down their weapons and lie close to the steep banks, wanting to fight no more. But for a while the wagon guns continue to seek them out. Then these are silent, too, and there is only the scream of horses hit and the moan of wounded and the smell of gunpowder and burning canvas. And soon, too, the ones left can hear the crows begin to caw once more from the far pine ridges to the north.

22

OMAHA BEE —

A BLOODY BATTLE

CAPTAIN WALLACE AMONG THE SLAIN

Tomahawked in the Head by a Treacherous Red Assailant!

— EVEN AS I WRITE THESE WORDS, I CAN HEAR THE HOTCHKISS GUNS POURING SHOTS INTO THE GULLY!

Quinton Tapp is close enough to hear the Hotchkiss guns when they open fire, their racket muffled by distance. But he knows at once what it is and kicks the mare into a long lope. His head aches and his mouth is brassy. The horse has an uneven gait when she runs, and each stride jars him, the shock going up his spine to the base of his skull like gentle but persistent hammer blows. He swears but keeps jabbing the mare with his heels. She fights him for a while, then resigns herself to the pace, but even then each stride hurts him.

It takes a long time to top the last line of ridges before the valley of Wounded Knee Creek, and by then the firing has stopped. Smoke drifts overhead on the breeze, and as he pulls up to take his first look he can hear the sounds from it. Indian women are keening, and it reminds him of winter wind blowing under the eaves. From somewhere there is a high-pitched scream that makes the hair stand on his neck. A horse, Quinton Tapp thinks. Then there is the flat report of a pistol, and the screaming abruptly ends.

In the valley, horses are running or standing head down for a distance of two miles in either direction, some with blue-clad riders up and others running alone or beginning to graze now with the din of fighting past. He watches soldiers trying to gather what is left of an Indian pony herd, the gray and spotted horses looking at this distance like large dogs beside the heavy Army mounts. Off to his left, ranged along a ridge, are the cannons, gunners swabbing out the bores with ramrods. Near the guns are horsemen in a tight group, and Tapp takes that to be the regimental staff. Forsyth is likely sitting there, with his little spade beard stuck out into the breeze.

Running into the valley from the south is the gulley that bends eastward finally and cuts directly across toward the agency road. There he sees people on foot, many with blankets thrown over their heads as they are moved along by cavalrymen. Farther along, near a cluster of buildings, is a growing group of these people, and he recognizes them as Indians, mostly women and children. But, he thinks, maybe some men, too, because at a distance it's hard as hell to tell the men and women apart. There is the encampment, too, shredded with artillery fire, debris, and broken wagons, and dead horses scattered among the tipi poles that stand black and crooked. And there, too, Quinton Tapp sees the smallish bundles on the ground, like old faded laundry bags, and he thinks, There was some killin' there.

Tapp rides down to the agency road and north along it past the gulley and the village site and sees the council circle. There the dead and wounded are lying thick, and on two sides of the circle are uniformed figures on the ground. Moving among these are other soldiers, bending down, lifting some and carrying them to the tents farther along the valley. As Tapp rides closer, a surgeon with a detail of troops has begun to move out into the circle among the fallen Miniconjous. The man called Little Bat is there, shouting in Lakota.

"Anyone alive raise your hand. We won't hurt you. The fight is finished. The white *pejúta wicasa* comes. The white doctor is here. To help you."

A few hands are raised from among the figures on the ground, and the surgeon guides his men toward them. Some of the wounded are lifted and carried away toward the tents as the soldiers have been. There are ambulances drawn up near one of the larger tents, and the flaps there are rolled up and tied. Men hurry in and out, and the wounded are carried inside or aligned neatly in rows just outside.

"Field hospital operation," Tapp mutters.

Some of the Sioux in the council circle rise unwounded, and one of these, an old man, is shouting.

"Where is Yellow Bird? Where is that terrible man?"

"Over there, father, in the burned tipi," Little Bat says.

In the smoldering ruins of an Army tent, Tapp sees a human form, a hand thrust out with blackened and clutching fingers. He understands little of what the Sioux is shouting as the old man points with his fingers toward the form lying beneath the slanted and burned tent poles. But he hears enough.

"He is our killer," the old man shouts. "He is our killer."

My God, thinks Tapp, is that Forsyth? Or maybe Whitside?

A man with a large bandage across his face runs past, and Tapp reaches down and grabs his coat. The man is in civilian clothes, and Tapp recognizes him as one of the Seventh Cavalry interpreters.

"Who's the dead man in that tent?"

"What? Goddamned horse got away on me, have to catch him up."

The front of the man's shirt is soaked with

blood, and it is dried and caked in his moustache, too.

"Who's the dead man in the tent?"

"That? Some old medicine man. How the hell should I know . . ."

"What happened here anyway?"

The man has started to pull away but stops and touches the bandage on his nose, and somehow through the bloody moustache he smiles.

"One of them red bastards cut off my nose," he yells. "Like a Kiowa woman caught sleepin' out with another man, and her husband takes blade to 'er. One of the docs sewed it back on."

The man with the cut nose turns and runs on, looking for his horse, dodging between the parties of soldiers carrying off wounded. Nearby, mounted troopers are assembling the survivors, milling them into a bunch like drovers working restless cattle. Some of the women look across the road at the dead in the council circle, and Tapp hears them moaning. A few children cry, but most stare with wide, black eyes, silent and clinging to the skirts of the women.

Tapp dismounts and moves among the bodies, pulling the mare behind, looking down at naked backs, bloody and turning tallow-colored. A fight here, one helluva fight, he keeps thinking. Two soldiers trying to carry a limp form ask him to help.

"Appreciate a hand, mister," one says.

Tapp tries to find a handhold. The body of the

man sags, a blanket draped across the middle. His eyes are open, dusty-looking.

"God, he stinks," Tapp says.

"Gut shot," says one of the troopers. "Innards are leakin' out."

They carry the Miniconjou to the tent area, where a line of wagons has formed, most of them still filled with sacks of grain. The wounded are being loaded into these, laid out on the grain, and Quinton Tapp can see the deep red splashes on the burlap sacks. As they lift the Indian into a wagon bed, the blanket falls away from his body, exposing an exit wound where Tapp can see a kidney and intestines bulging. He steps back and wipes his hands on his trousers.

"He looks dead to me," he says, pulling back and walking away from the hospital, pulling the mare behind. If I wanted this, I'd hire on to clean out the slaughterhouses in Omaha, he thinks. Along the road now, he sees soldiers loading their own dead into wagons. There are a number of bodies in a row, face-up, their skin the color of blue parchment. Tapp counts over twenty of them. He walks over and finds Fitzpatrick squatting beside one of the bodies on the ground. The face is covered with what was once a white handkerchief but now is soggy red. Tapp sees the captain's insignia.

"Fitz?"

The first sergeant looks up, his eyes puffy and red-rimmed. He wipes his nose with the back of his hand.

"Wallace?" Tapp asks.

Fitzpatrick nods.

"You got a drink of whisky?"

Tapp shakes his head. "I wish to hell I did. What happened here, anyway?"

"They tell me it was right at the start," Fitzpatrick says. "At the very start. One of the bastards shot the cap'n right through the head."

For a while they are silent, Fitzpatrick staring along the valley, his face unmoving. Along the line of dead, the soldiers lift the bodies and lay them like ricked wood in the wagon beds. Quinton Tapp can smell carbolic and the still-lingering scent of burned powder. Everybody tells me his own little troubles, he thinks, and nobody acts like they know what really happened. But that's pretty near right. In a fight, a man usually don't know what the hell happened but only puts it together after, however he wants it to be.

"Fitz, do you know how this all started?"

"Hell, it was just like a poker game brawl. Somebody started shootin', and all joined in. How the hell do I know what happened? Except these sneaky bastards said they was comin' in to surrender, then they wouldn't turn loose of their weapons."

"It looks like it was close business."

"It was. We was close enough to see the dirt under their fingernails."

"Well, anyway, it looks like Captain Wallace didn't suffer any."

"No, he never. But his woman and sprout will

suffer enough for all three, I guess."

"Well, it looks to me like you boys dealt out some misery your own selfs."

"Not enough," Fitzpatrick says, looking across the road toward the group of women and children. Tapp sees that Fitzpatrick would like to shoot the whole lot of them.

A trooper comes up and says they can load the captain, and the three of them lift the body. The body seems slight, as though all the weight had run out. When they lift it, there is a dark circle on the ground where the head had lain.

"You find any whisky in this place," Fitzpatrick says, "save me a drink. I've got to start roundin' up these mud-heads and get ready for the march back to the agency."

"Fitz, I'm sorry about the captain," Quinton Tapp says. "I know you set a store in him."

For a moment the first sergeant says nothing, his face expressionless, as though he has not heard. Then he shrugs.

"You find any whisky, you save me a drink."

Tapp, still pulling the mare along by the reins, finds Major Whitside along the road near the Wounded Knee post office. There are a number of mounted officers there, taking instructions for the march back to Pine Ridge agency. Tapp waits at the edge of this party until most of the officers have ridden off to appointed chores, then moves to Whitside and touches his stirrup as he looks up, eyes squinted against the lowering sun.

"Major, sir, could you tell me what happened here?"

For an instant he thinks the officer will pull away, but then he speaks.

"You're from the *Omaha Bee*, aren't you?"

"Yes, sir, I am."

"Your other man is over there in the trader's store. Let him tell you."

Quinton Tapp still holds tight to the stirrup.

"Sir, I'd like to hear somethin' from you on it."

"When we were disarming one of the young bucks, he fired a shot and they all began firing. We returned their fire."

"Well, you say the Sioux shot first?"

"Yes, they did. I'd guess maybe fifty rounds before we returned their fire. You can print that."

"How many casualties have you got, major?"

"I don't know yet; maybe as many as twenty-five dead, forty wounded. But that's a rough count."

"How about the Miniconjous?"

Whitside pulls his mount away now and scowls.

"How in Christ's name would I know? Count 'em yourself."

As the major rides off, another officer pulls his horse close to Tapp. He says his name, but Tapp pays little attention to him. Wants his name in the newspaper, he thinks.

"It was absolute treachery," the officer says. "We took their word in good faith that they wanted to come in peacefully, but they wouldn't give up their weapons."

"Yeah, well, it's a hard thing to take a weapon away from one of these people, ain't it?"

The officer's face mottles with red. His words are almost a shout.

"You appear to have a strange attitude, mister. Just where do your sympathies lie?"

"With those people over there," Tapp says, waving toward the wagons with the soldier dead and on beyond to the council circle where the Indian bodies still lie. He pulls away as the officer continues to shout, paying no attention, shutting out his words. He can see Cleaborn now, on the porch of the trader's store, motioning with both arms, like a Nebraska windmill, Tapp thinks. All right, I'm coming, you little bastard.

Cleaborn disappears back inside the store, but as Tapp ties the mare to a porch railing, Akins comes out, face serious, sucking on his cold corn-cob pipe. He offers his hand and Tapp shakes it briefly, thinking it a strange gesture.

"It's been a great tragedy," Akins says. "I suspect somebody will be court-martialed for this."

"I hear the Sioux got itchy and started shootin'."

"Quint, I was right there, and I swear I couldn't tell who shot first. It's a great tragedy."

"Well, I'm glad to see they missed you anyway. Whoever started it. I got the feelin' everybody was primed for somethin'."

"All it took was a small spark. The troops were

standing so close to the Indians. I don't understand that."

"Well, I'm glad they didn't get you."

"Come inside away from all this bedlam," Akins says. Inside, Tapp thinks, it's anything but calm. A group of civilian men are throwing merchandise from the store shelves into wooden boxes and hurrying through an open rear door where a wagon stands waiting.

"They're scared as hell," Krenshaw says, and Tapp sees the tall redhead for the first time, behind the counter with papers scattered in front of him, a stub of pencil in his fist.

"Quint, is that mare of yours still good for a ride?" Akins asks.

"She's no easy chair, but I think she's stout as an oak barrel. I reckon she could go a ways yet. Why?"

"Dispatches," Cleaborn shouts, rolling a number of notebook pages into a neat cylinder. "We've got to g-g-get dispatches to R-R-Rushville."

"I'd still like some slant on what took place down there in front of those tents."

"It'll be called a lot of things," Akins says. "Mostly it was stubborn pride and fear and trigger-happy, all rolled in one."

"The goddamned Indians," Krenshaw says. "They started it all, and they damn well paid for it, too."

"Yeah, I saw some of the accounts that got squared," Tapp says. Looking at Krenshaw, he thinks, I'd like to give him an elbow in the teeth. I ain't any kind of Indian lover, but that bastard grates on my quick.

"I got two of 'em, myself," Krenshaw is saying.

"Yes, we've heard about that," Akins says. "Five times. Quint, we need to get this stuff into the wire at Rushville, Wilmot's right about it. If you got started right away, it would make most of the morning newspapers across the country."

"What's wrong with you folks takin' your own copy to Rushville?"

"Now look here, Quinton," Cleaborn starts, but Akins cuts him off.

"Some good reasons. You've got the best horse. Cleaborn can't even stay on one of the critters. We need to stay with the Army. There's no telling what might happen in the next few hours. Besides, you're a better rider than any of us and could make better time."

"Well, hell . . ."

"That's a good horse you got," Krenshaw says.

"She ought to be. I paid dear enough for the bitch."

"You could probably reach Rushville before solid dark."

"Yeah, if some face-painted bunch of wild bucks don't catch me," Quinton Tapp says. Then he shrugs, thinking of the saloons. "All right. But I need a little fodder money. Say ten dollars apiece."

The two younger men set up a clamor, but Akins waves them down.

"It's worth it. After all, we were the only ones of the whole press gang who saw this thing to-day."

Each of them digs out silver and notes, and Tapp grins as he takes it, along with the rolls of paper with each reporter's scribbling.

"I hope I can read it all," he says. "But I can't file it three at once. Which goes first?"

"Krenshaw's," Akins says. "We flipped coins. Krenshaw's, then Cleaborn's, and finally, mine."

"Now you do it in that order," Krenshaw says from behind the counter, waving a finger.

"He will," Akins says. "Let's don't have any more ruckus. There's been enough blood let to-day."

They all walk out together, and for a moment Quinton Tapp looks across the valley. Activity at the council site is finished now, and they can see all the Army tents coming down, tied in bundles, and thrown into wagons. The wounded and the Army dead are all loaded. But the Sioux dead lie where they fell, scattered across the flat. The lumpy forms cast long shadows, making each look bigger than it is.

"They plan to leave them Miniconjous out for the birds?"

"No. As soon as they get to the agency, they'll contact some civilian outfit to come out and bury them. Forsyth told me he was anxious to get his wounded and the outfit back to Pine Ridge. So those will have to lay there until tomorrow."

"If I know these Army contractors, it may be

later than just tomorrow," Tapp says. "And in this weather, it won't be a pleasant job."

He goes to the mare, slides the dispatches into saddlebags. She grunts as he tightens the cinch.

"Well, here we go again, you spraddle-legged old whore."

"Be careful," Akins calls.

"I'll see you at the agency. After dark awhile, I'd guess." Tapp grins again, feeling the money in his pants pocket.

As Quinton Tapp reins away and rides south down the valley, the Army column is getting underway. Troops are forming, and the wagons have already begun the trip to Pine Ridge agency. Officers ride up and down, shouting their instructions. The Sioux, all of them walking and flanked by soldiers with carbines across their knees, move south along the agency road. Off to one side, the Miniconjou pony herd is driven along. The newspaper correspondents with their buggy and horses join the march; the trader, with wooden boxes stacked crookedly in his rig, is already far ahead.

As the last of the long column winds away to the southwest, the dust begins to settle in the deserted valley. The low ridges have begun to cast their shadows across the flats, and darkness creeps in, hiding the broken fences, the destroyed tents, the dead horses. Along the western hills, the last of the sun's light touches the short grass with gold. The rear door of the trader's store swings in the evening breeze, banging softly, the only sound once the crows on the ridge to the north have gone to roost. Then far to the east, a single coyote starts its yammering cry, a sharp, whining bark. Cold creeps across the land, and soon the temperature will drop below freezing, but it will not be enough to form ice on the surface of Wounded Knee. The morning sun will find and quickly dissipate rabbit ice thrust up along the banks of the little stream.

At the place where the council circle had been, all the dark forms are still, like clusters of sagebrush in the growing night. Except one, and it rises slowly and stands, then painfully stoops to lift a blanket up against the cold.

PART FIVE
THE SPACE WRITER

23

LONDON TIMES — The latest accounts of the battle at Porcupine Creek describe vividly the fury, inspired by racial hatred, with which the combatants on both sides fought. The hand-to-hand melee was an early feature of the fight. It did not last long. When the Indians took to flight, the artillery opened a deadly fire with Gatling and Hotchkiss guns.

Talks With Horses stands, the blanket held around his shoulders, knowing for the first time that many of the People have fallen. They lie around him in the night like obsidian pebbles at the floor of a dark stream. The sky bends over him sparkling with stars, and in their light he can see the valley deserted except for the dead. The Army tents are gone, and where the Sioux encampment had been only jagged poles stand, a few with tattered canvas shreds blowing out in the wind like the white soldiers' guidons, only these are black and do not have the soft whisper of silk as guidons do. The pony herd is gone and all the Hair Mouth wagons, along with the cannons that had stood along the western ridge. Far along the road, in the night he can see the darker shapes of buildings, but there are no lights from the windows, although he knows it is still early in the evening, and if white men were there, the kerosene lamps would be making their yellow shine.

His left arm hangs numb against his side from a wound high in the shoulder. Feeling it, he knows the bone at his collar is shattered. But the bleeding has stopped, and he knows this wound will not kill him. Nor will the gash across the base of his skull where a white soldier bullet split his scalp. With the fingers of his good hand he touches the wound and finds it is already crusted with dried blood and not dangerous. But the hole in his side is not so good. Blood still oozes from the swollen flesh, and at his touch a pain runs all along his ribs and seems to touch his heart, making him catch his breath. This is a dangerous wound, he thinks, although he feels little pain from it except when his fingers probe it.

He is numb from lying so long face-down in the sand. But most of all, he is thirsty. His thirst is so great that standing there with the wind moving about him, his mind hears the rush of water in Wounded Knee Creek, although he knows the stream is too far away for his ears actually to hear it. He recalls a well curbing behind the trader's store, seen yesterday as the People rode past. I will make myself walk, he thinks, because if I do not, I will die standing here.

He moves among the fallen ones, looking at

each in the starlight. It is hard to recognize any of them. They have been dead and under the afternoon sun for too long. With all the tents and the wagons and the lines of soldiers gone, it is hard to remember where the old chief was when the shooting started. But soon he finds Big Foot. His side gives a quick little pain as he bends down and looks into the lined face, upturned, with a scarf still tied about the jaw and ears. For a long time he looks down at the old man, and the bitterness rises from his stomach like the rush of sour vomit.

"*Até*, I am sorry," he says aloud, and his voice is harsh from long silence and lack of water. He straightens and walks toward the road and the trader's store, his feet dragging in the dust, and after a short while the pain comes up from his side where the blood still runs out to wet his leggings. The store seems a long way off. He drags one foot after the other, holding his wounded side with the good hand and feeling the wetness coming through his fingers like honey, sticky and thick.

It takes a long time, but finally he is at the well curbing. A wall of sandstone has been made around this well, and there is a wooden scaffold above with a pulley and rope, the bucket sitting on the sandstone. He drops it into the hole and hears the hard splash of water, sounding clear and cold, and he licks his cracked lips. With his good arm he heaves up on the rope, holding it against the ground with a foot after each pull until he has gained another hold. With the brimming bucket back on the sandstone, he lowers his face into it, shivering with the bite of coldness against his teeth and lips. But he can drink only a little before the pain in his side increases and he stops, leaning against the stone curbing and looking up at the stars, waiting for the pain to leave. Then he drinks again.

I am all that is left, he thinks. Of all the People who came to Pine Ridge reservation from Cheyenne River, I am the only one. To make peace between the Oglala and Brulé and the others, we came, and now I am all that is left. The soldiers have gone and taken the ponies and the wagons, and I am alone. In this dark place, alone where fools and hotheads and brave men met while the sun was still warming the valley.

He thinks of Big Foot's daughter and looks toward the valley where the tents have stood, but in the darkness does not see that the one where he last saw her has burned. His thinking is blurred and his wounds begin to make stabbing pains along his sides. He tries for a few heartbeats to think of her, but no more.

He hears the door at the trader's store banging in the wind, and he goes toward the sound, his movements now beginning to make him light-headed. For a time he leans against the wall of the white man's building, then goes inside, stumbling at the sill, but not falling. At first he can see nothing, but soon his eyes make out the dark shapes of table and chairs and a butcher's block.

He crosses the room and in the store begins to feel along the shelves. He bumps against the counter and gasps with the pain it makes. Then his searching fingers find small metal cans and he thinks, I hope this is not the white man's sneezing tobacco because I am hungry and cannot eat sneezing tobacco.

Back in the trader's rear room, he finds the metal tools the white man seems to set such store by when he prepares his meat and corn. Forks and a ladle and finally a knife. The blade is long and slender like a skinner, and it is very sharp. Near a window facing out toward the valley, he puts a can on the floor and with his good right hand drives the knife into it. At once there is the smell of salt and oil, and he knows he has found sardines. After great effort, he has one can open enough to finger out the small fish in chunks that crumble between his fingers. Sitting under the window so he can see out to the valley south of the building, he eats. But only a little, because the sardines make him thirsty again and he does not feel able to go back for water.

The wound in his side has stopped hurting sharply. There is only a dull ache, there and across his neck where the soldier bullet split his scalp. Leaning against the wall with his eyes closed, he tries to think of what has happened and what it means, but his mind is slow to work and soon he sleeps.

In his mind he sees pictures in vivid colors, red and yellow flashing in the sun. There are dancers around a drum, each dressed in the old way with cured skins and feathers and with paint on their faces. The drummers sit around the drum with long switches of willow, beating the stretched hide slowly, never looking up as the dancers move past them. Each time the door slams against the frame in the night wind, his mind sees the old men around the drum bringing their switches down. There is chanting, but he does not understand the words.

Often he comes fully awake, and then he can hear mice running through the debris of the trader's store, making a soft whispering across the floor. The little brothers are hungry, too, he thinks. But they will find little because they cannot open the white man's sardine cans. And each time, he drifts back into sleep. He dreams of Big Foot's daughter coming toward him, a gourd of cool water in her hand. She laughs, and he laughs, too. They touch hands, and her skin is soft as the belly of a young puppy and equally warm. They walk toward a wooded streambed, where he will touch her again with his fingers and speak of things men speak of to young women who are beautiful and soft and have golden shoulders in the sun. But he never touches her again because the pain comes in his side, growing larger now, and he wakes for a moment and hears the mice.

Sleeping again, he sees Cheyenne River, too, and Deep Creek, and the village of the People. But even in dreaming, he knows there are no

Miniconjous at Deep Creek now. And even if there were, he could never go there because he has no horse. Riding a horse would kill you, his dream says. And even asleep, he knows it is true. Then he is awake again, and his skin feels dry and hot, like white man's canvas that is old and stretched before a fire too long. And what if I went to Pine Ridge agency? he thinks. Who would greet me? The Oglalas, who stood yesterday in the white man's Army uniforms and on the white man's horses and with white man's weapons, just beyond the Miniconjou village and the gulley? Or would only the white man be there to hang me for shooting the corn silk Hair Mouth? It doesn't matter. I cannot go anywhere from this valley.

Again he sleeps deeply, with no dreams, nor does he hear the banging of the door or the mice moving over the trader's store floor. By the time he wakes fully, it is midday, the sun bright once more in a sky that is cloudless. His thirst is so great it hurts him, and moving slowly he goes back to the well. This time he does not draw fresh water but drinks from the bucket, even though the water is not so cold now, sitting in the sun, as it was the night before. He is stiff and all his wounds ache. In the light of the sun he sees the hole in his side, where there is a black swelling. The blood comes from it slowly, dark red, and he knows that somewhere inside is still the lead slug. This is a very bad wound, he thinks, but there is little I can do about it except splash the water against it.

Somehow the bright daylight makes him afraid, and he goes back into the trader's store. There he finds ants in the first can of sardines, and he opens another with the skinning knife. He eats all of these, then pushes the can still slick with oil away from him, for the little brothers who need it too. Sitting against the wall, he can look out across the valley, made by the sun almost like the season of *blokéta,* of summer. He can almost hear the flies humming in the shadows of the room, but he knows there are no flies now in the white man's December.

There are crows among the fallen People, and he wishes he had the old chief's rifle. He would fire at the birds and drive them away. Yes, he thinks, and bring a troop of white man's cavalry back into this place. He watches the crows, strutting among the bodies, stopping here and there to peck and tear. His eyes lift to the ridges beyond the killing place, but everything there is dimmed. It is the wounds, he thinks. They make me blind.

Death is not so far away, he thinks. It was always a wonder to me that the old ones knew when to sing their parting song. But now, it is clear to me. Death has been in this place for a long time, and now he is watching me. He is unkind to take me with him like this, like a muskrat wounded by dogs, crawled off to die in his hole. The rest of the People died there, on that flat place, as brave people are supposed to die, resisting. Death should allow me to be one of the People and die like them, brave and with a weapon in my hands. Talks does not know of those who were killed while trying to run and hide.

Maybe we killed a lot of the Hair Mouths, he thinks. But there is no way to know because the ones surviving would carry off their dead. There are so many of them, it would be impossible to kill them all. But we killed one, and he thinks it with some satisfaction. We killed the one with corn silk moustache and white teeth, and blue eyes like a summer sky. Because I killed this one myself. He begins to understand why it was important in the old days for a man to be a warrior and count coups against an enemy in warfare. Of course, killing is not the same as counting coups, but in such dangerous games a few are going to die. After the white man's weapons came, more than a few died in such games. Not so many as died from the white man's diseases, but more than a few.

That corn silk Hair Mouth was maybe a fine man in his own tribe, Talks thinks. He had been gentle to the women and children of the People, laughing and joking with them. But there must be no remorse at his death. Good men must die in war along with the bad, and maybe even more of them.

"It was good that I killed him," he says aloud, his voice grating across his throat like sharp gravel.

Pain grows in his side. His head is hot, but dry. Once, as he sits by the window, he thinks he hears firing far to the west, brought to him on the wind that has shifted to blow from the place where the sun goes to sleep. Maybe all the others are fighting the Hair Mouths now, he thinks. The Oglala and Brulé and the others. He does not know that what he hears is a small skirmish north of Pine Ridge agency where Seventh Cavalry soldiers are caught by a number of young warriors and almost destroyed until the black soldiers come and drive the Sioux away. He does not know that he hears the last fight of his people against the yellow-hides — the Hair Mouths — and that after this, it will all be finished. The resistance to new ways, the hopes and dreams and yearnings, the People as a nation, all finished. Soon all will come in peacefully to the parched corn and the tough beef ration that is never enough and the indignity of being told what to do.

But if he does not know this last battle, there are bigger things he does know. He knows that the Messiah dream, started among his people in the fall, has turned to cold ashes. He knows that the People do not know the white man's heart, nor does he theirs. And between this misunderstanding of both, they stood face to face yesterday and killed the last dream of the People. Each killed it together, the white man maybe more than the People, but still, both killed it. We were the hope killers, he thinks. And it is a bitter thing, even though he knows that without the killing the hope would not have been realized anyway. Maybe we all run together now in our misery, the white man and the People. But the white man's misery is much smaller than our own.

The blood still leaks from his side, blackish and thick. I will not die in this way, he thinks. I will die with my people, not in a white man's wooden hole. But before he thinks anything else, he sleeps once more with the sun lowering toward the western ridges, and he dreams nothing.

The stiffness and aching in his wounds and the cold blowing into the trader's store waken him. It is dark and cloudy, the wind has shifted once again, and now it comes out of the north. He rises without making any sound of pain although the pain is very great.

"I will spend no more time in a white man's lodge," he says aloud.

This is a long journey, he thinks, as he leaves the building and starts back along the road to the killing place. And I have dropped my blanket and the wind is cold. As he moves along slowly, his left arm hangs wet and useless against his wounded side, and in his right hand he still holds the skinning knife with the blade that is sharp enough to shave the hair from a white man's arm. It takes a long time, but he does not fall. He knows that if he falls, he will never rise again. His fever burns his face, even in the cold wind. Finally he comes to the place where the council was held and moves out to stand among the dark bodies. At the edges of the place he sees moving forms and knows these are brothers coyote or wolf. But he has no time for them. He tries once more to find the body of Big Foot, but only for a little while because his strength is gone.

Let me recall some of the old songs, he thinks. The songs old people sang when they were about to die. He tries to remember the words, but it is difficult. He goes to his knees among the bodies and loses his grip on the knife. After a great effort he finds it in the dark, and holding it tightly, looks at the sky, still kneeling. The wind is sharp against his face, and it is the only thing about him that feels good. Drawing a deep breath that causes his side to hurt, he begins to sing. It is not a loud song, but it is loud enough to make the dark shapes of coyote or wolf at the edge of the council circle bolt away into the night.

> The yellow-hide, the white-skinned man, I
>   have put him aside.
> I have put him aside.
> I have no sympathy with him now, he has
>   always been my enemy.
> I have put him aside, fathers, forever!

He coughs and his belly pains him and he bends over, still on his knees. After a moment the pain leaves, and he straightens. I will sing this death song through, he thinks, here among my people and near my father and chief. A man needs to sing his death song with his own people near. A man needs to show death that he is not afraid. I will sing it for her, the daughter of Big Foot, with the bold yet soft eyes and the fountains of life that will never be for my children. I will sing it for her and for myself and for all my people and for my unborn sons.

> Fathers, I come, fathers, I come,
> The People are good, beside clear water and
>   herds of game.
> The People are good.
> Fathers, I come.

He can remember no more and for a long time kneels in the hard wind among the dead. Finally he brings the point of the knife up to his belly, pressing until he feels the sharp point just below the ribs. He looks across the council circle, toward the place where he thinks Big Foot lies.

"Good-bye my father, good-bye from this world."

With all the effort he can command, he thrusts the knife inward and upward, grinding his teeth. He makes no sound and feels little more than a pinch of pain deep in his chest as he settles slowly to lie like the others, a shapeless bundle.

It has begun to snow. Soon, the flakes cover his shoulders and his sides, his head and his wounds, even the one where now shows only the handle of the skinning knife. Around him, as the night goes toward dawn, growing colder, are the silent and unmoving figures, covered in a blanket of white.

24

WASHINGTON STAR — It is being claimed as fact in many quarters that since the battle of the Little Big Horn in Montana Territory in 1876, the 7th Cavalry has been thirsting for revenge against the red man. The regiment of Custer, it is said, went to the battlefield at Wounded Knee with that intent and carried it forth against all they could find, men, women and children alike, having first disarmed them.

⬦

The New Year had come. And with it the last spasm of what was called but had never been an Indian war. After Wounded Knee, there had been frenzied activity among the Sioux. More than anything else it was a manifestation of fright and uncertainty, and few real threats developed. The baggage trains of one cavalry regiment had been fired on by a small group of young warriors. The Pine Ridge agency at one time was under an attack so feeble it hardly deserved the name. There was a skirmish north of the agency, near a Catholic mission, where elements of the Seventh Cavalry were once again badly deployed and pinned down by Sioux rifle fire until the arrival of the Ninth Cavalry, the Brunettes. And in the Stronghold, if the dream of a coming Messiah persisted at all, it was no longer a burning flame but only a candle's faint glow held secret in the heart. The dancers there sent word they would come in and give up their weapons. Much of this had been the work of agency Sioux who had gone among their brothers in the Badlands to persuade, to cajole, to point out the disaster brought on by resisting the white man's way and by bullheadedness. Always, the Sioux peacemakers were as pugnacious as any of the hostiles.

At Pine Ridge, Gen. Nelson Miles had arrived on the scene. The press gang made much of it, writing that a new hard-fisted attitude was at hand and the red devils would now be smashed for good. Very little was made of the contradiction in this and what Miles was actually doing. Like Brooke, he was keeping all the Army units under close control, hoping to avoid further bloodletting. His first act on arrival had been to relieve Forsyth of command of the Seventh Cavalry, pending an investigation of the regiment's deployment and actions at Wounded Knee. Serious observers said old Miles was after Forsyth's scalp for turning a demonstration of Sioux resistance into something more than a demonstration. And they were right. But those who had been at Wounded Knee and seen the flare-up of passions on both sides said old Miles would never be able to make anything stick, and in large part they were right, too.

After the snowstorm on the last day of 1890, which everyone was now calling a blizzard, the civilian contract party had finally gone to Wounded Knee to bury the fallen Miniconjous. With them went an escort of infantry and a photographer who propped up the dead and took Kodak pictures of them.

Still anticipating a war, the press corps at the agency increased after Wounded Knee. The copy going through the telegraph office from Rushville continued to carry sinister overtones and outright predictions of great battles to come; word pictures of painted fanatics, infesting the ridges in daylight, creeping close to the agency buildings at night with knives between their teeth.

Now the boom shows no signs of diminishing in Rushville. Each arrival of the passenger cars on the Fremont, Elkhorn, and Missouri Railroad brings more sightseers, freebooters, whisky drummers, missionaries, whores, loan sharks, gamblers, and all the others attracted by the concentration of an army and the promise of excitement carried in most of the country's press. A place to sleep, a good horse, and fresh eggs are scarce, and prices are higher than ever. Along the railroad siding military gear accumulates: stacks of baled hay, cases of canned food and ammunition, a brace of Gatling guns, tentage, beef cattle.

Because the hospital facilities at the agency are inadequate, a number of Army wounded are brought into Rushville for shipment on an eastbound train to military posts. Among these is 1st Sgt. Sean Fitzpatrick, hit in the leg at the fight north of the agency, now being called in the newspapers the battle of Drexel Mission. He lies on a litter at the railroad siding, on the loading platform, with more than a dozen others on a day that is not bitter cold but with a wind that blows occasional snow flurries under a layer of gray clouds. A switch engine backs a converted boxcar onto the siding where it can be loaded to await the arrival of the next eastbound passenger train, due in mid-afternoon. The car is equipped with litter racks, two iron heating stoves, firewood stacked across one end, and a field kitchen at the other. As soon as it is in position, soldier details begin to carry on equipment and covered metal pots.

"Potato soup tonight," Fitzpatrick grumbles.

He is strapped onto the litter and blanketed, made almost immobile. It doesn't matter. He has no desire to move. He lies watching the soldiers work, his thoughts critical of the Army surgeon supervising the detail for allowing the troops to dawdle. One soldier, with an armload of white enamel bedpans, drops one of the bedpans onto the platform and it makes a loud clatter. All the others laugh.

Someone squats beside his litter, and Fitzpatrick turns and looks into the face of Quinton Tapp. He blinks and licks his lips.

"You got a drink of whisky on you?" Fitzpatrick says.

"You asked me that the last time I saw you. I doubt that bone cracker would let you have a drink. What the hell happened to you, anyway?"

"A passin' nip in the leg," Fitzpatrick says. "Some damned red nigger at Drexel Mission. One of the last shots fired, I think. It don't amount to much. Have you got a drink this time?"

"Maybe. We'll see about it." Fitzpatrick watches Tapp walk over to the surgeon and they talk for a long time and Fitzpatrick scowls. Damned doctor'll be tellin' him all about the leg, he thinks. His face is pale, blue veins showing in jowls usually beet red. His wound is a serious one, a bullet shattering the left knee. He has already made up his mind that he will lose the leg and face the prospect of becoming a pensioned cripple. He closes his eyes but hears the sound of Tapp's boots along the platform as the big man comes back to the litter.

"Doc says you might could use a little stimulant," he says, and takes a pint bottle from inside his coat. A little of it runs from the corners of Fitzpatrick's mouth as he chokes down a drink, and Tapp wipes the first sergeant's chin with his fingers.

"Where you been?" Fitzpatrick asks.

"I came to town the night of that Wounded Knee fight," Tapp says, "and started wonderin' about goin' back to the agency. No women and no whisky. So I decided to stay here awhile. I don't think I'll go back at all."

"You look like hell."

"Well, I come into some money, as the sayin' goes, so I spent me a few days at Lottinvale's Recreation Hall and Domino Parlor, down the tracks a ways." Tapp laughs and takes a drink himself.

"By God. That pig ranch. I heard of that. Big Lottie's, they call it."

"That's the place."

"I hate to leave here without seein' it.'

"It ain't all that delightful. But they got card rooms where I managed to increase my holdin's a mite, and they got a player piano like that one you and me wrecked in Bismarck that time, and they got fair to middlin' steak and potatoes, and the beds are all right."

"And the women?"

"Fair to middlin', as the sayin' goes."

For a long time they are silent, Fitzpatrick with his eyes closed. Down the platform, soldiers have begun to move wounded into the car. Snow blows across the litters, and Tapp moves around to shield Fitzpatrick's face.

"Doc says you boys are headed for Leavenworth. That's a nice place."

"Listen, Quinton, I'm thinkin' about leavin' the Army. After thirty-two years I think I'd like to get me a nice livery stable in Junction City, just take 'er easy, and when the boys march out, stand on the street and wave good-bye."

Tapp doesn't say anything. Fitzpatrick opens his eyes and looks at the bottle in Tapp's hand.

But he shakes his head when another drink is offered.

"You come on down there with me, Quinton. You and me together. Have a little blacksmith shop right in back. I even know a place we might buy."

"Hell, Fitz, I'd have to hold up some bank to have enough money to buy anything," Tapp says. "Besides, I've got accustomed to big towns. And all this empty country has finally got on my nerves."

The soldiers have come to Fitzpatrick's litter. They bend to take him up, but he speaks first, looking at Tapp still.

"You got any cigars?"

Tapp shakes his head. Then as the soldiers lift the litter, he quickly slips the bottle under the blankets. As they start across the platform with him, Fitzpatrick lifts his head and shouts.

"You come to Junction City, Quinton. You ain't got no business doin' all this other shit. You ought to shoe some more horses before you die."

The interior of the car is dark, but Fitzpatrick feels them lifting his litter to a rack. He can still see out the open side door. There is straw on the floor, and it blows in wisps out across the platform. The smell of it reminds him of cavalry stables, clean and crisp. He thinks of Fort Riley and the rimrock behind the rifle ranges, the willow thickets along the Republican like green smoke in the springtime, the rows of neat sandstone officers' quarters across the Junction City road from the barracks and stables.

"Just a short trip, men," the doctor says as he comes into the car. He moves along the rows of litter racks, checking each man, then returns to the far end of the car where soldiers are rattling pots and pans.

This has been one sour campaign, Fitzpatrick thinks. Bad things bein' said about the regiment. And we lost twenty-five or so dead at Wounded Knee, a couple more at the mission. Only good thing, we killed a few of those red bastards. Some say as many as a hundred forty, wounded another fifty. Some women and kids among those, he thinks, which you got to expect if the women and children get caught in a fight among the men. But the thought does not sit well, and he turns his mind to other things.

When it is a long way off, he can hear the eastbound passenger whistling. Just about now passing Big Lottie's, he thinks, and smiles. He feels the ground tremble as the moving train approaches and passes close alongside the box-car; then there is the squeal of metal brakes, a whistle blowing, and a bell clanging. He can hear the stationmaster shouting.

"All passengers to Valentine, Fremont, and points east."

The boxcar moves with a sudden lurch as the switch engine backs it onto the main line, then pushes it to couple at the rear of the passenger. There are two more sharp whistle blasts, a conductor up ahead shouts " 'Board!" and they have started to move, gaining speed rapidly. As the car passes the loading platform, Fitzpatrick looks through the open door and Quinton Tapp still stands there, the snow beginning to swirl thickly around him. Fitzpatrick watches as long as he can see the big man standing on the platform in the snow, then presses his head back against the litter, eyes closed.

"I wish he'd had a cigar," he thinks.

25

CHICAGO HERALD — When I saw an Indian man crying after having lost a loved one, for the first time I realized that the soul of a Sioux might possibly in its primitive state have started out on the same road as did the soul of a white man. (The Widow)

Thelma Hanson Duncan returns to Rushville with a retinue of admirers. There are two officers from General Miles's staff, four male correspondents from among those who have overflowed the Hotel de Finley for almost two months, a reservation policeman, a Sioux woman acting as a kind of lady-in-waiting and chambermaid, and a half-blood interpreter. The Widow has decided to write a Sioux-English dictionary once she returns to Chicago. But first she plans a number of color stories on the citizens of Rushville and the accumulation of camp followers attendant to any army's campaign in the field.

Already she has interviewed old Red Cloud, has walked among the Sioux encampments around the agency — always escorted by a large detachment of cavalrymen — chastised the press corps for their sensational reports, and created her own philosophy of the red man and his place in a white society. She had once written, and it was widely circulated, "The greatest crime for which the government must answer is sending the educated Indian girl back to her tribe, where virtue is unknown."

Through all of this, she has retained the close friendship of agency employees and Army officers, both collectively and individually. In confidence, Miles has told her that the Indian trouble in Dakota has ended and all that remains is to wait for the last dancers to come in, have a grand review of troops, and leave, with, one hoped, Forsyth's military career hung out to dry like an old scalp. This last, of course, Miles has not said, but like everyone else, Thelma Hanson Duncan knows it is one of his hopes.

She rides into town at the head of her column, sidesaddle on one of Miles's own chestnut geldings, acting, as many townspeople say, like Queen Victoria without a consort. Thelma Hanson Duncan, first American lady war correspondent, they are calling her. Especially her own paper. The only gunfire she heard was the scattered shots sent in the general direction of the agency boarding school by a few young warriors during the hours immediately after Wounded Knee. But General Miles himself is only slightly more renowned than she, and his passage through the town toward the agency a few days earlier had attracted less attention than her entry. The day is overcast and cold with a threat of snow, but people come to the sidewalks, waving as she passes along Agency Street toward the town's only hotel deserving of the name, the Fremont, where two lumber salesmen have been rousted from their rooms to make place for the Lady of Pine Ridge and her Indian handmaiden. There is some talk that the squaw should be kept in one of the horse stalls behind the hotel, if indeed kept at all. But because the arrangement is only temporary and then will become the problem of Chicago or wherever else the Widow chooses to take the red heathen, the grumbling is not serious even in the back rooms of saloons and barbershops.

From a pool hall window, Quinton Tapp watches the little cavalcade pass down Agency Street. Since taking a few days at Big Lottie's and then seeing the Army wounded off, he has remained in Rushville, indecisive about everything except that he will not return to Pine Ridge and the press gang there. Behind the dirty window, a pool cue in one hand, glass of beer in the other, he watches the Widow pass, noting the small ankle of her right leg showing beneath the skirt as she sits high on the sidesaddle. Look at all the he-dogs tagging along, he thinks, tails up, in hopes she'll come into heat. He is a little surprised to see that neither Cleaborn nor Krenshaw is among the reporters in the entourage.

Then the baggage wagon goes by. On the box beside the driver is an Indian woman, blanket over her head. And there's the little squaw this

Duncan woman is rescuing from the savages, he thinks. But the blanket does not conceal the fact for long that this is Ruby Red Hawk.

"Well, I'm damned," he says aloud.

"Are we gonna finish this game?" one of the other players asks.

Back at the table, Tapp can neither keep track of the balls nor figure the angles of shots, and he loses three dollars before the string is out.

"You ain't quittin'," someone says as he places his cue in the wall rack. "You must be a twenty-dollar winner here already."

"I didn't contract to quit a loser," he says, and moves out to the sidewalk. Damn, she didn't go to Valentine after all. She backtracked on me, went to the agency, and got herself hooked up with that widow woman. He stomps along the street toward his own room, scowling and bumping into people. Through threats, a promise to pay twice the price, and playing hard on his Union Pacific experience, he had obtained a small room in one of the railroad boardinghouses near the depot. He has to share the bed with two other men. Neither of them is in the room when he arrives. He flings his hat and coat into a corner and flops heavily onto the bare mattress, happy to be alone. He thinks for a moment about the damned squaw, wondering what she might have told the Widow about the goings-on in the shed behind the Pine Ridge boarding school. Then he forces his mind to other things, but it does little to cool his temper.

Even though he has already decided against returning to the press gang at Pine Ridge, he mulls it over once more. If I went back, he thinks, I'd likely end up killing one of those peckerwoods. Except for Akins and maybe a couple more, they're mostly jake-leg liars. But you're no better than they are, he says to himself. The hell I'm not. Creating a little excitement in the columns to keep the readers' interest or to put Old Man Goodall's daily circulation above the *World-Herald*'s is one thing. But after a man sees heads shot half off, he ought to start taking it all a little serious. But they're all just as wild-eyed as they were before.

The whole mess is like waiting to go sit in the dentist's chair, he thinks. Nothin' really hurts, but somethin' is all-powered uncomfortable. The damned fool Sioux and the damned fool agents and Army and all the rest, turnin' this into something it wasn't supposed to be. Not that I give a shake in hell about a few red heathen gettin' theirselves killed. But then he thinks about Fitzpatrick and Wallace and the men lined up in neat rows, toes pointed toward the sky, at the hospital tent at Wounded Knee. And he thinks of Old Man Goodall and his kind, off safe in a warm bed every night, feeding on it because of politics or profit or God only knew what else. The hay merchants and gun drummers and Republicans and Democrats, the whores, card sharks, and brick makers, all the way from Baltimore to Rapid City, feeding on it somehow, all with an ax to grind.

And you were just like the rest, he thinks. No, by God, I wasn't. It is getting dark when he rises from the old bed and finds some rumpled copy paper and a pencil stub in his overcoat pocket. At the dry sink he sits and frowns, the pencil between his teeth. I'll send Old Man Goodall one more piece from this place, then head back for Omaha. He bends over the paper, frowning with the concentration of it, licking the pencil between every few words. He tries to erase a number of times, but it tears the thin paper, so he scratches out what he doesn't like and starts over. After almost an hour, in very nearly total darkness, he finishes it. Only then does he stop to light a lamp and read what he has scribbled.

There are some things need saying about this Indian war in South Dakota and the kind of man who helped make it happen. I will call him the space writer.

The big eastern newspapers generally had no regular correspondents here, but the reservation groaned under the tread of the space writer. Like Job's horse, he sniffed the battle from afar. To him, there was an outbreak in every breeze, a bloody encounter in the rustling leaf. The deep bass of the bullfrog and the hum of the tiny sand fly suggested to his hot head the massacre of settlers and the burning of a thousand happy homes.

The space writer sent his columns of blood

to any newspaper that would buy it, and next day contradict what he'd written. What he wanted was money, and he'd do anything to get it.

Those and all like him who have been here have to stand some of the responsibility for what has happened, good, bad, or indifferent. And you would have to say that I am one of them.

All right, he thinks, does that satisfy you? He reads it a second time. Yes, it satisfies me. He licks his pencil again and adds one line: "Personal note. I will be on my way back by morning train. Tapp."

It makes him feel better, walking through the growing night toward the depot and telegraph office. He has a few moments' trouble with the telegrapher trying to transcribe the message, some of which he has difficulty reading himself. But finally they have it down on the yellow Western Union form, and the key begins to click it out over the wires.

Quinton Tapp settles into one of the churchlike pews in the station waiting room, stretching out and crossing one foot over the other. The room is warm and dry, and he enjoys sitting there going over his assets. There is a draft in his pocket for two weeks' pay, he has won a little at pool and cards, and he has sold the mare and the other unused field gear for almost as much as he paid for it — as much as the *Omaha Bee* had paid for it. He has the clothes on his back and the Smith and Wesson, because he believes a man never knows when he might suddenly have use for a pistol. So there's a good deal of cash, he thinks. If I can just keep from drinkin' or gamblin' or whorin' it all away, I might buy me one of those new mail-order tailor-made suits of clothes, or maybe find me a better room in Omaha.

There are a number of people waiting for the westbound passenger, and their conversation is punctuated by the constant click of the telegraph key. With one couple is a small boy who tries to pet the depot cat dozing in an empty pew, waiting for the time to hunt mice in the baggage room. The boy reaches out and the cat spits and slashes a paw and the child backs away, pulling his hands tight against his belly. Watching the boy, Quinton Tapp thinks, I didn't see that whelp of Ruby's today. I know damned well she's got a kid, but something must have happened to it along the way. Maybe that squaw sold it to somebody. To some Army officer's family. At the agency they had all tried to outdo one another adopting red-nigger kids left orphan by Wounded Knee. There had been three or four of those, and maybe the squaw had pawned her own off as another one of the little ones found alive on the field by the burial party. There's no way of figurin' what those people might do, he thinks.

People are beginning to rise from the pews and take up their baggage. Tapp hears the westbound coming in as the stationmaster walks out and snaps open his vest-pocket watch and shakes his head, glancing up at the large wall clock over the telegraph cage. The depot windows rattle when the engine goes past, the whistle blasting. Tapp goes out on the platform to watch the people board. A baggage truck is pulled along to the mail car where two trainmen stand in the open door. The telegrapher runs out with a handful of dispatches for the conductor, whose brass cap plate shines in the depot lights. The passengers press against one another, shoving children ahead of them, and soon they are all in the cars. The conductor waves his red lantern, and down the tracks the engineer blows the whistle once and the coaches lurch forward with a loud rattle. Tapp sees the boy who had tried to pet the depot cat, his face pressed to the window. He waves, and Tapp lifts a hand to him.

The lights at the end of the last car move away from the station slowly at first, then gain speed and are lost in the darkness. There is only the smell of cinders left and the truck being wheeled back into the baggage room. Down the tracks, a switch engine is working cars into the Army loading platform, the engine's light a dirty yellow. Tapp can hear the engine bell clanging monotonously. A few snowflakes pass across the beam of the depot lights like white chicken feathers blown along before the wind. Tapp, alone now on the platform, leans against the wall, feeling the cold seep into his clothes. He fishes beneath his coat for a cigar, but finds none.

Old Man Goodall ought to have that wire by now, he thinks. He'll still be in the office, gettin' the mornin' edition into line before goin' off to bed for the few hours of sleep he always gets each night. Then he'll be back again, before first light, standin' at that window and cursin' the *World-Herald* news butch across Farnum Street under the lamp, defyin' the *Bee*.

His thoughts are interrupted by a movement at the end of the platform, where it is dark. Not even a movement, but a presence. He sees a dark figure there, familiar in some way, and he watches for a few moments before walking along the platform. As he comes close, he sees the face beneath the blanket.

"I'll be damned," he says. "Where'd you come from?"

"I come to see you," Ruby Red Hawk says. Beside her, bundled in a blanket too, is a smaller figure and Tapp can see a face, eyes wide and looking at him.

"What's that you got there?"

"This here is Emma," she says.

"Emma? Well, that's a good white name," he says. "Let's have a better look at her."

"She ain't very big," Ruby Red Hawk says, pushing the child forward. In the lantern shine from behind him, Tapp can see gray eyes and a thatch of straight, auburn-colored hair. He reaches down to touch the child, but she quickly moves back against Ruby Red Hawk's leg, her eyes watching.

"Well," Tapp says, straightening. "I see you never got to Valentine."

"Too far to walk. Now we gone to a big place where Emma can have a nice dress and learn reading."

"Sure she can," Tapp says. That damned Widow has got herself a regular red heathen pet and somebody to make her bed thrown into the bargain. "I thought you wanted to get to Valentine."

"Not now. Mrs. Duncan is better than anybody at Valentine. Mrs. Duncan gone get Emma in a school and buy her a nice dress. It's gone be a bigger place than Omaha."

"I suppose you told Mrs. Duncan all about me not wantin' to take you so she should."

"I never told her nothing about you."

The switch engine bell still rings. In the increasing snow, the headlight makes a yellow halo behind the woman.

"How long you been out here in the cold?"

"I followed you from that room you got," she says. "I couldn't catch up. So I waited."

"You been out here all that time . . . ?"

"I wanted you to see. Before Mrs. Duncan takes us to the big place. I wanted you to see Emma."

"You took some pains that I didn't see her before."

"That was before Mrs. Duncan. Now I wanted

you to see her before we go to that place."

"Well," Tapp says, "I hope you get a pretty dress."

For the first time he can remember, Ruby Red Hawk smiles, showing large, white teeth.

"Sure," she says. "A pretty dress. But I wanted you to know, it don't matter, you not taking us to Valentine."

Then she turns quickly and pushing the child before her goes off the platform and around the corner of the depot, leaving Tapp standing. Now why would she want to show me that whelp? he wonders. All this time she's been tryin' to hide it, now she stands out here in the cold for two hours with the little red bastard just so I could see it. She's tryin' to rub my nose in somethin', but I'm not sure just what. By God, that old squaw ain't too bad-lookin' when she grins.

Behind him, the telegrapher comes out onto the platform in his shirtsleeves, shivering in the wind. He waves a slip of yellow paper as he comes up to Quinton Tapp.

"I thought you were still around here, Mr. Tapp," he says. "Got a reply to your message to Omaha."

"I didn't expect any," Tapp says, taking the paper and holding it in the lantern light.

"Quinton Tapp, Rushville, Nebr. You're fired. Goodall."

The telegrapher, shoulders hunched against the cold, watches Tapp and waits. Tapp reads the message again and smiles.

"That bastard," he says.

"Any reply, sir?"

Tapp shakes his head. He wads the paper and tosses it out toward the tracks where the wind catches it and hurls it along until it is gone in the darkness.

"Spearfish weather station says it's not supposed to get too cold again for a day or so. Feels right cold to me," the telegrapher says, and Tapp grunts.

Down the tracks, the switch engine stands idle now, the boiler sighing but the bell silent. Tapp can hear horses in the Army pens and soldiers shouting as they divide the herd into remount groups for the cavalry regiments at Pine Ridge. Tapp walks to the end of the depot platform and looks along Agency Street toward the Fremont Hotel. He wonders if one of the lighted windows is the Widow's.

Well, he thinks, that breaks the tooth. I got no business in this shoutin' match anyway. The big place, she had said, where the whelp would get a pretty dress. Plenty of pretty dresses in Chicago, he thinks. And probably plenty of good smithin' jobs. They've got those street railroads there, and railroads mean horses, and horses mean blacksmith shops. Hell, there are probably more horses in Chicago than all of Nebraska, and Kansas thrown in besides.

High-toned civilization, that's what I need. Away from all this dust and mud and red-nigger worry, livin' from hand to mouth, drinkin' too much sour mash, smokin' too many bad cigars. Peaceful nights on my own bed is what I need, and some cool beer in summer and beefsteak smothered in onions without coal dust and cinders in it. Some honest, civilized work with a hammer and forge. And good horses. They say that Chicago is a civilized place, and they've got plenty of horses, too.

"Well, time for a little drink," he says aloud, and starts up Agency Street, the snow now beating hard against his face. He thinks about Ruby Red Hawk and that smile with all the big, white teeth, and of the little girl with gray eyes and auburn hair. In a pretty dress.

26

CHICAGO TRIBUNE — Miles says if we put ourselves in the place of the Indians, we might comprehend their feelings. We say this: The Indians have no better title to this land than the hunting bears and wolves that once roamed the plains!

A pair of coyotes, hunting, cross Wounded Knee Creek unafraid because they know that no man is near. They run through the shallow water with dainty steps, cracking the thin ice that has begun to form along each bank. They run with the wind past the trader's store and the other dark buildings, along the agency road, moving then into the camp areas and smelling the ground where bacon had been cooked, held over open flames on ramrods and sticks. At the council circle, snowflakes skate across the flattened ground as though it were a polished floor, worn smooth by the passage of many feet. Along the valley a few fence posts and tent poles still stand, knocked slanting now, with strands of barbed wire or burned canvas clinging to them. Where the Sioux encampment had been, blackened spots show where breakfast fires burned, and north of that, the outline of neat rows of Army tents is marked in the dead grass, beaten down.

The coyotes run silently up the ridge to the abandoned house, searching under the porch but not going inside because the smell of tobacco and man's sweat is still heavy there. The doors hang open, swinging back and forth in the wind. There are no leavings, no scraps of food. Even the prairie mice have gone deep into their burrows. The silence is complete except for the sighing wind and the squeak of rusty hinges.

Where the Hotchkiss guns had stood that day, there is a fresh grave. A mass grave where many of the People sleep. The patch of ground collects the snow in the turned soil not yet hardened in frost and rain and sun. For a while the coyotes nose about it, pausing uncertainly. Then the male lifts its head and makes the long, wailing howl that carries off and is soon lost in the darkness.

As they start back across the battleground toward the dead horses still lying there, the wind blows against their faces. It blows across the sharp ridges, whispering in the grass before going on westward. Blowing over the flat country, over the rolling prairie, across the Badlands and the Stronghold and the places where there had been dancing and dreams and hopes, but are no more. Like the powdery wisps of snow come in the darkness that with the morning sun will be gone forever.